I0662393

This book is a work of fiction. Any mention of named characters, businesses, places or events are purely for entertainment and not based on real people or places. Like any fictional story, any depiction of religious beliefs are for entertainment purposes only, and have no real bearing on the author's or publisher's political views.

Beyond the Desert Sun

A Jack Owens Series Novel

Wayne Lasner

Editor

Mark B. Goodman

Cover Illustrations

Brandon S. Lasner

I have many dreams, each uniquely bizarre. The one that stays with me day in and day out is the one I fear the most will come true.

Jack Owens

Satan looked down upon Jack Owens. No words came from the demon's mouth, but Jack heard what he had to say...

"Things have to change, Jack. I can't do this anymore. We are a family with nine lives, and eight of them have been taken from us."

Katie Claire Owens

Prologue

The sun began its slow rise over the vast Arabian desert. Shadows slowly move across the ripples in the sand that formed during the previous night's mighty winds. The atmosphere changing over from a frigid nighttime cold to a scorching heat. The amazing transition creates the appearance of a golden sea. Further to the north, this golden sea meets the rocky terrain that is home to several local tribes.

She was right, his beautiful wife Katie. She was always right. Jack imagined her warm body next to his as he reminisced. Their marriage had become one of extremes. From the first moment Jack Owens laid eyes on Katie Claire Evans, he fell in love with her; although, he didn't realize it at the time. Of all the crazy events in their short few years together, that moment in the college bar replayed over and over again, helping to keep his sanity intact. Her fair skin and blond hair whipping around as she gracefully slid the pool stick through her slender fingers into the shiny white cue ball. He remembered how angry one of her sore loser, male opponents got at her winning shot. He should have jumped in between them as things heated up, but Jack was sure she had it covered. Besides, he didn't want to lose momentum with the young lady he just met at the bar. His cocky judgment failed him. The lunatic guy started bullying the pretty female and poking his finger at her while slurring drunken insults and accusations of cheating. Jack's best friend William came to the rescue trying to negotiate a peace treaty. Suddenly, chaos ensued. They were in each other's faces resulting with William placing the guy in a choke hold. The asshole went down for the count but not before landing a solid fist into William's nose. William was the defender who won over the beautiful damsel in distress.

Unfortunate situations; those that lead to Jack's current dilemma, had resulted in William and Katie becoming estranged, and shortly after, William's murder. Years later, Jack and Katie would meet up again and eventually fall in love.

Jack yearned for her warmth against his body just one more time. He wanted to hold his twin boys and kiss them. He missed cheering them on at sporting events. As the days of captivity turned into weeks, and then months, his memories became clouded. Concentrating on a particular event from the past was difficult, at best. His attempts to replay those comforting moments would have been easier if not for the relentless efforts of his captors rousting him whenever they saw him resting.

They taunted him continuously with their subtle form of sleep deprivation; torture.

As Jack lay curled up in a fetal position, trying to keep warm, he thought about his final night with Katie and the boys. He had gotten a redo, a chance to bring normalcy to the Owens family. They had one glorious day and night celebrating their new beginning. He was finally home. *One incredibly intimate night with his beautiful Katie Claire.*

Jack had spent many years as a field operative, working very closely with his CIA associates and other law enforcement and intelligence agencies, to uncover a long-range plan to topple the US government. This nefarious terrorist plot was, by design, to play out over time. Decades, in fact. It involved a rather elaborate scheme, requiring many co-conspirators. Trusted members of terror cells from across the United States, mostly doctors or related medical staff, would report pregnancies of prominent government related or military families. The terrorist accomplices, doctors, would secretly take one of the newborn twins away telling the parents that the newborn did not survive childbirth. The purloined twin sibling would then be whisked thousands of miles away to a special camp in an undisclosed Arabian desert location, which was built to resemble a familiar American city. At the camp, the infant along with others would be cared for through young adulthood. These proclaimed *"Children of Allah"* were indoctrinated from birth to hate the western world, especially Americans and their *infidel* way of life. When one of the legitimate American twins showed promise for a political or military career, he or she would be closely observed, noting studies, passions, family, friends and intimate relationships. The "T2" or "Allah's Twin" would then go through rigorous training to match linguistics, personality traits and enough of their education to impersonate them. When the terrorist leaders thought it was the most advantageous time, they would abduct the legitimate twin sibling, and substitute the "evil twin" to carry out their destructive agenda. The havoc that would ensue would likely affect our way of life, as nobody could know who could be trusted.

Jack's current predicament made him ponder whether his abduction was intended to gain information, or for vengeance for all the damage that he had brought upon their cause.

Just when you thought, it was safe…

Jack had finally made the decision and resigned from fieldwork; taking a station job in Manhattan. It was the only way to save his fragile marriage. He and Katie remained separated for several months while he cleaned up his last bit of deadly business. Things finally calmed down enough to allow him and Katie to be reunited.

Their first night back together, Jack kissed his boys good night and returned to the kitchen. He and Katie drank wine and talked for a while.

"I missed you so much. You and the boys are my life."

Katie smiled; she had the most beautiful smile. She had Jack under her spell. Her magic also worked well for her in the courtroom, where she was an up-and-coming ADA. Jack often poked fun at her, saying that her smile was her secret weapon in winning cases by throwing off the defending attorney's game, and mesmerizing the jury.

"We missed you too, Jack." His wife glowed with a soft, sultry smile. He recognized that look, and was about to suggest heading to the bedroom but she beat him to it. "Let's go upstairs. I want to show you *just* how much I missed you."

Jack corked the wine bottle, which they had almost finished. "This is some powerful stuff." He looked at the label, trying to focus on the name, but his titillated wife took his hand and led him out of the kitchen.

They made love as if it was their first time together. Face to face, their bodies so close, each could feel the heat of their passion. No words were needed; Jack was back, and their family was complete again. They were happy.

Jack could only imagine what happened in the morning when Katie awoke. She would turn and slide over close, spooning her husband, as was their morning ritual of foreplay and sex. Only, Jack would not be there. She would slowly sit up in bed and scan the room. Her head probably ached from the poisoned wine. Panic would surely ensue shortly after her search around the house for him failed. His mind's eye switched gears. *What if Katie awoke during his abduction and they killed her and their boys?* Jack shook off that horrific thought. *That made no sense. They would want my disappearance to remain a mystery. No one will be looking for me here; not in this god-forsaken shithole.* He wondered if the authorities discovered the tainted wine that knocked them both out. He hoped they somehow figured out what had happened. Jack understood the answer, or at least the end result. Katie at first would think he disappeared as part of another secret mission. One of the many in their life together that he promised was over. She would be angry and disappointed in him for lying. She might never know that he would never leave her willingly again. She could not imagine his nightmare of waking up with his hands and feet staked securely in the blistering heat of the Yemen desert. His body infected with sun poisoning and his throat feeling as if he drank a cup of sand. He hoped that with Katie's access to Senator White and various high-ranking military leaders, she would soon learn that his disappearance was not part of any known operation. Time had no relevance to Jack. Not in this dimension, that he called Hell. Months passed as he endured intermittent but persistent torture and relentless questioning.

His cramped alcove inside a cave in an unknown location reeked horribly. The dampness left over from the frigid night air, now sizzled away as the torrid morning heat wave approached. He sat up quickly as one of his captors loomed close by the narrow entrance. Keeping his head down, Jack avoided eye contact. In the early days of his abduction, Jack resisted and showed contempt. The result lead to daily beatings. After a few weeks, he focused on what he needed to do in order for him to survive. Showing respect was the first item on the list. This he could manage even if it was not sincere. In recognition of what they perceived as the first step in breaking him, Jack's captors allowed him two meals each day. Prior to his concessions, he survived on six ounces of water and one meal consisting of what he hoped, contained boiled grains. He had lost over twenty pounds and had severe stomach distress. Familiar with only a smattering of basic Arabic phrases, Jack had to work hard to understand the unfamiliar dialect of these radical offspring of Al Qaeda. He wasn't sure of his location, but from their use of what sounded like a Yemen dialect, he assumed Yemen was his place of captivity. As he learned more of their language, they became less abusive.

About two months had passed before the questions started. Each time Jack ignored them, they thrashed him with a knotted coarse rope.

"We know you are CIA, Jack Owens! Tell us the names of your commanders."

Jack would explain that he no longer worked for the CIA.

"I am retired and no longer privy to any sensitive information."

"Who are your leaders in the CIA, and where are they planning to invade our sacred country next?"

"I am retired and no longer privy to any sensitive information."

More thrashing. Blood splattered everywhere. One of his interrogators wiped Jack's blood off his own face, and shouted in broken English, "I will drink your blood, Jack Owens; before this day is done!"

Then on cue, prayer time, one of five, saved the day, *or at least the moment*. One of Allah's soldiers placed a sajjāda prayer mat at his feet. Jack knelt on it and leaned over so his forehead almost touched the rug. He felt the itchy oozing of warm sticky fluid as blood trickled down his cheek and dripped onto the rug, staining it forever. At that moment, he had not noticed the residual stains of those who came before him.

Wayne Lasner

Chapter 1

The 6AM alarm rang loudly, as it did each weekday morning. Ritualistically, Katie Claire slowly opened her eyes, followed by a yawn and a stretch of her arms above her head. "Ooh; Ah. Good morning, Sir Oliver Jones. How's my little man this morning?" The cat gave his good morning "meow" and then proceeded to rub his cheek against Katie's face. "I love you too, little buddy. And I love you too, Lacy girl." Without so much as lifting her head, the dog grunted. "You are such a bed hog!"

After a quick set of stretches, fifty pushups and two sets each of fifty sit-ups, she headed down the hall toward the kitchen. "Ten minute warning, boys."

Jack's mysterious disappearance unnerved not only his wife, but also those closest to him. The events of the past few years had thrown Jack and Katie into a mix of high-level government and military officials, and eventually the president of the United States. No one had any idea what had happened to the invincible Jack Owens.

Around the time of her short marital separation from Jack, Katie received an offer to meet with Boston's District Attorney to discuss his need to fill the top senior

ADA position. Despite the temptation, she still had faith that her family would be reunited again. She declined the offer with no regrets. A few months later, after Jack's still unresolved mysterious disappearance, she received a call again. The position was still open, and they hoped she might reconsider. With all the past turmoil and threats against her family, she decided, in the interest of her family's safety, to accept the position. She had to be ready to start work in Boston by the beginning of September, when the courts came back in session. That gave her only six weeks to put her house up for sale, pack, find a place to live in Boston and arrange school for the boys. All of which, seemingly insurmountable tasks.

Katie tapped her foot nervously as the phone rang. She needed reassurance that this move was OK.

"Hi, Katie. How are you sweetie?"
"I'm doing alright, Rebecca. How are you and John?"
"Oh, you know. Getting older and not much wiser.
What's going on? You don't usually call so early; and during the work week."
Katie paused, before answering, which worried Rebecca.
"I need to run something by you. Do you remember the Boston offer? They called me again. It is so tempting. Financially, they made a generous offer and we really could use it. Besides, getting away from New York, a

change of pace, might make it easier for the boys. And me."

Rebecca laughed. "You silly girl. I couldn't imagine what disaster befell you. Of course, you should take it. You deserve to be happy. Jack would want you to be happy and he would think it made sense; from a safety standpoint." Katie was sure Jack would think it was a terrible idea.

"But what if…"

"You need to tell only those of us in your inner circle, and do not list your phone numbers. Keep a low profile for a little while. I know you still hold hope that Jack will show up. We all do. But sweetie…"

Rebecca stopped short of saying, *don't hold your breath.* Instead, she calmly and diplomatically said, "When he does resurface, he will find you. For god's sake, he's a spook. Besides, John and I will be right here for him and we'll know where you are. Take the job and move on with your life. John and I will come north for the weekend and help you pack; if you'll allow us to."

"I will. I did; accept the position. And, I would love to see you both. I love you, Rebecca. Tell John the news."

Katie was quietly excited and enthusiastic at her decision. She and the boys needed a change of scenery.

Rebecca simply and convincingly reinforced her decision to accept the job offer. Rebecca and John are the twins' godparents, and as much parents to her and Jack as their own were. Their son William and Jack had met when they were little boys while playing on the beach in South Carolina. They remained best friends through college. In their senior year, William's behavior changed radically, and he abruptly broke up with Katie who he had proclaimed to be "The love of his life." Around the same time, a beautiful and seductive young woman named Jane came into the picture and befriended Katie, only to betray her later. Jane was ultimately responsible for William's murder and his replacement by his "T-2", a highly trained terrorist doppelganger. This uncanny imposter was actually William's identical twin brother, Carlton. In accordance with the terrorists', carefully thought out plans, Carlton had been kidnapped at birth, with the White family believing that their son died in childbirth. William was the first *known* casualty resulting from the first wave of home grown killer terrorists transported from Yemen back to the States after almost twenty years of hostile brainwashing. Jack unraveled the mystery and he, along with Senator White and several covert operatives, including military officials, launched a crusade to destroy that plan.

Jack and Katie never really got along during her time with William. Later, both she and Jack would understand why that was. By happenstance, they met again years later and ended up falling in love. Individually, it was a slow and somewhat emotionally painful process. William would always be a part of their lives. They both had loved him, and understood that the horrible version of William was really his evil twin brother, Carlton.

Katie dealt with her own share of tragedy brought on by the crazy reign of terror surrounding Jack's war. There was even a time when Jack's case intertwined with a drug lord on trial that Katie and her New York team were prosecuting. A violent courtroom assault and the escape of the drug lord almost got Jack killed, as a high-speed chase ensued, leading to a disastrous ending.

Yes. Moving to Boston... a good decision. This, Katie was now certain of. She smiled; a rare event these days. To herself, she whispered, "Oh, Jack. Where the hell are you? We need you!" Her mind echoed what her heart felt. *I know that somehow you will find a way to come back to us.*

Lacy came running back into the room, tail wagging, and rested her head on Katie's lap. "You snuck out on me, little puppy girl. Where did you go?" Lacy panted, offering no clue.

"I love you, girl."

Chapter 2

"Of course. I'll give him the message as soon as he gets in. Yes, of course. I am so sorry he hasn't returned your messages. He has been crazy busy with his caseload." She paused a moment to let the mayor bark an earful at her. She understood his frustration at being put off by his top gun DA.

"I promise, sir. As soon as he gets in. Yes. You too."

Robin sipped her very hot, but deliciously satisfying, cappuccino. She routinely stopped and picked up one each morning on her way in for herself, and a large regular for her boss and good friend, ADA Katie Owens. Receptionist and executive secretary to the senior staff of the Manhattan District Attorney's office, Robin kept things running smoothly. Experience over the past two years taught her how to appease angry government officials. DA Johnson really had his hands full with a hospital mass shooting case that topped his other dozen or so "priority" cases. The mayor wanted a conviction, and his demeanor indicated that he didn't care who took the fall for it. The press hounded both of them relentlessly and in return, the mayor called three times a day.

Eventually, DA Johnson asked Robin to act as a buffer between them.

Robin held up the aromatic coffee as she routinely did each morning. "Good morning, ADA Owens." Katie took the beverage and lifted it to her cute little nose, inhaling slowly. "Yummy. I love you, girl. Thank you."

"You look different this morning, boss."
"Really, Robin? How so?"
"Like a load has been lifted. You seem happy."

Katie's grin gave it away.

"Oh, my god! You accepted the position!"
"I did."

Robin jumped out of her chair and hugged Katie. The coffee Katie held almost spilled with droplets beading down the side of the cup. "I'm so happy for you. I am... going to miss you so much! But, this is such a smart decision. You need the change and a new challenge." Katie and Robin chatted for a few minutes before they both returned to their desks.

Katie sat in her comfortable swivel chair and spun around slowly, taking in the view. The windows that surrounded her posh corner office exposed the most incredible panoramic view of New York City. She would miss this, and all of it. Not just the view. She and her colleagues had been through a lot the past two years; she more than any of them. Moreover, for the hardships she and her family endured, they were there, supporting her. She dreaded telling her co-senior ADA, Jason Albright, of her final decision. He had been supportive of the offer and even encouraged her to take it. She was sure he really hoped she would turn it down. Their friendship had developed early on, and after Jack's disappearance, their bond seemed to become even stronger. She and Jason shared a special intimacy and trust. He was there for her whenever her spirits were low, and there were plenty of those times. Katie was well aware that Jason wanted more from their relationship; he wanted physical intimacy. Knowing she was not ready, he avoided making her uncomfortable. She was sure that her move to Boston would be hard on him, and her, but she hoped their friendship was strong enough to survive the distance. She knew it was healthier for both of them as well. She would also need to call her friend, Michelle, with the news. Michelle Adams and Katie had a rough start. Jealousy and competition sent ripples throughout the office back then. Eventually, through a series of events, she and Michelle overcame their differences and forged a strong friendship. Last year, Michelle had accepted an offer, and is now working for the Suffolk County New York DA.

Recently engaged, she was planning a wedding for early next year. Katie was excited for her.

So many things have happened over the past few years. So many changes. This is a good move for my boys and me.

Katie closed her eyes and daydreamed of her and Jack on the sandy beach at Montauk. *He held her close as they lay on a blanket in the sand. The boys were making a sandcastle a few feet in front of them. She could feel his arms around her. She imagined his hands moving slowly over her back while applying sunscreen to her fair skin. She felt her breath leave her body as a dark shadow suddenly appeared in the sand where she now sat alone. Jack was gone.*

The ringing of the phone brought Katie out of her reverie, just in time before the onset of a panic attack. It was her new boss, Boston DA, James Mahoney calling. He wanted to check in on how she was doing, and give her a "heads-up" that he was sending a case file for her to review. He wanted Katie ready to hit the ground running as soon as she got to Boston. "We are very excited to have you joining our team here in Boston. I'll put you on with Angie Rodriguez, who has your initial itinerary. She also found you a temporary apartment until you find housing that is more permanent. We are all looking forward to your arrival; hold on for Angie." Angie sounded young; probably mid-twenties. She was very sweet. They spoke for about twenty minutes, mostly about the people in the office Katie would be working with. Angie also described the month-to-month apartment lease she arranged for Katie and her boys. "The apartment has three bedrooms and two bathrooms. There is a concierge, which is really nice, too. DA Mahoney asked if I could assist you; at least until you are settled. I told him I'd be honored. I hope you don't mind." Katie was confused. She asked, "Why would I mind? I am so appreciative of your help with arranging my move to Boston." "Honored? Why? Oh my god, Miss; I mean Mrs. Owens. We all know what you and your husband went through; and, all he did to help prevent such a horrific assault on our country. We all owe a huge debt of gratitude to both of you." There was a moment of silence to allow the awkwardness of the conversation to settle. Angie's comment took Katie off guard. Most of Jack's "Ops" were of a covert nature. He took no credit, publicly. "I'm so sorry, I shouldn't have…" "It's OK, Angie. Say or ask anything you want to, and then let's not bring it up any more. It is very difficult for me to discuss publically. Also, please address me by my first name, Katie. We can leave the formalities for meetings and courtrooms; then, ADA Owens will do just fine."

After hanging up, Katie tried holding back tears. She snatched a tissue from the box on her desk and wiped her eyes. To herself, she mumbled, "This is the right move for us. I hope this is the right thing for me and the boys." In her head she thought, *Where the hell are you, Jack?*

She decided it was now or never.

"Hey Robin, is DA Johnson in?" Robin smiled and nodded. Robin and Katie had already discussed the move over coffee earlier that morning. Robin was happy for her friend's brave decision and proud of her strength during the horrible ordeal she had to endure. "Go right in. I think he's expecting you." Katie smiled and knocked gently before entering her boss's office. They spoke for a while about personal issues and then DA Johnson cut right to the chase. "So, when is your last day?" Katie grinned, embarrassed, and said, "The end of the month, if that works and doesn't interfere with any cases you need me to clean up. I want to get settled in, and give Ryan and Kyle time to adjust to their new home before starting school." "I see. That should work out. Besides, I hear there's a high profile case they want you to head up. Nothing like getting thrown into the pond to break the ice of a new position." Her boss grinned. "You are incredible at what you do. I have no doubt you will be successful in Boston. I hate losing you, but I understand your need for a change. You will always have a place here, should you want it." He put out his arms; Katie reciprocated. They hugged for what seemed like an eternity. She wiped a tear from her eye and thought she caught Johnson doing the same, but he was quick to cover it up. "Thank you for everything, boss."

Her "partner in crime" (literally) or at least in prosecuting it, was sitting at her desk, in her chair, when Katie returned to her office.

"Jason, I was just going to call you to see if you wanted to do lunch."
"Oh, sounds good. Did you want to tell me something? Perhaps, that you're leaving New York?"

Katie was stunned at his attitude. "Well, yes. But, Jason, we discussed this. You agreed it made sense for me and the boys." He looked away from her and softly said, "Yes. But we never discussed what was good for me and you." Katie expected this conversation to be a difficult one. She walked over to him. He had stood up as she approached the desk, but did not move from behind it. Katie walked around to him, and took his hands in hers. "It has been a great run, and we have been through so much." He chimed in, "As colleagues." "No, Jason. More than

23

colleagues; as friends. But, you know how it is. I believe in my heart that Jack is alive, and will be coming home. I have to; I want to, hold on to that. Can't you understand what that means to me?" Katie put her hand to her heart. Her facial expression begged him to say he understood and accepted the situation. They now had direct eye contact. Katie kissed Jason gently on his cheek. He turned his face so their lips were only millimeters apart. Katie slowly let go of his hands and took a half step back. She tried to smile. She wiped a tear with her sleeve. "I'm sorry."

"If you need anything, Katie. Anything at all." He looked at the phone.

"I know."

Jason switched gears, hoping to lighten the mood. "I'll see you at the afternoon meeting. Don't forget the case briefs you took home last night. Raincheck on the lunch?"

Katie smiled and said, "Sure." His return smile said that *they* were OK. The reality for Jason, he was *not*, OK.

Chapter 3

Time passed slowly in the high desert. Each day, Jack would use a small sharp rock to etch a tiny line in the wall near where he slept. This was his only way to keep his sanity. Although he missed days here and there, his makeshift calendar was mostly accurate. By his account, today was day 241. Eight months of torturous living. But, he was surviving. At first, Jack tried figuring out the day of the week. Anything to keep his mind sharp. After a few weeks of sleep deprivation and pain consistently inflicted upon him, his days melded together in one great big blur. Prehistorically motivated, Jack started etching those lines in the rear wall of his cramped cubbyhole, crossing every seventh line with what he thought was a Sunday. His bed consisted of a small rug laid over a mostly smooth area of compacted sand and stone. His modest bathroom, a deep copper washbowl in the corner that they allowed him to empty once each day. Amazingly, his captors provided real toilet paper. Rough to the bottom but welcome all the same.

The daily routine never changed. He would be kicked awake or just kicked or shoved if already up and waiting for them. He would have a prayer mat placed at his feet along with a small bowl of clear water. Jack would thank them, "shukran." His guards, being creatures of habit, ignored him, and left him with his few minutes of peace. Before washing his hands, as is customary before prayer, Jack would drink half the bowl. Prayer time was also the only time he would be provided with clean water during the day. *Clean* being an exaggeration. After a week of cramps and diarrhea, the definition of *clean* improved. Following prayers, Jack would then leave his domicile, shit-pan in hand, and armed guard in tow, to make his way down the hill to a makeshift cesspool. Upon his return, he would find a tray placed alongside his *carpet bed* consisting of a small cup of sweet strong tea, and a petite wedge of bread made of sorghum.

Afterward came more time-wasting and useless chores, followed by an occasional beating and another round of prayers. The brutal sun would be directly overhead by this time, making it around high noon. Early on, Jack's face blistered from the intense Arabian sun, now his skin was just red-hot and leathery. The workday started with the pointless activity of moving heavy rocks from point "A" to point "B." In the afternoon, they made him reverse the direction. Jack was aware that his captors' methods were designed to torture him; to break him. The evil ones who took him from his home and family, they should have known better. They knew almost everything about Jack and his ability to survive. These grimy morons they dumped him on had no idea of what this CIA trained terrorist survivor could endure. They did not know that the cruel exercises they put him through made him stronger. Jack saw the daily grind as training for his mind and body. He supplemented all this with secret exercises of his own; sit-ups, pushups, and so on. On some days they had him cleaning rifles under careful watch and with no ammunition anywhere close. But Jack, being trained as a spy with acute observation skills, discovered where ammunition and other tactical explosives were hidden. Often, while laboring through his senseless duties, Jack would observe one particular sandy area among the rocky terrain that always had a guard stationed near it. *Guard* seemed like an undeserved term for one who slept with his eyes open and mind closed. Every so often, Jack would wander closer to the *guarded* area. Often, it would be one of the other sand devils to yell at him. Ib'd! Ib'd! He figured out it meant, "Get away! Get away *from there you American Pig!* Occasionally the lame-ass guard abruptly awakened from his half-asleep stupor. In an attempt to impress his superior, he would run up to Jack and kick him while yelling some curse words at him. Jack kept his cool; always. *The time will come for payback*.

As the sun slowly dipped below the higher peaks of the rocky hills, prayer time approached along with the evening provision of his bowl of slop and four ounces of tea. His mind working hard on a plan to escape, and his body worn from the heat and chores of the day, Jack closed his eyes for a moment of rest.

She walked into the bar, he couldn't remember if it was before or after they were married. His ability to organize events in time diminished daily. He clearly visualized her removing her long overcoat to expose her sexy, above the knee, pleated pencil dress. Her silky, blouse, opened to the third button. Her hair had been pulled to one side over her left shoulder. Everyone in the bar took notice as Katie Claire, glowing brighter than any celestial body in the galaxy, made her way to meet him. *Oh how he longed to kiss her neck and hold her tight in his arms.*

Chapter 4

Everyone attending the event seemed to be having a blast. They were all drunk, due to a long evening of partying. Young men, he surmised most in their early thirties, danced sloppily with their half-buttoned, half-open white shirts. Some held a bottle of beer in one hand while strategically planting the other on their dance partner's bottom. Sweat dripped off the foreheads of others as they maneuvered between the dance floor and the bar. One guy in particular caught the killer's attention with his two fisted drinks splashing as he moved across the crowded dance floor. He was obviously on a quest to find his female partner. Although, he seemed hell bent on flirting with every other female as he made his way through the tumultuous crowd.

The one who did not belong looked on, wondering what it would be like to be happy and carefree like these inebriated imbeciles. His inability to comprehend any of this drove his frustration levels to an all-time high. He needed to be in control, to set the stage of perception. He had to show them he was the director; the puppet master.

He thought to himself, "*There's the bride. She is quite the looker. Ooh, and the dress, very revealing. She wears it well. She obviously wants to attract more than just the attention of her new husband. In her drunken stupor, she is probably fantasizing about being ravished by the entire entourage of groomsmen.*" He watched as she dirty-danced with the groom. He fantasized that it was *he* who whispered dirty things in her ear. He imagined all the sensual things he would do to her. Her aggressively slutty responses to her dance partner's moves seemed so obvious by the variety of teasing touches on her man's body. But her face, the sultriness of it, added much more to the story. His twisted mind began conjuring up a plan for her abduction.

It won't be long now.

The stalker had a plan, he always did. As expected, ten minutes later the bride took hold of her new husband's hand and pulled him in the direction of the exit.

She's a sassy little bitch.

Chapter 5

The after hour party was still in full swing when newlyweds Ed and Tina Santiago quietly snuck away. Her silly giggles echoed in the hotel hallway as they arrived at their honeymoon suite. The six foot two inch groom easily swept his gorgeous bride up into his arms as he pushed the suite's door open with his foot.

"Wow, Mr. Santiago. I'm speechless." Ed looked at his new bride with a grin that said it all. She smiled, then burst out laughing as she said, "No, really. You have outdone yourself, mister." Red and pink rose petals were scattered all around the room and trailed their way to the master bedroom, where they culminated on a luxurious canopy covered, round bed. Champagne already in a bucket of ice, two long stem glasses sat ready and waiting.

As he gently lay Tina on the bed, the over-anxious groom methodically slid his hands downward, along her sides, stopping at her waist. She asked shyly, "Why are you staring at me like that?" "Because, you're so beautiful. Lying there like that, you are angelic." Tina turned her head so her cheek met the soft bedspread. She gently inhaled with her eyes closed; the scent of the rose petals was euphoric. With her eyes still closed, she told her new husband, "I suppose we should consummate this marriage. Take me Mr. Santiago. Take me now!" She stretched her arms over her head and looked up at her new husband. Her moist and inviting ruby red lips glistened. Ed continued his motion downward as he began inching her dress up until he again held her hips. But now, with only sexy under garments between his lips and her silky smooth flesh. Tina moaned at his every touch. He stopped once again, quickly removing his tie. She giggled, "Now, we're making progress. Are you going to strip for me?" "Not exactly, my love. Not now, anyway." She squealed with anticipation. "I love when you play dangerous and dirty games with me. Ed covered his bride's eyes with his tie, tying the makeshift blindfold without catching any of her soft hair. He then continued his methodical pleasuring of her body.

At first they tried to ignore the loud knocking on the suite's door, but after three times, Ed told his lady-in-waiting, "Don't move. I want you exactly where you are. You cannot deprive me of this moment of slow, maddening seduction." "Maddening; is that what this is?" Tina grinned. Ed commanded in a very serious tone, "Don't remove the tie, either."

"Room service!"

The muffled voice from the other side of the door repeated, "Room service!" Ed yelled through the door, "We didn't order anything! There's a 'Do not disturb' sign! Can't you read?"

"I'm so sorry, sir. There is no sign. It must have fallen off. I'll be sure to replace it for you. The hotel sent you a complimentary late night supper, and what appears to be very expensive champagne. It would be a shame to waste it, but I'll send it back to the kitchen. Again, my apologies, sir, for disturbing you."

"No. Wait." Ed did not want the poor guy to get into any trouble. From the other room, Tina called out. "Come on. I can't wait any longer." "One minute, babe. I'll be right there."

"Thank you, sir. And again, so sorry. Please sign here." Ed signed the proffered receipt and added a generous tip. Tina, impatient and eager to get on with the nuptials, slid out of her party dress, which was a much shorter and lighter version of her wedding gown. She resumed her position, lying on her back on the bed, blindfolded with her hands above her head, and her thighs spread, just as her husband had left her. She wanted him to continue where he left off. Her body ached for him. Tina was about to call out when she heard his footsteps. "I almost took things into my own hands. You had better take good care of me, mister. That is, if you still want to be married in the morning." She expected Ed to comment about her expedited removal of her dress, but he said nothing. His breathing was audibly heavy; his excitement aroused her even more.

At first, his hands seemed cold but as he moved them over her body, things heated up. Something seemed odd though; his movements, his touch was different. She considered that the blindfold allowed her mind to play tricks on her. He undid her stocking clips and his fingers found their way to all the right places. Her body arched and quivered. His strong hands, unrecognizably strong, now gripped her hips. The hold on her body felt like a vice clamping down on her. Without warning, he lifted her and flipped her onto her stomach. He had never been so aggressive. She was startled, yet incredibly turned on. He said nothing. Made not a sound, except for the heavy breathing. She remained anxiously silent, awaiting his next highly anticipated move. Again, his strong grip took hold of her hips and pulled her bottom upward as he swiftly entered her from behind. The assault lasted nearly twenty minutes. Tina felt at times as if she would black out. She was sure she had pleaded more than once for him to ease up, or stop altogether. She could not be sure.

When he was through, he abruptly let go of her, and she fell face down onto the bed. Her mind was racing. What had come over him? They had been together for three years, living together for the last one. Ed had never behaved so aggressively. "Ed? Are you OK, babe? What came over you?" She tried to turn over to face him. Her body was so numb and fatigued that she couldn't even move her arms to undo her blindfold.

POP–Fizz

Her mouth was so dry and the crisp pop of the champagne cork made her put aside what she just went through. She tried again, and this time, successfully turned over onto her back. His hands were immediately on her again, his mouth on her breast, his tongue working her most sensitive body part, aggressively. She moaned as she frantically removed her blindfold. The light from the overhead chandelier blinded her for a few seconds. For a split second, her mind questioning Ed's kinky behavior, including why any lights would be on during their lovemaking. As her vision cleared, a shock wave ran through her entire body. She froze as if rigor mortis had set in. Tina screamed, but no sound came out of her mouth.

Chapter 6

Between hiring a broker for the Dix Hills home, arranging mail forwarding, schools for the boys and transfer of knowledge to her NY team, six weeks came and went quickly. Katie Claire Owens made sure the two other Assistant DAs that worked with her picked up the caseload. She also met with Jason to bring him up to speed on all the important details. She had concerns, more like guilt, for burdening him with so much. Jason assured her he could handle it, reminding her it was just him only a year ago when she and the other ADAs reported to him. He wished her all the best; both promised to keep in touch.

"We have been through quite lot, Jason. You have been an awesome friend and mentor. Thank you, for everything."

Jason had a lot to say to his associate, none of which he could actually verbalize. His heart pounded, but he held back. *Restraint... Not the time to tell her how you feel.*

"I'll see you when I see you."

He extended his arms, and Katie accepted his genuine embrace of friendship.

Excited for the 4th of July holiday, the boys insisted on seeing the fireworks show in person. Katie, through one of Senator White's contacts, got tickets for the waterfront viewing in Long Island City. They had a spectacular time watching as the barges floating on the East River launched computer synchronized colorful explosions into the night sky. Katie held her boys close. She wondered if Jack knew what day it was, and if he was looking up at the sky at that moment. If he saw fireworks, they would be of a different nature and certainly not for a celebration of American independence. Katie kissed each of her boy's heads and smiled. "Are you guys ready? We have a big day tomorrow."

Early in the morning on July 5th, with her car packed to the brim, Katie Claire Owens and her twins began their epic journey. Goodbye, New York. Hello, Boston. The Owens trio plus two were northeast bound for a new city, a new school, and for the beautiful, superstar lawyer, a new job.

"Mommy? How will daddy find us?"
"Stupid Ryan. Daddy can find anyone. He always knows where we are. Right, mommy?"

The dog yawned and licked Kyle's face. "Yuck! No! Lacy." Ryan laughed. Katie wondered if the dog really intended to help change the subject. Ryan's question turned Katie's stomach to all knots.

"Phew! Ryan farted!"
"No, I didn't! It was Lacy."

The boys both laughed and so did their mom. Sir Oliver Jones stretched out beneath the back window, uninterested in any of Lacy's or the boys' antics.

Upon arriving in Boston, the Owens family, minus one, settled into their temporary apartment overlooking the city. They would call this home for at least the next few months. Pleasantly surprised, it was nicer than Katie had imagined. The apartment had three bedrooms and two full baths. Two were comfortably sized rooms. A master suite with private bath for Katie, and the other for the boys to share. The third and much smaller bedroom, she considered for use as her home office. Katie was thankful for the two bathrooms. Thankfully, the building allowed pets, which caused a big concern during the apartment search. So many property owners refused to allow pets; especially dogs. Katie figured she would need at least an extra thirty minutes in the morning for Lacy's walk. She already missed her beautiful Long Island home with its huge backyard and beautiful in-ground swimming pool. She would look into hiring a dog walker for Lacy's afternoon needs.

Excited to start day camp at the local tennis and swim club, Kyle and Ryan seemed to adjust fairly well to the move. With the two of them settled, Katie Claire Owens could focus as she readied herself to walk into her new office. Being unfamiliar with most of the legal staff, Katie took a deep breath. *You got this, girl.*

The building at One Bulfinch Place, even with its modernization, had that special New England charm. Katie would be joining forces with 140 other lawyers and another 100 or so administrative personnel. She, as a senior ADA, would have a large staff working alongside her. Aside from prosecuting cases, one of her departments handled assisting victims or providing protection for witnesses of crimes that her office prosecuted.

After a moment's pause, Katie entered the office suite. It seemed larger and more intimidating than during her earlier visit for the *big* tour during her second interview. She smiled as she approached the receptionist. "Good morning, I am…" The young lady interrupted Katie. "Senior ADA Owens. I remember you from your visit last month. Besides, you're pretty much famous in this office." Katie was certain she blushed from embarrassment. *Jeez, I guess my personal business bears no privacy.* The receptionist continued. "I'm sorry; it's just that you're my hero. Your New York reputation precedes you. Please sign in here, just for today. Once payroll and HR processes your first paycheck, this won't be necessary when you enter the office. You understand it's our protocol; there's a lot of them. By the way, I'm Jan. Please let me know if you need anything. She smiled and pointed across the room, Down the hall and through the doors is an extended suite. That is where your office is. Angie Rodriguez will help get you settled in." Katie thanked Jan, and with attaché in hand, marched forward, ready to start her new adventure.

As if she had radar perception, and just like her New York friend and assistant Robin, Angie was standing and waiting for her as she entered the suite. She had met Angie as well, on her last visit, and spoke with her several times during the planning of her move and the apartment search. Katie found her to be very sweet but felt assured she was no pushover. Angie would be efficient and dependable.

"Well, good morning ADA Owens. I trust you had a most excellent transition to our lovely city." Her smile was sincere. Angie seemed to be the type of person that kept everyone's spirits up during the toughest of days. Katie said, "The trip up was fine. The boys are in camp and the animals have what they need, for now. I will have to find a dog walker for the afternoons." Angie never stopped moving, Katie wondered if she took "uppers." "I can help with that. Give me an hour and I'll set up several interviews for you here in the office. You can do the callbacks and hiring at your home, so they can meet the animals. Does that work for you?" Katie chuckled. "You are the best, Angie. Thank you. And, please call me Katie." Angie smiled. "Of course, I forgot. Thank you, Katie."

Katie and her assistant Angie discussed a few of the more important things needed to help get Katie transitioned into the daily grind, while Katie explored her new office. It wasn't quite the corner office looking out over central park, but it was nice enough. Her desk was a good size, and solid mahogany; there were an abundance of drawers; Katie smiled. *How cool is this desk?* The conference table had six chairs positioned around it. She thought that was awesome for quick departmental meetings. Or, a good place to pile up case files. Katie sat back in her new black leather executive swivel chair and took a deep breath. "So, here we are. Now what?" Angie laughed, "You asked... Get ready to dig in first thing tomorrow. DA Mahoney assigned six case files to you.

Don't get too comfortable with them because more will follow in the coming days. As for these bad boys, five are easy, that you or one of your team can handle. Each is probably no more than a day in court. One, this one, is a major case that DA Mahoney wanted you to take the lead on." Angie handed two packed manila file folders to Katie. Katie flipped through the top few pages from inside the folder marked Case 0010387.1. She looked at the other folder that was marked 0010387.2 and said, "DA Mahoney sent me a summary profile of this case before I left New York. It certainly looks interesting." Katie paused as she placed the folders on the corner of her desk. "This looks like a huge case for only two folders." Angie made a serious face and shook her head. "Are you kidding?" She stepped outside Katie's office and disappeared. Katie leaned back against her desk and waited for two minutes. Her heart began to beat faster as she recognized the sound of squeaking wheels that guaranteed one thing; a forest full of documents. Angie rolled the file cart in with what looked to be about sixteen folders. "Here ya go. The boss didn't want to over burden you *before* the first day." She smiled. "Sorry, Katie; but you know how it works." Katie grinned and shrugged her shoulders, mumbling to herself, "And so it begins." "And so it does. I arranged a meeting with your staff at 10AM tomorrow. They can update you on where they are so far, and what leads the FBI and local authorities have."

"Thank you, Angie."
"You're welcome, Katie. Please let me know if you need anything."

An hour later, Angie announced the first pet sitter interviewee had arrived. Ninety minutes later, number 3 won the prize. She was a forty-year-old woman with two kids away in college. She loved animals, and dog walking allowed her to interact with lots of them. She had impeccable references, one from the mayor of Boston who was still currently using her. With that settled, Katie checked her watch. It was just shy of 5PM.

"Good night, Angie; and thank you so much for all your help. Got to get my kids." Angie asked, "Do you need help with that?" Katie laughed and told her "No thanks, I got this one." With a big smile and a giggle, she added, "New York, Boston, no difference when it comes to taking work home."

"Good night, ADA Owens."

"Good night, Angie."

Chapter 7

Jack carefully snuck a peek outside his less than spacious "hole in the wall". One of the leaders argued with another and pointed in several directions. The dialogue between them often too fast and angry for Jack to decipher any worthy details. He did notice that the other leader sporadically pointed in his direction, apparently cursing. Jack was certain that their almighty Allah forbade derogatory language. But then again, the same would logically apply to rape, murder and blasphemy. So much for the rules of faith.

For months, they had tried various forms of torture. Jack held strong. They could not break him, which made them furious. He could not understand why they hadn't killed him yet. Even the methods of torture they employed were relatively endurable. He would have done a much better job if the roles had been reversed. The finger pointing unnerved him. It appeared that trouble was brewing somewhere, and they were planning to clear out, cutting any unnecessary baggage. That likely meant Jack's time could be running out. *Be careful, Jack*. His subconscious alert came too late. The power behind the impact of the rifle's butt as it made contact with Jack's face sent him flying backward into his stinky little cave.

Still conscious, he wished he had been knocked out. A tremendous amount of pain coursed throughout Jack's head. Against his better judgment to remain lying down, Jack attempted to sit himself upright. "Aleaql eamluka, alkafr!" As the guard yelled at Jack to "mind his business", he raised his firearm to a ready state, his finger firmly planted on the trigger. Jack prepared himself by staring boldly, showing no fear, or pain. The guard then said, "Nayafruminida, waqatak sayati qaribaan bma fyh alkafayat." Rough translation… "You'll be dead soon enough." He lowered his rifle, spat onto the rocky floor of Jack's dungeon and left. Jack sat back against the damp wall while applying pressure to the side of his head. Sticky warm moisture coated his hand. Blood had started to ooze out of the wounds. The side of his face had also swollen to almost twice its normal size. He would have given anything for two, or ten aspirin.

Just seconds before being blindsided, Jack also heard them say, "Hasalat alkhanazir jiman ma yastahiquwnah." He picked up enough in translation and figured some terror attack in Germany had gone badly. Based on all the crazy commotion in the camp, it appeared that their plans might have been compromised. He thought, the German security forces or police must have caught at least some of the terrorists. Probably low-level sympathizers trying to get into the big time terror game. Those types are the first to break and tell all.

Time and space all but blended together these days. Jack constantly practiced mind-strengthening exercises that he learned years ago while in training. He tried thinking back in time to his days in college. Only a few months into his first year at Atlanta's prestigious Emory University, Jack was approached, and soon after, inducted into the United States government CIA training program. His training involved interrogation techniques. Some, actually most of them, involving some form of torture or duress. He and his fellow trainees had to endure limited examples of what they practiced, in order to understand what their subject was going through, both physically and mentally. Those painstaking years of hard work, is what had kept Jack alive all these months. The other very important lesson learned back then, was how to keep secrets. Jack essentially lived two different lives. In the beginning, he found it difficult not to tell his friends, especially his closest friend, William. As time passed and he learned how to lie professionally, it got easier.

When it came to romance during his college years, Jack's reputation had him pegged as a player. Still, women came and went all the time. Jack's friends stopped trying to keep count. His cool, "holier than thou," persona didn't fool his best friend. William often made remarks to him that he would eventually find the perfect woman, as William did when he met Katie. Then, shortly before graduation, something in William changed. His seduction by Katie's new friend, Jane, transformed him into a cold-hearted person. Or, so they all thought. Actually, Jane's terrorist associates kidnapped and killed William. His twin brother, Carlton, stepped in as him. The "new" William had hurt Katie emotionally, and alienated the rest of his friends; including Jack.

Carlton White, first born by one minute, son of Rebecca and Senator John White, was declared stillborn at birth and taken away by the doctors. He, along with hundreds of others, were secretly raised and brainwashed as killer assassins in a mock-up of an American city, hidden deep in the Yemen desert. Twenty years later, Jane would play the seductress who stole William from Katie. She would watch over the fake William to ensure he followed their leader's plan. Eventually, Carlton, posing as William, would gain strong governmental clout as he moved up through the political ranks.

Carlton would be the first of many successful terrorist imposters to infiltrate United States government and military institutions.

Carlton's leaders often referred to him as "T2," a code name for Carlton as twin number two, who now permanently replaced William who was "T1." "T2" had travelled to Washington DC to assist in lobbying a bill. He and Jack happened to run into each other at a restaurant. The encounter left Jack unnerved. Even though he and his longtime friend were estranged, he sensed something was just not quite right with his old pal. That was the start of it all, thrusting Jack Owens from a CIA desk jockey into an elite field operative.

Jack, still aching from the guard's earlier assault on him, let his mind wander back in time. He and William had just met at the beach in South Carolina. They were both barely five years old. The two boys became fast friends and "best buddies." Their parents also became friends and managed to keep in touch even though they lived in different states. The boys eventually agreed on attending the same college and became roommates. They had each other's backs until the evil seductress, Jane, came into the picture.

Jane's powerful personality and drop-dead beauty captivated anyone she came in contact with. She was cold and calculating and without a soul. She could seduce anyone into her evil web. Ironically, years later, Jane would become Jack's ally and help him bring down those who controlled her and commanded her loyalty.

Years later, a chance meeting in New York City brought Jack and Katie Claire Evans together again. Jack had just run into William, and he wanted to speak to Katie about it. She wanted nothing to do with that discussion or with Jack. Jack's persistence eventually won her over, and she agreed to meet with him.

Love is truly a mysterious concept. The moment Jack laid eyes on Katie in New York, he knew he had missed her; missed their friendship. Only, it was different this time. His heart spoke to him in silent words. He had fallen in love with his ex- best friend's ex-girlfriend. It would take some time and several future meetings before the feelings became mutual.

Oh, Katie. How I miss your warm and tender touch. Kiss my beautiful boys good night, and remind them how much I love them.

Chapter 8

Much like in the United States, additional security for public events had been increased all over Europe. With terror attacks on the rise, many sport and concert venues experienced a drop in attendance. This of course, was exactly the outcome planned by the terror groups. The killing of infidels took on a lesser concern to them. It was a benefit of the exercise, to negatively impact the economic well-being of the Western European nations. Of course, sending a message that these attacks are the consequences of being allies with the most contentious of Westerners, the United States of America, was the ultimate goal.

Alim turned off the television and called out to his brother. "Alyas, I am late for my evening class. Don't forget to clear your dirty dishes. I am tired of cleaning up after your messes." The elder brother folded his prayer blanket and gently placed it in the corner on a special stand that stood about six inches off the floor. He looked around the small residential flat, dismayed at the clutter. Alim shook it off thinking to himself, *it didn't matter, anyway. They had no friends and no family that would ever visit*. He opened the apartment door ignoring the annoying creak of the old hinges. From the other room he heard his brother say, "OK, Alim. Tosbeho 'ala khair." Alim shouted, "Yes, goodbye. And I told you, speak English; or German!"

Alyas carefully inserted the copper pin that he had just securely fastened to the red wire into the charge; a small tube of gunpowder. This was the last step, according to the numbered diagram he downloaded from the Internet. He checked the cell phone and made sure the green wire coming from the other side of it was not connected or touching anything. Following his leader's verbal instructions, he placed a good amount of electrical tape on the tip to prevent any chance of it accidentally grounding itself out. Alyas re-read the instructions highlighted in bold italics, "The phone should be turned on only before placing the device in its final destination." The green wire could be safely attached to the ground connection on the device as soon as the phone went into sleep mode. The plan for Alyas, or "The Brave One" as his dad always called him, was to place the device in a crowded area. His contact instructed him to get far enough away to avoid getting hurt. The plan was set in stone per instructions received anonymously via a secure email message. Alyas would wait for the end of the concert. Then, as the crowds began to exit, he would make a call to the cell phone. If all worked as planned, the phone would wake-up, completing the grounded connection and igniting the charge. In the center of the six by twelve inch pine box, two pounds of C4 explosives would detonate. Thousands of tiny shards of shrapnel that completely enveloped the explosive material would pepper the unsuspecting crowd, causing mass casualties, panic, and mayhem.

The "Brave One" took a good look around his home of almost two years. He could not be sure if he would be back. "Goodbye, my brother. "nergo an ykon sallam alla makm."

****

As the concertgoers made their exodus from the Frankfurt stadium, Alyas did his best to control his breathing. There were herds of security and police. They seemed to be everywhere. He hoped it was only paranoia making him sweat so profusely, and that the authorities were not actually watching him. The possibility of incarceration had never crossed his mind until this moment. The "Brave One" feared nothing; except being locked away in a western prison; any prison. *I could not bear it.*

The plaza now had masses of young people heading for trains and other modes of public transportation. Alyas surveyed the landscape until he spotted the section of flower boxes that forced people to pass left or right, controlling the flow of the crowd as they made their way toward the exit. At that point, people would split off between the public parking field and the fenced in area that lead to the various transportation terminals. He placed the device just inside and along the wall of the floral divider. People scrambled to make their trains. He hoped no one would notice his actions. After placing the box and waiting for the phone to go dark, Alyas took a deep breath and connected the green wire to the ground source. He exhaled as he replaced the cover and quickly walked away.

Once he safely distanced himself from the explosive device, he found a safe place to observe his work. Alyas could not see the floral planter where his killing machine lay in waiting. He did however, have a clear view of the plaza filled with people. He reached into his jacket pocket and pulled out the "burner" cell phone. For about one minute, he waited. He took one last look around. The crowd of young people seemed to be growing rapidly. Alyas surmised that the concert must be close to ending and people were heading out of the stadium. With trembling hands, he uttered to himself, "Lak ya allah." *For you, Allah*.

About five hundred miles distant, at about the same time in Manchester, England, sirens screamed as heavily armed police and military troops stormed the concert venue where an American pop artist had just finished her last set. Dozens of security officers rushed people out of the arena, directing them to another fenced in area where police yelled instructions to sit down with their hands clasped together and placed over their heads. They were told to wait for the "All Clear." The loud music inside shielded the concertgoers from the commotion outside. Most were spared the bloody outcome resulting from a terrorist detonated explosive device placed near the exit. Nineteen people sustained injuries, three of them died before reaching the hospital. An alert rang throughout all major European governmental security agencies as well as the United States and Canada.

"Entschuldigen Sie, haben Sie ein Licht"? The nicely dressed man dangled an unlit cigarette between his lips. Alyas shook his head, "Nein." He realized, too late, that his mission had been compromised. The pain in the back of his head was fierce. He was hit with the butt of a police rifle so hard that his legs immediately gave out. As he fell, the man who initially approached him grabbed the cell phone and immediatey popped open the back and removed the battery. The plainclothes agent placed the phone into a specially lined evidence bag, and handed it to one of the uniformed police officers.

Men in suits whisked Alyas away, shoving him into the back of a black SUV, heading to an undisclosed location. Unknowingly, he had been on a "Watch List" for two years. German agents maintained surveillance on him and several others that had traveled to Yemen and other known terrorist homelands. From afar, others who had been anxious for a successful jihad looked on as all this played out. They quickly sent word to their leaders. Alyas' elder brother, Alim, was tracked down and arrested by German authorities. After a thorough interrogation and the surrender of his passport, he was eventually released.

By the time Alyas's elder brother arrived home, it had already been ransacked by police and security agents. Alim put his hands to his head and shouted, "Allah, what has he done?"

Chapter 9

Word spread throughout the various factions across the Yemen desert. The new president of the United States began the first deployment of an extra 4,000 troops. He made good on his promise to assist in training and advising the Afghan forces. The recent wave of terror attacks hitting Europe, along with several failed attempts here in America, prompted the president's swift decision for deployment.

Unlike the rough and rocky terrain of Afghanistan, the mountains of sand were scattered with Taliban camps. This Al-Qaeda controlled area of the Arabian Peninsula known as Hadhramaut, had sympathetic tribes spread across its vast desert terrain. It was harder to invade them. With political lines changing at a moment's notice, America's allies could never be certain who was a friend and who was not. Jack, in his confined quarters and limited outside exposure, had no idea how close he was to an actual city. His captors, followers of whoever paid the highest bounty, divided their loyalties between the Isis factions and the Al-Qaeda troops dispersed among the city and its outer regions. Hadhramaut was home to Alyas while going through his induction into the terrorist group. He trained for several weeks while studying at the

University. The young man was very bright and boasted publicly at home, in Germany, and pretty much everywhere, of his loyalty to Allah. To those observing his travel back and forth between Europe and Yemen, he seemed to be the average young radical college student who wanted to study at the core of his roots.

As joint interrogators from both German intelligence and American CIA began laying out their specialized tools for the interrogation, the young terrorist began to sweat. The slow and methodical placement of tools, obviously chosen specifically for bringing unbearable pain, kept Alyas' attention sharply focused on his interrogators. Behind him, the drum-like pinging of water hitting the inside of the large tin decanter as it was filled, sent chills throughout his body. He had heard of the cruel American methods used to obtain information. The leaders spoke of these American scare tactics. "The Americans are weak and non-committed to their beliefs. They will threaten you, even start to practice some form of torture on you. But, they will stop before actually harming you. Be strong and you shall prevail." The investigators asked several more times, but Alyas said nothing. Without warning, one of the men guarding the door grabbed his forehead and held it down using a leather belt. His arms and legs were already in restraints.

The other guard threw a damp smelly towel over his face. *"Remember, The Americans are weak and non-committed to their beliefs. They will threaten you, even start to practice some form of torture on you. But, they will stop before actually harming you. Be strong and you shall prevail."* The leader's words echoed in his head as they poured water over the towel cutting off his air supply. He could not inhale. His lungs felt as if they would burst. His body began to shake violently. *Allah, they are mistaken. The Americans may appear weak but they are not! Please, Allah, make them stop.* The American torturers swiftly removed the saturated towel. Alyas' vision took a moment to clear and his lungs burned as he drew the first somewhat, waterless breath. He whispered to himself, "Thank you, Allah." The interrogator held up the towel. "Allah cannot stop this. Only you can, by telling us what we need to know." The pinging of the water quieted down, clearly indicating the bucket was full and ready for round two. All went dark as the soaked towel again covered his face. His interrogator poured water slowly over the towel suggesting, "Why not make this easier on yourself? Tell us what we want to know. Alyas' lungs began to fill with water; he was drowning. His body began to convulse as the water displaced the last bit of oxygen in his lungs. He knew he would not survive another round of forced drowning. "OK, ok." Water gurgled and splashed out of his mouth as he spoke. "I'll tell you whatever you want to know." He spilled all he knew about locations and plans for varied attacks. During Alyas' training, they warned him of western torture tactics. They even practiced gentle waterboarding on the trainees to help alleviate the fear of it. The failed attempt to convince at least this one trainee of how easy survival would be, left him terrified.

In German, the lead investigator smiled as he said, "Well, my friend, you have chosen wisely. Why put yourself through all that pain only to end up in prison for the rest of your life anyway?"

Behind the one-way mirror, others listened intently to the interrogation. As details flowed from the mouth of the insidious fanatic, they began scrambling to alert the various military and law enforcement agencies of the potential terror threats planned against public venues.

As the story unfolded in the interrogation room, outside at the east entrance of the small military base, a commotion ensued. A small Toyota SUV deliberately crashed through the security gate. The vehicle had looked innocent enough as it approached the security gate. Without warning, the car accelerated quickly; two men in the back seat leaned out of the car's windows and open fired using Russian made AK-47 automatic weapons. One guard suffered a wound in the shoulder before a member of a backup security team open fired using a German made M320 grenade launcher. The 40mm shell vaporized the Toyota, instantly killing the three terrorists inside. The attempt to silence Alyas was thwarted with minimal allied casualties.

Jack sat back against the jagged wall of his cubbyhole and closed his eyes. His mind raced with new ideas for survival. His head ached from the tedious plotting for a strategic escape. He no longer felt the pangs of loneliness. He was numb to the discomfort of the sharp and uneven rock wall he leaned against as he closed his eyes. Jack allowed himself a rare, thoughtless moment of peace. His mind shut down so tight he did not hear the augmented commotion just outside of his *hole in the wall*.

The early arguing among his captors now turned to panic. Jack cautiously peered outside to see the chaos. His eyes hurt while they adjusted from the dim lighting in his cave to the bright sun reflecting off the sandy area in front of him. A loud pop followed by an even brighter flash caused an involuntary reflex in Jack's body, thrusting him backwards. His head hit something hard. As he tried to regain control of his senses and stand on his feet, another blast exploded just outside his cave. Rapidly followed by another on the other side of the camp, and then several more. Then, silence. Jack could not tell if the deafness was from the extreme compression caused by the exploding missiles or if perhaps everyone was dead. With great effort and just the right amount of fear, Jack cautiously made his way back to the small opening and looked around the camp. In an animated, slow-motion effect, things seemed to return to normal, along with his hearing. Rebel troops had seemingly overrun the camp. Most of the bastards who had previously starved and tortured him appeared to be dead. Those who survived had their hands and feet bound. The unknown aggressors dragged his bastard captors by their feet, throwing them into a ditch that had likely opened up after one of the missile strikes.

Click–Click

Jack knew that sound all too well. He froze and slowly put his hands over his head. As he said, "American! 'ana 'usir alharb al'amrikia. I am an American Journalist. Please, help me."

A third rebel, Jack assumed was a leader, approached.

"Rayiys alqarfi, al'amrikia!" The leader, dressed in fancier but certainly not cleaner attire, spat at Jack's feet. Jack assumed whatever verbal crap came out of his mouth was not "Praise Allah, we're here to save our American friend."

Chapter 10

The intense workload, at first seemed comparable to what she dealt with in New York, but now appeared more like *overload*. Katie had a team of junior ADA subordinates to work the seventeen cases that her new boss had unceremoniously *dumped* on her desk. For the most part, many were minor cases. Any one of her underlings could easily review the case and settle or go to trial within a few days. One of the cases involved a situation where a sixteen-year-old teenager jumped to his death after months of "cyber" bullying. Katie hated how computers, cell phones, and social media had become a vehicle for all kinds of cruel acts. Especially when a pack of young peers single out and attack one individual, or even a group. Justice needed a stern hand. She would handle this one on her own.

"Oh, lord. Here it is." Katie spoke as if there were someone else in the room. She picked up the thick file folder labeled "CASE # 904567 (2 of 9)". She scrambled to find the other seven folders. One of nine was still in her attaché case. Katie glanced over to the far side of her office to the beautiful red roses centered on her small conference table. It made her think of those tough times she experienced last year. She had people there, back in

New York, to rely on; *friends* she could vent to in a moment of need. There was no one on that level with her here in Boston. Not yet, anyway.

During the scheduled early morning meeting, DA Mahoney re-introduced Katie to the managing group. He went over, in detail, each active case and asked the responsible senior ADA to present a summarized status. Katie was up last. She was the "new kid on the block," but certainly not the least experienced. She figured he had saved *the best* for last. Katie addressed the group, making a point to mention her limited access to the complete set of case files. "I did, however, have the opportunity to review the summary overview for case 904567, the Santiago murder. From what I read, we have a good deal of detailed information regarding the crime scene; but, none of which, leads us to any possible suspects. I will need to dig in deeper before making any further conclusions." She paused for a second, taking in a slow breath. "Apparently, the investigation thus far, has not found much in the way of witnesses, or collected any substantial evidence. At least not from what I have read so far. I will arrange to meet with the investigative team as soon as possible to get the latest on their progress. I'll follow up again with them after I have thoroughly reviewed the entire case file." She thanked everyone and took her seat.

"ADA Owens, when you get back to your office you should find your cases piled high, and waiting." Katie expected her new boss to flash a grin but there was none. Apparently, he was quite serious. He continued, "In light of your vast experience with violent cases," he paused, knowing she would need a moment to digest his intentional reference. DA Johnson's lack of empathy for her past personal situation was disappointing. He continued, "The Santiago murder is turning out to be one of the hottest cases of the decade." Again, he glanced in Katie's direction, "At least in New England. We are holding a suspect, Edwin Santiago, in the county jail. We managed to have bail denied at pretrial. The evidence we have so far to prove premeditation is weak at best. His lawyers are sure to have the "no bail" order overturned within the next 48 hours." Katie shyly raised her hand. DA Mahoney acknowledged her with a nod. She remarked, "At first thought, and without having the opportunity to review the entire case history, I'd suspect this to be a crime of passion. However, once I read the notes taken of the interviews with family and friends, and the resulting profile regarding the couple's carnal escapades as the couple's normal demeanor, I see no indication of unorthodox sexual behavior, or any tendency for violence. None of which appear to be part of this couple's relationship. Kinky foreplay is one thing, but a total and complete personality change on their wedding night seems to be way out of character. The husband was found unconscious by a housekeeping maid who immediately called her supervisor. The poor thing then ventured into the bedroom to find Tina Santiago laying in a pool of blood. The supervisor and security found their employee trembling just outside the bedroom door. The husband's blood alcohol level was fairly high, but not enough to knock him out for hours." Katie paused before continuing. "I don't see anything in the Medical Examiners report comparing the wife's assault and time of death to the husbands' time unconscious. Aside from his alcohol levels, there is no toxicity analysis listed. I'll need to follow up on all of this with the medical examiner. Non-the-less, I would say we are probably holding the wrong guy, and the killer is still out there." The new boss neither smiled nor frowned at her short and obvious response. "Let's not lose sight of the goals of this office, ADA Owens. We are here to prosecute and convict. Leave the prospect of his innocence for the defense team. We have, what appears to be, a crime of passion. The husband cannot even swear he didn't do it. He claims to have little memory of the events. All he can provide is a sketchy, unsubstantiated story about room service he never ordered. This should be an easy conviction." He looked around the room and then at his new ADA. Katie felt as if he disregarded every word that came out of her mouth. "This is an extremely high profile case. The media will over-publicize their newscasts and the families of the Santiago couple will be watching closely. They will be talking to the press too." The meeting ended on that note. Katie stopped at the small kitchen area and poured herself a cup of coffee. She was upset. DA Mahoney completely sidelined her analysis for which he charged her with conveying. She would give it more time, but she hoped politics did not completely control this office. Prosecuting another human being required true and honest intent on getting to the truth. Katie was so preoccupied; she failed to acknowledge two staffers sitting at the nook on the other side of the room. Katie said "Hi." They both nodded; one replied with a "Hello." The warm and fuzzy welcome had not come forth. She had a feeling that acceptance into this family might not be so easy.

"Hey girl, how was the meeting?" Katie did her best to smile as Angie walked over to her. "Oh, Oh. What happened?" Katie smiled and said, "Nothing. It's all good. Just testing the waters, or rather the water is testing me." Angie said, "It will get easier. Patience, lots of it. Anyway,

I have two things for you. First, you have a one on one with ADA Mahoney tomorrow to discuss the Santiago case at 12:30. He asked me to order in sandwiches." Katie shook her head, "Really? Tomorrow? I haven't even had a chance to review the case." "Welcome to Boston, ADA Owens. I guess it's going to be a busy night for you." Katie asked, "You said two things, what's the other *good* news?" "Not good news; good something though. It's in your office.

Centered on her office conference table, was a beautiful hand blown glass vase swirled in pastel colors, and filled with ruby red roses. Katie said to herself, "Oh, my. They are gorgeous." From behind her, Angie remarked, "So, you have an admirer. They are really beautiful." Without turning around, Katie reached for the card. "They are beautiful!" She opened the small envelope marked "for KC" and pulled out the folded mini card. She could sense Angie's somewhat intrusive curiosity behind her.

"Dearest Katie,
Wishing you good luck in Boston. Thinking of you; missing you."

The mysterious but obvious sender signed the note with one letter. "J"

The flowers included a hidden message; Jason was subtly trying to seduce her. His concept of "Friends" evidently had a different meaning to him than it did to her. Katie had to admit to herself that Jason's pursuit for her affection was flattering. At the very least, it was a good distraction for her. She needed to fill a void in her heart. What she really wanted was for Jack to magically appear.

"Wow, Katie. Your face is redder than the roses. Are you OK?"

Katie flashed an embarrassed smile. "I'm OK. It's from my New York office wishing me good luck."

Katie gathered eight of the nine heavy folders and packed them in a banker's box. She took the folder labeled "Santiago # 904567 (1 of 9)" and sat on the couch that lined the wall to her right. As she perused the table of contents, she shifted a bit to sit up straight. She thought, "T*his is a very comfy couch*." Katie prepared for a long day, followed by an even longer evening.

"Crap!" File 904567 had ADA Owens' full attention. As she got deep into the background of the killer's MO, she thought how much it was like reading a work of fiction. A glance at her watch reminded her that she was already late picking up the boys from their after school session. Her stomach ached. Already the pressure of work versus family was upon her. With her pocketbook slung over her shoulder and behind her, Katie picked up the heavy box with all nine folders and headed out of her office. "Good night, Angie. Gotta run." Angie scanned the atrium, all was quiet; most of the staff had left already. "Good night, Katie. See you in the morning. Don't work too hard tonight..." She smiled, knowing it would be a very long night for her new friend and boss. Without turning to look back Katie asked, "These are all scanned in the system?" Angie answered with an affirmative "Of course." Standard policy was that interoffice or off-site transport of case documents required a senior ADA or higher approval, and all must been scanned into the secure electronic data system.

Katie's arms ached as she quick stepped her way to her car. She would pick up the boys and take them for pizza before going home.

Chapter 11

Hey, asshole. "'alsifarat alamrikiat, mukafa'a." Jack raised both hands in unison; painfully joined together with thick cord; very tightly. He rubbed his thumb and index fingers together hoping they understood the universal gesture for money. He also hoped they would not know the embassy *could* not, *would* not, pay for his release. Yemen had fallen far from the United States' graces and vice versa. The embassy ran on a skeleton staff. Basically, there was no representation for U.S. citizens in the region. Jack laughed to himself, knowing that as an agent of the U.S. government, *they* might not even acknowledge him. He would be officially disavowed. Still, he hoped that if a message found its way to those who would help him, it would happen before it was too late; *for him*.

For a moment, Jack saw possibilities as the leader seemed to ponder his suggestion. *Money first. Allah's jihad second.* The boss man blurted something too fast and sloppy for Jack to decipher. One of the rebel underlings grabbed Jack's hands by the rope and yanked hard, causing both of them to stumble. As they approached a dented and timeworn Humvee, Jack responded to the command, "wekf"! He abruptly stopped in place and stood at attention, as he did numerous times on a daily basis, since his capture. Another meatball joined the party. The first guy held Jack by his ripped shirt while the newbie blindfolded him. By the amount of force that thrust him into the back seat, he figured both took pleasure in shoving him into the vehicle. They conversed for a moment and then one of them told Jack in broken English, to remain quiet. "Stay down, no words! Or, sa'aqtae lisanak" The two of them laughed. Jack understood "lisanak" as tongue and figured out the rest. The air temperature was already over one hundred degrees. Jack's escort team showed no mercy as they tossed a heavy rancid tarp over him. He prayed that he would pass out. Suffering the smell and heat would be as agonizing as anything he had already endured during his captivity.

After about three torturous hours that felt like an eternity, the vehicle came to an abrupt stop. His captors argued for a moment, then cursed each other jokingly. Jack was all too familiar with that nonsense. "ygeb an atbol! Ahamk." Jack also understood the idiots' need to pee. His own bladder ached horribly. He could not call out, so he repeatedly kicked his feet hard against the vehicle's door. His feet could no longer find their target as the door opened. The tarp was pulled away allowing the torrid air to rush over him. It actually felt good. There were no words spoken, while one of them pulled him out of the vehicle and removed his blindfold. "Alzahab!" He pointed to a large rock about ten yards away. The other skell held his rifle at the ready. His creepy look indicated his desire for Jack to run, so he could shoot him in the back. Jack waddled to his *piss* spot and maneuvered his fingers as best as possible to help ease the painful task of relieving himself. As he made his way back to his *limousine*, he made a panoramic sweep of the backdrop. He thought the road and surrounding terrain looked familiar.

Blindfolded and covered again, they were on the move. The roads in general were bumpy, but these were downright painful. Jack considered that out of cruelty, hitting some potholes and harsh swerves had to be intentional; mostly based on the constant laughter from the front seats. He also considered that several of the erratic moves might have been in avoidance of IEDs. Jack tried to imagine where they were headed. He had traveled these remote Yemen roads several times. It was a few years back. He was not bound and gagged or blindfolded and had armed guards that were there to protect him. Vague as it all seemed, and from his two-minute survey of the land during the pit stop, he figured they started out somewhere on or near the N5. The bumpy turns might be the N17, which would lead them to the intersection of 515. If he stayed alert long enough, he might be able to tell if they made a turn onto 5621. The urge to puke came and went, along with dizziness. The sweltering heat under the tarp was slowly suffocating him. About an hour had passed when the Humvee again came to a halt. One of the idiots up front quietly commanded, "Hadaeh!" Jack thought, *like I have options, my mouth is gagged*.

From arguing, to abrupt silence, followed by some additional conversing, and then salutations, it sounded as if a payoff to a security patrol was transpiring. That likely meant they were at the N6 or already at the 621. *Nah, probably the 5621 or N6, it would be at least another two hours to the 621 interchange*. Jack's mind wandered out of control. He could be completely off on his geographical supposition. He thought, besides, I'll probably be dead before making it to Aden or even the 621.

As the vehicle resumed its bumpy trek toward one of the possible crossroads, the awful acid that accompanies nausea began flowing upward, burning his esophagus. He fought hard to keep the agita within from coming up. His efforts resulted in the acrid fluid backing up and into his sinuses. With his mouth gagged, he began to choke. His head spun, as he passed out from severe dehydration and lack of oxygen.

As Jack regained consciousness, it felt as if they lifted a hundred pound lead blanket off him. "anhed!" Two hands grabbed Jack by the shoulders and yanked him out of the Humvee. He was off balance and neither of the two idiots cared enough to assist him as his legs buckled beneath him, causing him to crash to the ground. Jack's head pounded. He thought perhaps that he had suffered a mini-stroke or brain damage from the unbearable heat and lack of oxygen. Despite the sizzling outside temperature, the air felt almost refreshing once Jack was out from under the tarp. As his vision came back into focus, he caught the debasing grin as the taller one pointed to a rocky ridge about fifty yards away. "Astyqz!" Jack flipped off the arrogant bastard as he obeyed the command to get up. The shorter one aggressively pulled out a short bladed knife, making Jack flinch. He cut the rope on Jack's legs, and then freed his hands as well. After one more gesture, Jack understood that they were telling him to go take care of his personal business again. *Or, they wanted to take target practice.* After puking, more like dry heaves after a raging night of drinking, Jack tried to take care of business, and empty his bladder. His mouth was too dry to talk himself into peeing. *Mind over matter...* Finally, he managed to relieve himself. The throbbing pain and brown color further sickened him. Jack imagined sand as it passed through his kidneys.

"Thank you, my friends. Now how about some water? Ma'an fadlik." The taller one, surprisingly after being flipped off with the universal sign language, nodded and poured a few ounces into the metal canteen cover. He held it up and nodded to Jack. As Jack cautiously approached him, the other one grabbed the cup from his partner's hand and took a small sip. He licked his lips, his face expressing how refreshing it was. He, like the taller one, held it out for Jack to take. As Jack reached for it, the slimy asshole pulled it back, and spat in the cup. He swilled it around for a thorough mix before offering it once again. Jack took the cup, nodded, and said "Shakar, asshole." Desperation makes men do what they must do to survive. Jack closed his eyes briefly as he drank the tainted beverage. He wiped his mouth with the back of his hand and winked as he handed the empty tin cup back to its owner. Suddenly, his captors seemed distracted. Jack turned to see dust rising into the sky.

The next few moments were a blur, as Jack had not yet recovered from the extreme heat exhaustion inflicted upon him during the earlier road trip. His current escorts had no time to run. They raised their weapons ready for a fight. Jack considered his two options. One; running *for his life,* but figured he would take a bullet for sure, so he chose option two, and dove behind his Humvee. His heart pounded as he waited for the ear shattering pops as the shooting started. He waited for seconds that felt like minutes but there were no rounds of gunfire, just the quiet gentle lilt of a momentary desert breeze; and one commanding voice. Before he knew it, he was again in the hands of yet another militant group. His cruel travel mates were now bound, gagged, and on their knees at gunpoint.

Three Humvees expelled a small platoon of uniformed soldiers; about twelve from what Jack could see. Three of them held their guns in a "ready" position, pointed at Jack. "Amerakish! American Journalist." As Jack blurted out what seemed to be another futile plea for help, his voice cracked and faded at the end of his sentence. His legs began to wobble, but he fought hard to stay standing at attention. Jack did not want to create any additional concern that he might be a threat, or try to run. One of the soldiers, he presumed the leader of the unit, approached a little closer. "Amerakish?" Jack nodded, "Yes. Yes, Amerakish." The leader rambled too rapidly for him to catch any part of what he shouted to his small band of soldiers. He heard a few of them repeat as they laughed, "Amerakish, Amerakish." The leader put up his hand, commanding instant silence. Jack's stomach began to churn more acid, followed by another round of nausea. He thought to himself, *here we go again*. The leader reached under his vest; Jack envisioned his swift hand motion as he sliced Jack open with his jambiya. His mind flashed images from a few years earlier, when he battled the assassin twins scattered throughout the American governmental agencies. Those crazy brainwashed fanatics ran amuck, leaving pools of blood and bodies in their wake. Instead, a small flask appeared as he held it out for Jack to take. He also pulled a small salt stick from his pocket and handed it to Jack as well. He nodded and walked away. His troops remained, keeping a watchful eye on Jack. *OK, so water and salt, survival tools of the desert; I guess they are not ready to kill me yet.* Jack looked over to his ex-travel mates just as their captors shoved them into the back of one of the trucks, still bound and gagged. They did not look happy. Another soldier signaled for Jack to get into the second Humvee. As Jack passed the two Assholes in the third Humvee, he put his face against the glass. "See how *you* like it, Mother-Fuckers!" As he angrily thrust out his middle finger in their direction, one of the soldiers shoved him forward to keep him moving. Jack raised his hands indicating all was OK and to signal his willingness to comply.

Once again, bound in such a way that he still had some ability to hold a cup or walk in small steps; Jack held onto some hope for better treatment going forward.

From what he could tell, these guys were some faction of Sunni troops. Possibly Saudis. After being placed into the Humvee with his guard, the convoy continued with no further conversation. As far as Jack was concerned, that was perfect. He still had not fully recovered from the effects of the heat exhaustion that overcame him earlier that day. He hoped his previous captors were suffering the same or worse.

Seated upright and with no blindfold to obscure his view, Jack surveyed the lay of the land confirming what he previously imagined was the planned destination. Exiting onto the 621 allowed for some comfort in knowing that they were, in fact, headed towards Aden. That meant a port and more likely US troops or other friendly possibilities. The convoy passed through two checkpoints, being waved through with little or no fanfare. Again, some additional comfort to Jack.

After three kidney-crunching hours of non-stop bouncing on rutted roads, signs in both Arabic and English began to appear, "Shaykh Uthman." The English translation indicated a somewhat tourist friendly municipality. *OK, I know this place. We are two hours outside of Aden*. Jack asked, "Hal natawajah 'iilaa edn?" At first they ignored him. A minute later, the driver replied without turning around, lest he hit a camel or a cactus, "No. la, edn." Again, Jack's mind, riddled with confusion, began to fantasize escape methods. He considered trying to outrun them. If he didn't get shot, then perhaps he could make Aden in two days.

After another twenty or so minutes, scattered mud-brick houses appeared. As they neared the city, the population became denser. A few minutes later, they were in the center of the city, with lots of locals roaming the streets. Some appeared to be having shady meetings in alleyways. Others patronized vendors who were selling various items, including food. It reminded him of the L.A. beggars market. Half the items soiled or spoiled, the other half, stolen or non-functional. *Hey, there's where my custom mags went!* Jack silently laughed to himself. He considered the fact that he could even smile, a very positive event. Off to the side and at almost every corner, small ragtag groups of uniformed men stood with some fairly heavy fire power. It had been over eight months; he could not remember if Isis or Al Qaeda held control here, or had the Saudi allies regained control? He hoped the latter. As they pulled up to one of the larger multi-dwelling buildings, the armed militia showed a tense reaction. Jack noticed the same reaction from his escorts. His escort seated in the passenger side in front of Jack slowly got out of the vehicle, his hands held in clear view in front of him. Some undefinable words were exchanged and then the finger pointing. First at Jack, then to the Humvee behind his. One of the soldiers raised his automatic machinegun while another opened the door and removed the two tied and gagged shit-heads. With the butt of his weapon, he nudged them toward a doorway far to the left.

Jack's escort commanded, "Kharj!" and again in English, "Out!" As Jack exited his transport vehicle, he stood at attention with his hands extended in front of him, still tied together, ready for additional restraints or a lead rope. The driver was now out of the vehicle and standing next to Jack's other guard. Both men stared at him, and while mimicking Jack's extended hands, began laughing. The driver drew his dagger and in one quick motion sliced the rope between Jack's hands. He then smacked Jack's hands downward and then lightly shoved him forward and gestured toward a door.

Chapter 12

"A toast to Dave and Carol. May you have ten more perfect years so we can celebrate together again in 2028. Cheers to the perfect couple." Everyone at Lucio's Italian restaurant raised his or her glass. The couple picked this place to throw their own ten-year wedding anniversary party. The restaurant had the most beautiful view overlooking Boston Harbor. The invitations noted an after-dinner walk down Congress Street, to the Boston Tea Party Ships & Museum. The celebratory couple thought it would be a fun and memorable way to end the evening.

"Would you like another cup, Miss? I believe you prefer decaf." Carol smiled as the handsome waiter poured the freshly brewed beverage. "Thank you." The waiter caught the smile of the busty ten-year veteran of marriage as her eyes met his. The waiter let his imagination run wild, *"Ten years; she must be starving. I can surely satisfy her hunger."*

The two servers dedicated to Carol and Dave Loring's party cleared the rest of the three tables occupied by the celebrating guests. Carol kissed her husband's cheek and excused herself. She giggled like a little girl, "Nature calls, darling." She paused as her eye caught the waiter repeatedly trying to make eye contact with her again. She whispered in her husband's ear, "I'm fine, but my stomach is feeling a bit queasy. Don't worry, I might take a little time to let it settle. I'll be back for our exploratory mission to the museum." She brushed her finger on his earlobe. Dave considered grabbing her hand and telling her that he wanted to skip the museum for a more exciting adventure. As usual, he did not. His impromptu fantasies would have added some spark to their monotonous relationship had he ever summoned up the nerve to actually express them aloud to his wife. He watched as she walked to the other end of the room and disappeared through the red velvet curtains. His sister's kids diverted his attention. "Uncle Dave, show us some card tricks. Please..." Dave always carried his magic cards with him.

Destiny has a funny way of setting a path for destruction. The door labeled "Le Signore" was locked, indicating it was occupied. The men's room was definitely not an option. *Ah, the family restroom is available.* Carol pushed down gently on the latch. Magically, the door swung open. "OK. Not occupied." She felt his body heat behind her even before he placed his hand above hers, taking control of the heavy lavatory door.

His cologne was intensely erotic. Carol had no idea her subconscious fantasy could actually become a reality. What followed next seemed so natural, as if it was supposed to happen.

"Allow me, Miss."
"Thank you."
"Is there anything else perhaps, I can take care of for you?"

With not a word spoken, her ten minutes of ecstasy could have written an entire erotic story. Several times, as the waiter satisfied his patron, he had to hush her up by pressing his lips hard against hers. One of the times, as he relaxed his kiss, Carol bit his lip, and drew blood. Her she-devil grin drove him into a sexual frenzy. He ravished her hard, and she moaned loudly. Again, he hushed her, and she laughed quietly whining, "OK. OK! Oh, my god. Help me!" "You have to keep it down... You'll get me fired. Oh, Hell!"

"Ooooh, ahhhh, Oh; yes!" ...*Holy Jesus*.

The handsome gigolo wiped beads of perspiration off his brow with his sleeve. They were both out of breath.

 "Thank you for allowing me to service you this evening, Miss. It has truly been a pleasure."

"You are so getting an awesome tip."

As Carol went to stand, her legs began to buckle. She steadied herself, waving off her lover's offer of assistance.

"Um, we have an audience of one out here." His look of concern unnerved Carol, as she paused for ten seconds before following her paramour out of the lavatory. She gestured for him to *get lost*. Carol's six-year-old niece sat squatting against the far wall. She looked terrified.

"Oh, sweetie; it's OK. Auntie Carol just needed help; I slipped and twisted my ankle." The little girl eyed Carol's leg and then focused her eyes upward. "The nice man helped me get up, but it hurt really badly when I tried to stand on it. But, see here?" Carol dangled her foot and then stepped down on it. She squatted next to her niece. "I'm all better now." She took the child's little hand in hers, and they both stood. "I need to pee." Carol waited for her niece to come out of the bathroom. "Do you want to walk back to the party with me?" The little girl's smile indicated, *yes*. Carol wondered why her sister had allowed the child to wander off alone. She thought it best to leave it be, and not bring it up.

Dave wanted to know what had taken Carol so long to return. Carol explained to him that she found their niece by the bathrooms and was talking with her for a little while. Dave said, "Well, I'm glad you're feeling better, shall we get going?" Carol smiled, "Lead the way." Dave stopped before they reached the restaurant exit. He touched her left ear. "You're missing an earring." Carol felt the heat of a deep flush coming across her face. "Oh, my. I must have knocked it out of my ear while washing my face in the ladies room. I'm fairly certain I'll find it on the side of the sink. I'll meet you outside." Carol did not wait for a response from her husband of ten, rock-solid years. She rushed off to retrieve her missing earring and to catch her breath.

Extreme guilt overcame her.

Chapter 13

"Ryan, can you please help mommy?" Katie held out her pocketbook and her attaché. Ryan made a face. "No. Only girls carry that." He pointed to the pocketbook. "Actually, Ryan, a real man is secure enough to not care what others think and help where help is needed." Kyle ran up to his brother and pushed him aside; "I'm a real man, mommy." He grabbed the pocketbook. Ryan screamed, "No! She asked me!" "Here, Ryan. You take this." She held up her lunch bag. "And, do you think you can hold the door open for me and your brother?" Ryan smiled and nodded as he snatched the empty lunch bag. The little man ran ahead and waited by the apartment building's garage door. Katie reached into her back seat and retrieved the heavy banker's cardboard box filled with her case files. "OK, Kyle. Let's go upstairs." With care, Katie balanced her various items on top of the box and followed Kyle across the garage floor. "Mommy?" Katie did not have to ask Kyle what he wanted. "Where is Ryan? Ryan!" Panic ensued as she dropped the boxes and all the items balanced on top of them. With Kyle in tow, she raced to the door that lead to the building's elevators. "Ryan! Where are you?" As they reached the door, it magically swung open. "I'm here, mommy." Ryan pointed to the gray steel fire door. "It was too heavy, and I slipped and I fell." Tears rolled down his cheeks. "I'm sorry I yelled like that, sweetie. I was scared too, my baby boy." Kyle made a manly face and said, "I wasn't scared. Daddy wouldn't have been scared." Katie hugged them both. "You're both my brave little men. How about, we go pick up mommy's stuff. I'm hungry."

Kyle said, "Me too, mommy."

Ryan agreed as he wiped his cheeks dry with the back of his hand.

"Lacy! Lacy!" Katie's boys jumped up and down while calling the dog's name. The dog playfully nipped at their feet, almost tripping Kyle. They each took their designated seats at the small kitchen table. Lacy circled around them a few times before settling down, beneath the table.

"Mom. I hate chicken." Ryan mimicked his brother by mouthing his words. Then said, "Me too." "Well, my darling little men, you need to eat healthy. You want to grow up big and strong like your daddy, don't you?" Katie's heart ached as she spoke the word "daddy." The boys had a keen sense when sadness overcame their mother. By now, Katie's emotional response was expected anytime they or anyone else mentioned "Dad;

or Jack." "Mommy?" "Yes, Kyle." "When is daddy coming home?" Ryan shoved his brother, "Shut up! You're making mommy sad."

Lacy played secret agent by hiding under the kitchen table and eating the evidence as Ryan slipped her his leftovers. The boys declared they were full and headed to their room to watch TV. Lacy chased after them, this time nipping at Ryan's heel. Katie had strict rules for the boys, to keep their routine flowing smoothly. She usually cooked dinner during the week. It was her downtime, and the only time the boys did their homework without an argument. During dinner, they would discuss what they learned that day. First grade was much more intense than what she remembered it being, back in *the day*. She and the other moms would talk from time to time, and discuss how the kids today are so much smarter; doing math and reading already. After dinner, the boys had playtime, or would watch a TV show. Then off to bed, no complaining permitted; *by order of Mom*.

She allowed herself five minutes of contemplation. Katie thought, *how am I going to manage this new position and not neglect my boys?* Her heart was heavy with guilt and sadness all the time, and now she had second thoughts over the move to Boston. These were all new people. She had no history with them. Back in New York, her associates knew Jack. Some of them suffered the wrath of his enemies; enemies of the United States. Her husband was a hero, and so much more. He humbly touched so many lives. *These new coworkers, they are aware of some of what happened; as much as any regular citizen could know.* "What the hell am I going to do? I need you, Jack! Where the hell are you?" Katie didn't mean to shout out her frustration.

"Mommy?"

"It's OK, boys. Mommy is just looking for her work stuff."

Lacy had no reaction; middle age made her the most laid-back dog. Sir Oliver Jones strolled into the room with confidence, and authority. He rubbed back and forth against Lacy's face. The dog moaned, and then sneezed.

Three hours later and four volumes down, Katie stretched and reached for the phone. She glanced at the clock. She hoped 11:15 was not too late to call Rosa. Either way, this was an emergency of the soul.

"Hi Rosa, it's Katie. I hope it's not too late to call." Rosa and Katie talked for an hour. Katie loved hearing about Rosa's grandbabies, who aren't babies anymore. Rosa had twenty questions about the move to Boston. She asked, "How are the boys adjusting? And, how about you, Miss

Katie Claire? How are you *really* doing?" Katie started to say, "Good. Really good. The change was a *smart* choice." Her voice crackled on every other word. Rosa could tell that her friend was in trouble. "Oh no, Miss Katie. Tell me what is going on." Katie burst out crying. She reeled off a list of issues she had difficulty dealing with. "Wait a minute. After all that you have been through, you are the toughest woman I know. You just need a break. My daughter's kids are in day school now. They can spare me for a few weeks. I'll make arrangements and fly to Boston." Katie tried to tell her, "No." "I can't ask you to do that. You have given so much time to our family already. We're OK." She really meant; *oh God, thank you*. Rosa would not take "No" for an answer. In fact, she had not asked for permission. After they hung up, Katie cried some more. She cried happy tears. The cavalry was finally on the way. Katie decided to wait until the morning to share the wonderful news with the boys that Nana Rosa would be coming for a visit. She was sure they would get so excited. In her mind 's eye, she imagined them running around the apartment jumping and singing, "Nana Rosa is coming!"

Halfway through the seventh folder, sleep overcame Boston's newest ADA. When she awoke in the morning, she found that the box of folders had fallen to the floor. An assortment of papers randomly decorated the living room floor. The cat had curled up in the box, his paws clenching a folder. "Hi, Oliver. How about putting all the files back in the box?" The cat got up and walked over to Katie, purring loudly as he rubbed against her leg.

Chapter 14

Dave leaned against the right front fender of his car, waiting for Carol. Most of their guests had already left the parking lot. A few headed home while others walked ahead, down Congress toward the piers. The elated husband of ten years waved to the last of his friends to leave, as the valet closed her car door. "Really, Carol, where the hell are you?" The valet walked over to Dave, "Excuse me, sir?" Dave shook his head, "Oh, nothing. Just talking to myself. OK if I leave my car here? I need to run inside to find out what is keeping my wife so long." The valet said, "Of course. No problem." Dave handed him a five-dollar bill and thanked him.

"I searched everywhere. She was looking for this." Dave held up a small hoop style earring with one glittering diamond setting dangling from it. The police officer took it and placed it into a plastic zip-lock bag. "Did you two have an argument? Has your wife had any issues with someone else? A coworker, perhaps?" Dave shook his head indicating, "No." "Is it possible that your wife left with someone else? Perhaps a friend?" Dave knew what the officer was referring to and shook his head. "No, of course not. For God's sake; we celebrated our 10th anniversary this evening." The detectives showed up and asked the same questions again. Dave wondered if they were trying to trick him into changing his story. He realized they usually suspect the husband first. *This is crazy!* "Sir, we will need a list of everyone at your party and their relationship to you and your wife." The detective wrote down Dave's contact information. "Here's my card. Email the list to me as soon as you get home and be sure to call me if you think of anything else that can assist us in finding your wife. The faster we rule out those who had access to your wife, the sooner the chance that we figure out what happened to her.

Before leaving the restaurant's parking lot, Dave called his brother and sister-in-law to ask if Carol had left with them. Fortunately, they had just left the restaurant and had driven only a short distance down the road. Within five minutes, Carol's brother in-law pulled up. The detective was about to leave, but stopped and got out of his car. Jerry asked, "Hey, Dave; any news?" Carol's sister hugged Dave. Dave softly said, "No. But thank you both for coming back." "Well, I may have something." Jerry looked at the detective, "Hi. I'm Carol's brother-in-law, Jerry Bieselin. My daughter wandered off to use the bathroom a short time before the end of the party. She said both bathroom doors were locked, so she sat down on the floor in the hallway leaning against the wall trying not to pee herself. She heard what sounded like crying or someone getting hurt. She was frightened but could not move, afraid she might wet herself. She said, one of the bathroom doors suddenly opened, and a man came out followed by my sister-in-law." The detective asked, "Did Mrs. Loring appear hurt or crying when your daughter saw her?" Jerry shrugged his shoulders. "She didn't think so. My daughter said the man seemed very nice. He asked if she was OK. My daughter said Carol, my sister in-law, told him to go on. She waited for my daughter to use the toilet. Then, my sister-in-law walked my daughter back to the party."

The detective had an inkling that the wife might have been taking care of a ten-year-old itch. Possibly a spur of the moment erotic encounter. The encounter may have gotten too rough; the little girl most likely could not interpret what was happening behind the closed doors. He went inside and asked the restaurant manager to assemble all the staff in the dining room.

"I need the person who assisted Mrs. Loring earlier this evening, specifically in the lavatory, to step forward." The restaurant staff whispered among themselves. No one made a move to admit anything. Dave pleaded, "Please. My wife is missing. We need help." Still, nothing. The detective then said, "OK. We have a witness that saw a staff member and Mrs. Loring together. We will hold all of you until the witness arrives." He looked at the brother-in-law, "You may need to fetch your daughter."

"That won't be necessary." A young, good-looking waiter stepped forward, his eyes trying to avoid contact with Dave's. "The lady hurt her ankle. I heard her yelp in pain and offered my assistance." The detective thanked the other staff members and told them they could go home. He reminded them to call if they remembered anything that could help locate Mrs. Loring.

With everyone including Dave and Jerry out of the room, the detective began his questioning of the waiter. He quietly asked his first question.

"So, the lady celebrated the ten year itch, and you helped her out? I expect things got a bit rough. The little girl can corroborate this much so far. I see only two possibilities. You expected more, or at least a hefty tip for special services rendered. When she laughed at your pretentious demand, you threatened to tell her husband. Or, perhaps that wasn't the case. Then when she returned to the scene of infidelity, she panicked. Afraid that her husband suspected something, perhaps she wanted to come clean. You feared accusation of rape and took the opportunity to silence her first." The detective had a stern look on his face. The waiter stood up, his face uncomfortably close to the detective's. "This is total bullshit!" His words blurted aloud, and aggressively. Then, still in the detective's face, but in a quieter tone, "I fucked her! That's, all. It was mutual and damn good for both of us. Ten minutes of sexual bliss." He took a step back, his eyes not wavering from the detective's. "As far as I know, consensual sex between two adults is not a crime. All you have is a missing person and no proof that I was the last person to see her." He paused, cursing under his breath, "Am I under arrest? If not, I'm out of here." The detective told the perturbed waiter, "Sure; you're free to go. But don't leave town."

The detective instructed Dave to go home and stay by the landline phone. The detective also reminded Dave, "Make sure your cell phone remains fully charged and on. Call if you hear anything."

****

Darkness & Fear

As she slowly regained consciousness, Carol immediately began to panic as she realized a blindfold securely covered her eyes. The last thing she remembered was walking into the restaurant bathroom.

The lights were off and it was pitch black in the room. As she felt around for the light switch, someone grabbed her from behind, pressing a large damp cloth over her face. A strong, somewhat sweet odor made her gag and her eyes burned. She had no time to react or scream for help. Carol tried to take stock of her situation; she was good at that. Dave always made fun of her astute perception of things. *My hands are tied above my head.* She envisioned them tied to the bedposts. *I'm on a bed, so I'm no longer in the bathroom at the restaurant. I'm gagged.* A gag made from a course material tightly covered her mouth. The pressure inflicted pulsating pain. She tried moving her legs. *They are tied the same as my arms.* Carol realized that her legs were bound in such a way... she felt completely vulnerable. She envisioned the uncomfortably cold room as dark and dreary. Her skin tingled as if tiny beads of perspiration continuously formed and then instantly dried up. Her panic escalated, and she momentarily stopped breathing as she abruptly realized, *I'm naked!* Carol's mind blanked out for a second, either out of utter hysteria, or as a result of the drugs still in her system. Her mind's eye played out fantasy horror images of an anticipated sexual assault. The silence was deafening until there were footsteps, and she faced the fact that she was not fantasizing. She tried not to, but she had to take a breath.

He spoke softly. His voice not recognizable. "Hello, Carol. This is a special gift to help you commemorate your special occasion." Carol struggled to free herself. Fear now morphed into terror as she sensed movement close to her. He lightly brushed her exposed belly with the sharp point of what felt like the cold steel blade of a knife. It seared her delicate skin like a fuse burning toward gunpowder. "If you play nice, I can promise you, there will be less pain and more pleasure." The pressure of the knife increased; she felt the warm oozing of blood as her flesh parted. "Don't worry; it's just a little pain to get us started. You are going to have the most extraordinary sexual experience." Holding a firm and painful grip on each of her ankles, he slowly began his sexual assault that seemed to last for hours. Shock had already set in. Carol had no control over her body any longer. He methodically worked his way upward on her body. As his tongue reached her neck, he removed the gag from her mouth. "Promise me you won't scream." She could not tell if that was a question or a demand but the freer movement of air in her lungs allowed for some relief from the claustrophobia she had endured during the assault. She rapidly nodded her head in agreement. He kissed her lips gently, "Good," then bit her lower lip, drawing blood. His tongue followed. She envisioned a vampire fucking her to death. The knife found its way back to her body. He teased her, touching her sensitive areas with its sharp point. A slicing sound made her body twitch in fear; she realized he had cut both hands free. Her unknown assailant drew the knife along the side of her body and down past her ankles. Now her feet were free too. *Maybe he is done with me and I can go home.*

His powerful grip that had started with her ankles now took hold of her hips, forcing her over onto her belly. His assault continued with his one hand pressing down firmly on her lower spine to immobilize her. His other hand guided the knife down her back to her buttock. Again, she felt the sensation of a slight oozing of blood. His sexual assault continued. She prayed for death. His silence while doing this to her was as bad as the damage the knife had done. As he held her firmly with his arm around her neck, he maneuvered Carol onto her side with her back pressed against his bare chest. He continued his assault. He grunted loudly as his fluids mixed with hers, she fought hard not to lose control; then she exploded in orgasm. A cool stream of perspiration trickled down from between her breasts and over her belly, followed by a drastically warmer flow. All went dark as the nightmare mercifully ended.

Chapter 15

"Sharmuta!" The young rebel looked up as he raised his hands in disgust. "Avi, why do you speak to me like that? Have you no respect for your leaders?" "I call it like I see it. You use people for your own gain. I can't understand why my people asked me to help over here. You all are out of control. And, make no mistake; you are not my leader." The young man looked in his direction and sneered as he glanced to his associates for their agreement as he said, "You are a consultant to our cause Avi; that's all." "Consultant!" Avi stood up. "Ali? Was I consultant when I snapped the neck of that sharmuta Taliban who held a knife to your throat? I think I interrupted him as he promised to teach your wife how to be a proper subservient?" The other two laughed while making throat-cutting gestures. Avi grinned, "I'm going outside; it stinks in here. "Hadu'a, 'ant ghabi!" Ali commanded his two subordinates to be silent.

At first, Avi had not given any credence to the two men standing to the side of the doorway he had just exited. Instead, he focused on the small caravan of filthy, dust covered Humvees blocking his view of the dwelling across the road from him. His real mission directed him to keep any eye on what the inhabitants over there, the leaders of the rebels, were up to. One guard stood by the second vehicle. No one else occupied the streets. Avi turned to go back inside just as the two other men disappeared through the doorway, ahead of him.

"Hadir min alshra'. Alsahafiu al'amriki." The guard gently poked Jack in the back for him to take a step forward. Jack asked, "Don't you ever speak English?" He stopped short of saying anything else. He understood the rules for how things worked. Those rules applied in all cases for hostages. Jack considered his status as "hostage" at the moment, although most of the time, prisoner seemed more appropriate. The general rule being... Speak only if spoken to. From behind him the voice said, "He told the sharmuta that you're an American journalist. Hadiat min alsahra', a gift from the desert."

Jack's head began to spin. He had stopped breathing the second he heard the accent. The use of sharmuta confirmed it. He abruptly turned, "Avi!" The guards raised their weapons. Avi waved his hands, shooing them away. "Hadha al'amrikiu hu 'aswali." He looked at Jack. "I told them you are my asset. I'm sure this will be difficult for you, Jack, but try your best not to speak." Avi explained in Arabic how he had sent Jack on a mission in the desert to spy on the Taliban and how a conflict ensued between Isil and Taliban forces. He explained that Jack got caught in the middle and taken as a prisoner. The guard, who had brought Jack to the city in the sand, repeated his earlier remark, "Hadir min alshra'. Alsahafiu al'amriki." Avi thanked him for the present.

Avi arranged a shower and clean clothes for Jack. For more than eight months the only body cleansing Jack had, was what he could manage with a bowl of water and a filthy rag. He even welcomed the generosity of soap, even if it contained lye. He carefully washed the plethora of sores that had formed on the back of his legs, behind his knees, his groin and buttocks. Avi also gave him a handful of antibiotic pills from his own personal stash.

An hour later, Jack waddled his way back to the common area of the dwelling. Avi nodded with his approval. "OK. You look and smell much better now, my friend." Jack grinned, "I don't feel much better. As a matter of fact, I am seriously hurting. I was numb to the pain before cleaning the sores. Do you have any pain killers?" Avi regretfully told him "No. Besides, someone would probably kill me in my sleep for them.

"What about my family? What have you heard?" "I'm sorry, Jack. Last I know, Katie wreaked havoc at your agency trying to find out what happened to you. She did not trust anything they told her; especially that you were presumed dead. She still believes you went deep undercover, and everyone in the agency including the president, is lying to her." Jack had tears in his eyes. "I have to get word to her. You have to get me out of here." Avi put his fingers to his lips signaling Jack to hush. "Listen to me, Jack. These are not friendly allies. I am surviving here in this shit-hole of a country because they are convinced I can provide intelligence to assist in their battle here. I am really on an assignment to watch the leaders of this pack of morons. Israeli intelligence has uncovered information that a deal to move short-range nuclear capable missiles to Israel's enemies for money and guns is on the table. The only reason they will allow you to survive is if they think you are working with me and can prove useful to their cause. So, for now, that's how it is. Keep quiet and do as I say. And, for God's sake, do not expose them to your Jack Owens sarcasm.

Later that evening, just as Jack had dozed off, loud laughing, and shouting of vulgar remarks awakened him. Before he could reach the doorway to the main room, one of the highly intoxicated *sharmutas,* Avi's favorite word to describe them, came in and screamed something at Jack. He flailed his arms in a gesture that indicated, "Follow me." The lower ranking guards were nowhere to be seen. New faces that Jack did not recognize drank booze and passed gas freely. He assumed they were higher ranking leaders passing through on their way to raid a village or some other non-official tirade. On second thought, he considered they might be Avi's assignment from across the road. He would inquire of his friend later, when the opportunity for privacy allowed them to speak again.

Music played loudly. Bottles of whisky passed from hand to hand, and mouth to mouth. As Jack observed the disgusting swapping of spit with each pass of the bottle, it reminded him of 1920's prohibition. This obscene party could have been from an old movie. There were men with guns and illegal booze. Jack laughed to himself. *Who was going to bust them? The entire local law enforcement contingent were probably in the room, and they were trashed.* With a bang, the front door swung open. Avi and another of the group came in, followed by a harem of young women. Jack guessed the five girls ranged from sixteen to maybe twenty years old. The girls seemed to have come of their own free will; probably for a promise of money and food. Perhaps their fathers' lives were spared, as well. Avi patted Jack on the back. He *appeared* to be drunk too. "This is no time for morals, my friend. Be careful not to insult anyone." Jack grinned; "Don't they hang locals for consuming alcohol?" Avi put his hand on Jack's chest and pushed him gently against the wall. "What part of no insults or wise cracks did you not get? Eight months can easily be extended to forever. Keep quiet! Try to enjoy tonight. Tomorrows are always questionable in this place."

In minutes, it seemed that all the girls were engaged in various sex acts. The room resembled "Plato's Retreat;" one big orgy. Avi seemed to fit right in. As if Jack's paranoia had not reached an all-time high already, all eyes seemed to be on him. "Tuhibu?" There was a phrase Jack understood. In another time, and country, and if he was a single man, Jack would have *liked* what was being offered to him. A young woman, who Jack guessed barely reached the age of eighteen, shook her boobs in his face. "Aismi hu, Shaama." *Ok, her name is Shaama*. Jack did not reply with his name. He focused on her somewhat pretty face. She had a beautiful body and knew how to use it to entice him. Her pungent body odor reeked like camel dung. Her smile gave away her need for major dental work as well. "Shaama? Rhymes with llama." *But, smells like camel*. He laughed, and she laughed. Jack asked Shaama, "You don't have a clue what I am saying, do you?" She nodded and giggled. Jack figured, *these camel fuckers find the odor quite pleasant*. He had no desire to be involved in this repulsive orgy. Before he knew it, her hands pressed on his chest. His shirt was already open from an earlier attempt to find relief from the extreme afternoon heat. It had been eight months since sex even crossed his mind. Her back-and-forth motion as she straddled his lap caused an involuntary response. One, considering the atmosphere, or lack of it, he did not expect. Along with his unsolicited excitement, came excruciating pain. Her movements back and forth across his lap irritated the desert borne sores that covered his most sensitive areas.

"Kafia!" Jack's outburst commanded her to stop. As he pushed the young girl off his lap, his actions drew a fleeting glance from some of the others. In a split second, however, they went back to their own salacious business. Jack made a sorrowful face and quietly said in Arabic, to the best of his ability, "'Iinaa asif, 'ana'asheur bialmirad." He hoped that making the excuse that he was feeling ill would get him out of this awkward situation, and hopefully avoid a knife to his throat later. Shaama didn't seem to have taken much offense at Jack's rejection. She had already joined one of the other girls. They both voraciously worked on satisfying one of the rebel leaders.

"Jack; where are you going?" "Back to bed, Avi." Avi whined, "No. Stay, Jack. Have some fun." One of the other men shouted, "Mithli aljins." Then, in broken English, "Let him go. More for us!" Then he added, "Gay men are put to death in this country; for sure before drinking booze." Everyone in the room laughed, except Avi. The filthy cretin's remark calling Jack "gay" did not really bother him, but he felt as if it required a response. Jack considered asking him why he wasted his time with women when he preferred the company of a warm goat. He refrained, lest he added another reason to fear one of the desert rats cutting his throat while he slept.

Jack's sleeping accommodations consisted of a soiled mattress and a threadbare blanket on the floor in a room where at least five others would eventually join him. The stench of sex *and camels* followed him. He fought hard to keep from retching. His chest ached. He wondered if his diagnosis would be a broken heart, or a heart attack. Sleep came quickly to Jack's exhausted mind and body. He pushed aside the aches and pains for a little while so he could try to rejuvenate. He dreamt of the slender body aggressively moving back and forth over his lap. He imagined Katie's face and her feminine scent. Weightlessness sent him floating through time and space.

The sensual warmth that had engulfed his body now turned dark and cold. In his deep slumber, he dreamt of a slow death by drowning in a rancid pool of blood. He found himself back in the fires of hell once again.

Chapter 16

After examining nine massive folders of police reports, psychiatric evaluations, crime scene photos, and various other evidence, ADA Owens felt as if she understood her victims. In her sleep, she played both the victim, and the perpetrator roles. Her mind evaluated many scenarios based on her readings. She was the actor who played all the characters. When she awoke at around 4:30AM, sweat covered her body. She had the most disturbing sense of reality. Oddly, in the first few seconds of her awakening she remembered her dreams in detail, only to lose them a moment later. She could not remember anything except, that she did have nightmares.

With plenty of time before the morning rush of waking kids and all the other daily chores, Katie took a long, steaming hot, relaxing shower. She made herself a cup of coffee and sat for a little more than an hour reviewing some of her notes that she had recorded the night before. Knowing that Rosa would be there in a few days changed everything for Katie. A great pressure would be lifted from her overburdened daily grind. Her phone chirped, signaling the daily 6AM wake up alert. She laughed to herself, knowing the alarm was totally unnecessary. The dog walker would arrive shortly to take care of Lacy, and based on the commotion down the hall, the boys had already started getting themselves dressed. Katie put a lot of responsibility on her young men, and they always seemed up to the challenge. They had many attributes of both her and Jack in them. "Don't forget to tie your shoelaces, Ryan. Let's go boys. Mommy has to get to work on time today." In unison, Ryan and Kyle both said, "OK, mummy. Don't get yourself all wrapped up." They laughed at their own joke.

The office staff appeared quite busy when Katie arrived. "Good morning, Angie." Angie stood up, "Let me help you with those files." Without slowing her pace, Katie kept walking toward her office. "No. No thanks. You have enough going on here already. I've got this." As she used her foot to push open her office door, she looked over her shoulder and asked, "Please call Detective Lawrence. Ask him to come in for a meeting at 9AM." Angie smiled, "Good morning, ADA Owens. I'm on it." Katie tossed the box of files on her conference table, and then settled in at her desk. She stared at the stacks of open court cases lined up on her couch, and pondered how she would manage them all, especially given the major serial killer case. She shook her head and refocused as she started writing notes for her 9AM meeting with Detective Lawrence. She wanted to make sure that when this lunatic was caught, all the "i's" were dotted and the "t's" were crossed. The mayor already started putting pressure on the police commissioner and Katie's boss, DA Mahoney. The news media, as usual, loved these unsolved situations. They were already having a field day using the horrifying sensationalism to gain more viewership.

Before she realized how much time had gone by, Angie knocked on Katie's office door. "Detective Lawrence is here for your 9AM meeting." Katie stood as the detective assigned specifically to the DA's office walked in. She offered her hand and said, "Nice to meet you, Detective Lawrence." "Nick; please. Before we get started, I just want to say that your reputation precedes you, and I look forward to working with you. I'm a straight shooter and will always tell you like I see it."

"That's good to know, Detective. Thank you."

"Nick."

"Detective?"

"Nick. My name is Nick. I prefer us to be on a first name basis if that's alright with you." Katie thought, *"Dick" might work for me.* "Actually, I would appreciate if you would address me as ADA Owens. We need to keep things formal in this office. Besides, it's a bit too casual and we haven't even started working together yet. It's more professional; don't you agree?"

"Well, actually..."

"Great. Let's get started."

Katie sat back down feeling a bit uneasy about how she had to take charge in her initial encounter with Detective Lawrence.. She needed to keep it professional. Especially since she just started this high profile position; and as a woman had the added pressure to keep the respect aspect going.

"So, I spent most of the night reviewing the case reports. There is quite a large volume of paperwork for one attack." The detective squirmed in his seat. "Well, actually, ADA Owens, it's two. It's now two violent rapes and murders. It has not reached the press yet, but I'm sure it will in the next few hours. The commissioner will hold a press conference at the mayor's request. We can be certain the mayor will then follow up with DA Mahoney who in turn will be on our case immediately after." Detective Lawrence noted the senior ADA's expression indicating her surprise and said, "What? I'm sure the communication must have gotten misdirected or something. Your office is always the first to know in these situations." Katie responded with a shake of her head and said, "OK. I suppose it was just a communication failure. I'll investigate what happened, later. Can you please fill me in with whatever details you have?" Her hard facial expression revealed how pissed she was at being left out of the loop on what she understood to be *her* case.

The detective laid out the gruesome details for his ADA counterpart. As detective Lawrence spoke, he could see that she was horrified. "I know how this can affect you. When I got the call this morning that they discovered her tortured and mutilated body in a hotel room located just outside of the city, I wanted to throw up." Some color came back to Katie's face. She said, "Really?" Detective Lawrence laughed, "No. After fifteen years as an investigator in the Special Victims Unit, I'm numb to these details. But it worked." Katie almost smiled. The detective pointed his finger at her. "See, you're fighting it, but I caught you off guard and almost got a smile. I find that a little warped humor can help keep the sanity in an insane case like this." "Don't get used to it, Nicholas. I mean, Detective Lawrence." His laughter helped to lighten the conversation even more so. "It's Nick. Don't really like Nicholas. It, for sure, doesn't fit me. So, ADA Katie Owens, let's figure out how to stop this despicable bastard." Katie leaned back in her chair. "I'll make sure you have whatever is needed at your disposal. Just make sure you get it right, and play by the rules. I want a life term without the possibility of parole." Nick grinned, while mumbling under his breath, "I'd like to cut off his balls before sending one through his brain."

"What about this waiter guy? Do you think he is involved?" Katie sat back in her cushy chair, motionless and appearing pensive. The detective could tell she already knew the answer. He shook his head as if pondering the question, "I don't think so. He's a young stud getting his jollies off with a bored, hot cougar. His only offense is bad timing." Katie said, "OK. While he's still officially a person of interest, I agree; he does not appear to be involved in Carol Loring's abduction. I want you to speak with him one more time just... to be sure." "Yes, ma'am."

"Don't call me Ma'am."

"I like you, Katie. We're going to work well together." "We'll see Detective. Oh, and while you're over at central holding, kick Mr. Santiago loose as well. I'll make the calls. He obviously didn't commit the second murder from his five by nine cell. Let the poor guy mourn his bride. Let's get him in here for additional questioning too. I want to try to jog his memory. He could hold the key to identifying the real killer."

Katie stood and offered her hand. "Thank you, Detective; Nick. We'll work well together *if* you bring me this serial killer's head on a silver platter."

Nick thought to himself as he walked out of the office, *Hmm. I guess a kidnapping, two rapes and murders, obviously by the same fucker, probably classifies as a serial killer.*

"Enjoy the rest of your day, Detective."

"You as well, beautiful." He winked at Angie as he passed her desk, and strutted out the doors toward the elevators. Nick Lawrence reminded Angie of the "Dick Tracy" character. Hat on his head, trench coat, and as he walked, head partially down, as if the intent was for his posture to be aerodynamically correct.

****

DA Mahoney did not seem pleased with Katie's unannounced intrusion, but he had thrown her into the fire. She was damned if she would allow herself to be burned. She made her case for Santiago's release. Mahoney did not afford her the respect of her analysis and opinion; he simply based his approval on the fact that they didn't have enough evidence to hold him. He ended their short meeting with, "I have the greatest respect for how New York City handles their cases." His face drew some color. "But, ADA Owens, this *isn't* New York and things are done differently in this Boston office. I'm aware that you're just finding your way. You will need to catch on quickly so as not to adversely affect the continuity of this office. There's a reason we poached you from New York. You are a brilliant prosecutor. I don't want you to back off on your methods. Just get familiar with our ways, and adapt a little." He walked over to his office door, opening it in one smooth motion. He checked his wristwatch. "Almost lunch time."

Chapter 17

"I miss you so much." Her arms wrapped around him, keeping him safe. Her warmth was different now. Jack was no longer drowning; he was swimming in a tranquil sea of compassion. His words that were spoken aloud, but apparently unheard by anyone in his dream, still echoed in his head. He shifted his body, and it seemed as if his dream person, Katie, was there, and moving in perfect unison with him.

Still in his deep dream state, Jack mumbled aloud, "Hold me and never let me go. I miss you so much." The responding voice in his dream was soft but unfamiliar; yet, it *was* strangely familiar. "I missed you too, Jack. I once told you I would have your back if you ever needed me. I've got your back now, Jack." He thought he felt the pressure of soft yet firm lips against the nape of his neck. It seemed so real.

"Holy Crap!" Jack jumped up into a seated position. The room seemed to spin while his eyes fought to quickly adjust. He sensed movement behind him, and prepared to attack whoever was hovering over him. "Whoa! Easy, my friend." His eyes took another few seconds to focus on the goddess-like creature seated behind him. Her face partially covered by her hand as she rubbed her nose. "Dude, you nearly broke my nose. Amazingly, it's the one part of my body that hasn't been broken at one time or another." Jack stared, still not sure if he was dreaming. "Jane? What the hell are you doing here? How did you find me?" Jack began to panic, his eyes darting around the room. "There's no one else here, at least not alive. Except, Avi. He'll be back shortly. Jack had tears in his eyes.

"B... B... But... how?" He stammered with disbelief.

Jane smiled and put her arms around Jack and kissed his cheek. "There's a rather long and complicated story, and a simpler, more abbreviated one. I'll go for the latter. Your body gave out to infection and fatigue. You have been out of it for about three days. The first day you were checked-out, Avi got word to Senator White. As you well know, he has a lot of clout high up; and the president is seriously fond of you. It took some effort to get a team together and to find your exact location. My job was to recon the situation since I still have the accent and language skills. I worked my way into the rebel safe house. Avi thankfully recognized me and used his better judgment, trusting I was there as an ally, not as the enemy. Your military guys executed a precision drone strike away from any local innocents to create a diversion and draw most of the security forces away from the town. I took out the rest of the group inside." Jack looked at her in bewilderment. "Yes, Jack. The girl's still got it. Five bodies now gone, thanks to Avi. We still need to figure out how to get you out of here. Both rebel and Al Qaeda forces are all over this territory. Word of the drone strike must have reached them by now, and they're probably headed our way already." "I'll say, Jane, you are still a sight for sore eyes." In a weak and raspy voice, Jack asked, "How's Canada? Pete?" Jane smiled, "It's all good, Jack. I've been trying to lead a *normal* life; until today. I owe my salvation to you, Jack. Hence, consider my debt to you paid-in-full. Going forward, I think we'll call it *even*. I have to check on what's happening outside. I'll be back. You stay put." She said it with such authority that Jack made no argument.

Jack shifted closer to the wall and leaned back. He closed his eyes. His daydream brought him back a few years to when he first met the beautiful and highly dangerous Jane. She posed as a college student and with the most evil of intentions, befriended Katie. Eventually, Jane would steal Katie's boyfriend William who was also Jack's best friend. She ultimately had William kidnapped and murdered. Jane was part of the terrorist plot to unravel the United States government. She was one of many "Twins" kidnapped at birth from various prominent military and government leaders. She was one of just a few female operatives raised in isolation, void of any affection or sense of family. She was groomed to be sociopathic.

Jack, not long after his induction into the CIA as an analyst, ran into the William *number two* in Washington. Because Jack and the "real" William were best of friends since age five, Jack was able to spot minuscule anomalies in his friend's demeanor. This triggered an investigation, which lead him to Jane and William's diabolical plans. The years that followed involved extreme peril as Jack went on his quest to thwart the terrorist plot against our country. A bizarre twist in circumstances later put Jack and Jane on the same team. Jane had twins of her own, the result of an earlier affair with an innocent bystander to all the evil antics. Being responsible for two young lives released an inner conscience and eventually feelings of love for another human being. She and Jack traveled across the oceans and suffered torturous passage over the vast desert terrain. Eventually, this lead to a sort of truce and later a partnership to end the attacks on American soil. Jane managed a pub in Canada and eventually fell in love with and married the owner of the establishment, Pete. She managed to maintain a low profile with the appearances of normalcy.

Jack's rest period lasted less than an hour. Jane returned with Avi in tow. "Time to get moving. She pulled a 9MM Glock from her waistband and handed it to Jack. You up to getting out of here?" Jack pulled the magazine from the firearm and reinserted it with vigor. He then nodded, affirming his readiness. Jane handed him a backup mag and motioned for him to get moving.

Both men followed Jane out of the disgusting bedroom and into the main room where Jack's last memory was of drunken rebels and whores. Or, as Avi remarked that evening, "Sharmutas." Jack's keen observation skills kicking in, he noticed small amounts of blood splatter around the room. "So, where are all of our hosts?" Avi grinned and glanced at Jane. Jack nodded, and addressed his one-time female nemesis, "I see you haven't lost your touch." Jane covertly peered out the window, holding the grimy curtain to one side. "A girl has to do what a girl has to do." She turned to her pals, "The coast appears to be clear. It's now or never."

Avi signaled as he opened the door to an already running jeep that looked like it was from the Korean War era. Jane boldly took the front passenger seat and Jack jumped into the back seat; or, what was left of it. "Crap! Did a bomb go off back here?" Avi turned as he ground the ancient shifter into first gear. "Sorry. I had to shoot the fool as he reached for his weapon. I missed him and he jumped out the other side of the jeep." Jack immediately thought of him returning with reinforcements. "Come on, Jack. No loose ends. He would have been better off if I *hadn't* missed. Unfortunately for him, he landed in Jane's beautiful arms. He is in that barrel over there behind the water shed with a few of his buddies."

Avi's driving reminded Jack of a scene out of the first Mad Max movie; erratic and fast. Even more so as the dust settled, exposing an ominous plume of dust rising toward the sky behind them.

Chapter 18

"They're closing in on us!" Jack kept his eyes trained on the one vehicle chasing from behind as it gained on them. Jane yelled, "Two o'clock! Another one." Avi shouted for them to hold on as the rickety old jeep hit a small mound in the sandy road, sending them airborne. The less than gentle landing made Jack's upper and lower teeth gnash together. His dental health had deteriorated badly during his captivity due to a poor diet and lack of daily oral care. The pain was excruciating, but he had no time to complain with the two vehicles closing in on them.

Avi shouted, "I'm going to circle around to create some cover. You both know the drill. Avi gunned the engine as he aggressively turned the steering wheel, forcing the jeep into a hard and tight 360-degree spin. As if on cue, the engine cut out and they came to an abrupt stop. One could envision this scene as a script from the 1970s action show, Charlie's Angels. The three freedom fighters scrambled out of the jeep and stood back to back covering the complete 360-degree threat vector.   As the dust settled, the two chase vehicles came into view, along with massive incoming rounds of automatic fire. The loud pings as the bullets hit their jeep made Jack wince several times. *After eight months, had he had gone soft?* No. After eight months, he had had enough!

"Cover me!"

Jane screamed at him, "No, Jack!" Avi followed with, "Wait!" Jack ignored them both and stepped out directly into the hail of gunfire. The fast movement of the two assault vehicles and their sloppy aim sprayed stray rounds in every direction. Avi and Jane each repeatedly fired on one of the rebel Humvees. This allowed Jack the few seconds he needed to take solid aim on the driver of each vehicle. He fired two successive rounds at the closest Humvee and immediately moved his aim to the other vehicle. The first Humvee veered sharply to the right and rolled over twice. The second Humvee slammed into the overturned vehicle with a resounding crunch of metal. Stopped dead in their tracks, both vehicles slowly reappeared as the plume of sand and smoke settled.

Avi ran past Jack and toward the smoldering vehicles with his automatic weapon at the ready; Jane and Jack followed close behind. There appeared to be no movement from inside the first Humvee that had rolled over and landed on its roof. There was a flicker of flames as smoke rose steadily from the engine compartment. The muzzle of an automatic weapon slowly appeared, followed by an arm, and finally the rest of the body, as one of the assailants attempted to free himself from the wreckage. "I don't think so, Sharmuta!" Avi squeezed off one shot, and the weapon fell from the fingers of the would-be assailant. The emerging arm fell limp. One more shot into the fuel tank ensured there would be no survivors. Jack wiped his brow while gesturing toward the other enemy Humvee. "There's been no movement in that one." Avi started walking toward it, "I'll check it out." He stopped abruptly, noting a stream of what appeared to be gasoline saturating the sand at the rear of the vehicle. Without warning, the second Humvee exploded. Jane picked up the dead guy's automatic M16 and handed it to Jack. "Keep the handgun for backup." She sort of smiled; then winked. Avi turned toward both of them. "That was a foolish move on your part, Jack; and damn bold of you." Jack shrugged his shoulders. "My motto has always been 'Do or Die.' I figured we were likely going to bite the big one. Besides, I knew you two would have my back. We're a great team." Jack looked around and then towards Jane. "Can we go home now?"

As they got into the jeep, Avi sat back and said, "Let's see if this piece of shit will start." The engine whined. After the third attempt, he sighed. "There is something else, Jack. My mission is completed, but I ended up with more intel than I expected. Apparently your missions from the past years had not completely eradicated the doppelganger terrorist agents." Jack scratched his head, which itched horribly from insect bites and sunburn. "We never held the fantasy that all of them were discovered and destroyed. We expected the operation to be abandoned for fear of further exposure of their terror groups. Do you know where they are?" Jane answered, "We don't. Military, government, possibly the White House." Avi added, "Other forms of government, such as legal institutions. Could be judges, District Attorneys, anyone in a position of power. The situation is just as bad as before last year's fiasco." Jack asked, "Who have you told back home? What about your people?" "Jack, no one knows anything yet. I just got this intel yesterday before we, Jane actually, took out the rebels. Israel is just as vulnerable as the United States and may even be at greater risk. Don't forget that we have nuclear arms as well. I'll update my people, you need to take care of the business at home. We can work together and share intelligence as we discover it."

Avi tried the engine one more time with no luck. Jane got out and opened the hood. "Jack, look in my backpack and be careful not to blow yourself up. Hand me the silver duct tape." Jack unzipped the larger compartment. His sifted through several magazines of ammo and what looked like a mini hand grenade. At the bottom of the bag, he found the miracle tape. Jane closed the hood. "It was a broken fuel line. It was pinched, so it didn't leak. Lucky break for us." Avi tried again, and the engine went "Vroom".

After forty minutes of what seemed like going in circles, they found a main road. As they headed south-west Jane yelled, "Shit! Check your six. We got company!" About one hundred yards behind them, two Humvees shadowed them. As Avi sped up, they kept up the pace but made no threatening maneuvers or attempts to draw closer. Avi slowed down as he approached a crossroad. The sign read "Madinat ash Sha'b" with an arrow pointing to the right. Below it, read "Adan." Some of the locals had considerable literacy issues, even with the spelling of their own home town. The port of "*Aden*" would be where an exfil team would be waiting; or so he hoped. Jane boastfully exclaimed, "Our escort has abandoned us. I guess we are close enough to neutral territory." "I'm sure there's no such designation in this god forsaken place." Jack clasped his hands together and rested them on top of his head as he laid back in his seat. "Either way, it looks promising." Avi glanced in his rearview mirror that was hanging by a thread. "Listen, my boldest of bold friends, one of the largest bounties I've ever heard of has been offered for your capture; dead or alive. You need to keep a low profile and pray for a clear route to the extraction point." Jane added, "I think the price has doubled for your capture; alive. At least when I was hunting for you, it was something like fifty million Yemeni Rial." "Shit, that's like two hundred thousand US dollars. I bet with inflation it's upward of three hundred now." Avi laughed whole-heartedly. Jane looked at Avi and then they both looked at Jack. "Ok, OK. Cut out the banter; the two of you are freaking me out."

The town of Aden seemed to be operating in a fairly normal manner. Strategically positioned military vehicles, some with 50 caliber machine guns, lined the streets. If any rebels or al Qaeda soldiers were among the bustling crowd, they would likely remain well behaved. Jack considered this as he imagined his picture on the "kill" posters. Jane noted the ships in port and several more in the harbor, anchored in the not too far distance. "There are a lot of oil rigs over there", Jane pointed north-west of their heading. Jack said, "Hence the heavy fire power. I hope they see our transport as friendly. Those puppies can tear one in half." Avi made a sharp left turn into a narrow alley, barely missing two pedestrians and nearly hitting a wall. As they emerged from the alley and into a large abandoned schoolyard, there it was; big and beautiful. The Sikorsky Blackhawk helicopter sat idling but ready for action. As the trio stepped onto the pavement, the one soldier on the makeshift tarmac signaled for them to advance quickly in his direction. His aviator shades glistened as the sun reflected off them.

"Boy, you guys are a sight for sore eyes." Jack wanted to hug the soldier who greeted them, but refrained from doing so. They tossed their backpacks and gear into the storage bins along the front fuselage just right of where they entered, and settled into their seats. Jane pinched Jack's arm. "Ow!" "I thought *I* was your *sight for sore eyes*." Jack laid his head on her shoulder; she put her arm around him. Jack mumbled, "Who would have thought…"

"Buckle-up, boys and girls; headsets on." The massive eggbeater lifted off with force, and slid sideways for a south-west heading over the Gulf of Aden. Jane noticed Jack's watery eyes glowering in her direction, raising her curiosity as to the emotions running wild in his head. She asked in a soft voice, "What?" Jack responded with a warm smile. "You know; in the 1950's the Gulf of Aden was a hot tourist spot for Europeans and Americans alike. This place had so much potential. Beautiful snow-white beaches, crystal clear blue water. Back then, the

British had control. The locals seemed content. They prospered greatly from the growing tourism. Then a few aggressive local politicians began stirring up the pot. For the most part, the tourists were oblivious to the building tensions, and the British government did their best to keep it that way. The underlying unrest allowed for the more subdued radical factions to crawl out of their holes and begin a reign of terror to force their unholy way upon the people of this region. Such a fucking waste." Jane smiled sympathetically at Jack's brief history lesson but said nothing as he turned away and leaned his head against a large box labeled "Munitions." The pilots took notice of aggressive action on the ground below them. The government soldiers manning the 50 caliber guns stood by and watched as the US military aircraft exited their airspace and made its way toward the European continent. A few tracer rounds came skyward as the rebel forces made a futile attempt to shoot down the American helicopter.

Jack closed his eyes and imagined his boys playing while Katie called to them from the kitchen. "Dinner is ready, boys. GO GET YOUR DAD." The last few words rang so loud and real, Jack jumped in his sleep. Jane took his hand and whispered, "Shush. You'll be home soon with your family."

Chapter 19

The Blackhawk landed at Camp Lemonnier Naval Base for a re-fuel and crew swap. The base, which is located adjacent to the Djibouti's Djibouti-Ambouli International Airport, in the Horn of Africa, appeared unusually quiet. After all the trio had gone through, quiet was a blessing.

"I'm taking a walk outside. Be back in thirty." Avi grabbed Jack's arm. "Not a good idea, Jack. It's over one hundred degrees out there." Jane chimed in, "Avi, this is Jack... 'Mister Bold, shoot me if you dare.' Jack, there is a huge bounty on your head; you cannot trust anyone. Except us, for now. Stay put. We are wheels up in less than an hour." "Sure, then another 3 hours to Berlin. I need a drink." Jane said, "Sounds good. I'll see what I can muster up for us for the flight. Besides, the plane ride will be much more comfortable than the helo." Jack smiled, which made Jane smile. Jack seemed to be almost back to reasonably good health. He still looked worn out and very thin. "Captain, is there a coms I can use to make a stateside call?" The officer sitting across the room as a sort of guard and concierge looked up from his reading material. He seemed a little annoyed at Jack's request to do something, or anything. The "captain" stood,

"Captain? Would be nice, some day. I'm Chief Petty Officer, Smith. You can address me as CPO Smith. Follow me." Jack thought, *some personality this one has.* Jane waved, assuming he was calling the Senator. Avi reminded Jack, "Stay inside, Jack." Jack nodded.

The small cubicle had panels that were similar to what the level-1 NSA guys used to muffle sounds, affording them the privacy required for them to operate effectively. Jack's eight-month imprisonment took a lot from his memory, but not his family's information or John White's secure phone line, both of which were embedded permanently in his head. After three rings, a familiar and very welcome voice answered, "John White." Jack's heart pounded. He tried to speak, but no words came forth. "Jack? Is that you?" Jack took in a deep breath through his nose and then exhaled slowly out of his mouth. He learned this trick while training at the CIA. It worked when he was in desperate situations and needed to remain calm. "Yes, John. It's me." "Oh, dear God. She found you. Are you…" Jack cut him off. "I'm OK. I have all my fingers and toes. Although, I suppose, I'm half the man I used to be. Nothing to worry about that a few good meals won't cure." They spoke for a few minutes, mostly about his return to the states. John explained that the state department would debrief him in Germany and that it might be a week or so before he is able to return home. John teetered on the big question that Jack had not yet asked. Jack had not asked because he was completely unnerved over it. He finally blurted it out. "Katie, and the boys. How are they? Do they know that I... that I'm alive?" In the background, the sweet music of Rebecca's voice made his heart skip a beat. "Is that Jack?" There was a rustling and some whispering. "Oh my God, Jack. Sweet Jesus, thank you. Jack, please just say 'Hello, Rebecca', just say my name. Let me hear your voice so I can be sure it's real." "Hello, Rebecca." Those two words were all he could get out before starting to weep. She softly said, "We love you, Jack. We never lost hope that you would return to us. I'll see you soon. Here's John." "Hey, my boy." "What about my family?" Jack asked the question with authority this time. "Katie and the boys are fine. As of today, they are not aware of your situation. We wanted to be sure our intel was good, and that you were safe. I'll fly to Boston first thing tomorrow morning and deliver the news in person." As he said "Boston", he realized Jack had no idea of his family's move from New York. So much had changed in the eight months that Jack had been gone.

"Boston? What's in Boston?"

"Sorry, Jack. Just a few weeks ago, Katie accepted a fantastic job offer as an ADA in Boston. She and the boys moved into an apartment there." Jack sniffled and cleared his throat. "Is she happy?" "Jack, she hasn't had a smile on her face since the morning you disappeared. She simply needed a change. She never gave up hope. Her last words to us were, 'How will Jack find us if we move?' You need to get some rehab while you're over there and clean up any other business from the past year that you can. This way you can come home and ease back into normalcy; whatever that is, for you. I'll see you next week."

"Tell them, that I love them…"

"Of course."

Jack hung up the phone. To himself he said, "Boston? Hmm." Jack thanked the guard standing outside the door and headed back to meet up with Jane and Avi. The guard shadowed a few feet behind him. Jack thought, *Nice, eight months with those fuckers and they think that I might have been turned.*

They don't know Jack Owens.

Chapter 20

Jason caught the 6AM flight out of New York's LaGuardia Airport. He almost missed the flight as he forgot to allow time for the massive airport construction delays. The Uber driver must have cursed a dozen times, and Jason's nervous questions did not help calm the driver. "How much longer? I have a 6AM flight and its already 5:20. Please get past these *turtles*." The driver glanced in his rearview mirror, "These construction delays are not new. It has been going on for two years. You needed to allow more time, my friend. I don't have a magic carpet to fly you to your terminal."

With minutes to spare, Jason made his way to the gate and then onto the plane. The actual flight took all of forty minutes before touching down in Boston. His heart pounded as he instructed the cab driver to take him to Bulfinch Place, downtown Boston. He checked his phone for the time, noting how long it took to get to Boston. He mumbled to himself, "Jeez, 8:20; I could have driven here almost as fast." He knew that wasn't actually true, but who was he to argue with himself. Besides, he didn't want to arrive too early for his surprise visit. He hoped Katie would be happy to see him. He thought about waiting another week or two considering it's only been a few weeks since she left New York. He missed her, and needed to tell her so. He considered that she might see his reaching out to her like this as poor timing, but he did not care. As the cab navigated through traffic on the MA-1A, Jason checked the navigation app on his phone. The ETA said 8:45AM. He prayed Katie would be flattered and happy that he walked back into her life. He hoped *more than happy*. He knew she needed time, and a few weeks didn't really cut it. Selfishness ruled. He needed to do this. There was history between them, personal and business. They worked together on many high-profile cases. The biggest one involved the notorious Raul Espinosa, a Mexican drug dealer whose strong ties with Al Qaeda lead to major chaos. The DA's case intertwined with Katie's CIA husband, Jack's, who at the time, had his hands full thwarting a major terror plot. Jack played a major role in apprehending the Mexican drug lord. Things got ugly during the trial. Gunfire and the successful attempt to kill the judge. Raul's lover, Adeen, who was also a lawyer on his defense team, shad muggled a weapon into the courtroom. Jason remembered Katie as she fell to the floor taking cover. At first, he thought she had been shot. He was sure she stopped breathing until she abruptly sat up. In that crazy moment, he recognized his true feelings for her. Meanwhile, hero husband Jack ended up in hot pursuit of the Bonnie and Clyde pair. Raul and Adeen crashed their car into Jack's vehicle, causing a disastrous collision; both of them died instantly. Jack spent weeks in the hospital fighting for his life. Katie never left his side. Jason understood the situation and made the best of it.

Things are different now, so he kept telling himself repeatedly. Jack is gone. Katie needed to get on with her life. He would be the one to tell her, to show her that she can be happy again. Happy with him. Jason had no idea how delusional he would seem had he disclosed his feelings about Katie Claire to anyone else.

That'll be twenty-seven even, sir. Jason paid the driver and stepped out of the cab in front of the government offices on Bulfinch Place.

In the courtroom, he displayed nerves of steel. When it came to Katie Claire Owens, she always managed to break through the stronghold of defenses that allowed him to be so successful. The elevator ride seemed to take forever. He hoped the three other people riding up with him did not notice his nervous knuckle cracking. No matter how hard he tried to resist, he pulled one finger after another. It always amazed him how much it calmed his nerves. One last yank and the knuckle on his left index finger exploded in relief. Like magic, the elevator doors slid open.

"Excuse me, ADA Owens. You have a visitor." Rude by any else's standards, Jason leaned in over Angie's shoulder with the biggest smile on his face. "Surprise." Jason's voice gave a little screech at the end of his vocal exclamation. "Thank you, Angie; it's Angie, right? Thank you." Angie had the most awkward expression on her face. She had no idea how to handle his *insolence*. Katie's face declared her surprise as well, but the animated expression quickly turned into a huge smile.

"Oh my god, Jason! It's OK, Angie. This is my former boss from New York." Using boss seemed so out of place at the moment. "Jason was a senior ADA. We worked together, and he's a really good friend." Angie smiled, thinking to herself, *He's so good looking. Good friend, indeed.* "Nice to meet you, Jason. I'll leave you two to catch up. Let me know if you need anything." Angie fought off the urge to wink, simply smiling as she turned and closed the office door behind her. Katie opened her arms for a hug. "What are you doing in Boston? Wait. It doesn't matter. I'm so glad to see you." Her arms felt good around his neck. She smelled incredible. Her scent made him lightheaded with lust. Katie took a step backward breaking their embrace just as Jason almost leaned in for a kiss. He caught on quickly that she was not living in the same moment. He needed to use some restraint. *Calm,*

Jason. Calm. His heartbeat thumped like native drums before a jungle war. *Calm.*

After several minutes of catching up with small talk about this and that, Katie finally asked the question again that Jason prayed she would not. "So, what really brings you to Boston, ADA Albright?" The way Katie asked him the question struck Jason as *so adorable*. Jason seemed to blush, which bewildered Katie. Jason always came across as the "Ironman" of their team. She took his hand in hers. "Come sit over here with me and fill me in; I want to hear more about everyone in New York." As they sat on her office couch, she let his hand go. It felt to Jason as if someone turned off the electric current. Jason thought to himself, *its now or never*. After he finished speaking his mind, he considered that she might want to kill him.

"I'm here in Boston under the guise of research. But in truth, I'm here to see you. I've missed you every day since you left New York." He took a deep breath, ever so slowly, in an effort to mask his nerves. Now Katie blushed. He had caught her completely off guard. She should have realized based on their last few days working together that his *surprise* visit was of a personal nature. Oddly, Katie's blush sent waves of warmth throughout her body. *No. No. No!* Her mind told her to resist. Yes, she was fond of Jason. More than that, she was attracted to him. Lord knows she needed a distraction. *In a flash dream, she envisioned him kissing her under the moonlight*. Then; saved by the bell! Her phone rang loudly. "I'm sorry, Jason. I'll be just a moment. Stay put." Her curt order to remain seated added to his anxiousness. Katie got up and moved quickly behind her desk to answer the phone. Angie's voice in a whisper said, "Sorry to disturb you, Katie. You win the popularity contest this morning. There's a John White here, asking for you. He said he's family and I should interrupt whatever you're doing."

Chapter 21

The day had barely started and already it was exploding at her feet. She had no time for visitors, let alone from two people she cared so much about and wanted to spend time with. Katie apologized to Jason and agreed to meet him for dinner. She picked a restaurant close to her apartment and set a time for their *date* for 8PM. This would give her enough time to get her boys settled in and shower after what promised to be a grueling day. She carefully, not too intimately, kissed Jason's cheek and said with a warm smile, "I'm so looking forward to dinner. I'll see you later."

As Jason walked past the reception area, he thanked Angie and nodded to the distinguished white-haired gentleman standing with his coat draped over his left arm. As Jason got into the elevator, he had the sense that he knew the man. Then it hit him. *That was Senator White.*

Feeling a moment of Déjà **vu**, Katie said with the biggest smile on her face, "Oh my God, John. What a morning of surprise visits. What are you doing here?" Before he had a chance to answer, she blurted out, "Is Rebecca OK!?" John calmed her down, telling her

"Everyone is fine." He asked Katie, "Do you mind if I close the door so we can speak in private?" Katie suddenly remembered Rebecca White's last, reassuring words before she departed New York.

John and I will be right here for him and we'll know where you are.

Before pushing her office door closed, Katie called out to her assistant in a nervous, almost trembling voice. "Angie, can you please hold my calls?" Katie observed Angie's nod indicating her understanding. Katie called out, "Thank you" and proceeded to close the office door. A few people in the open work area looked over at Angie inquisitively. She simply shrugged her shoulders and went about her work. Behind closed doors, Senator White began the process of breaking the news about Jack.

The shriek made everyone in the common area and those in nearby offices take notice. Angie wanted to go to Katie but held back. After a few minutes of silence, Angie knocked and without waiting for a response, opened Katie's office door. She did not expect to find her boss sitting on the floor leaning back against her couch. Her visitor was holding her tight. Angie excitedly demanded, "What is going on here. Katie, are you alright?" Katie couldn't speak, but waved her arms

142

indicating she was OK. John suggested, "Perhaps some water would be helpful. Thank you, Angie." Angie stepped out without saying anything else. John continued, "This is shocking news, but very good news. Jack is alive and well." Katie still could not get any words out. She had so many questions; questions that she practiced for months in order to be ready for Jack's return. Now that reality had brought news of her missing husband, all those prepared questions remained jumbled and stuck some place out of reach in her head. "You cannot say anything to anyone or discuss Jack's re-emergence; for everyone's sake. You understand what I'm telling you, and how this works Katie. You have to get past the shock and go about your day. We can meet tonight and I will fill you in with all the details." Angie knocked on the partially open door. "Here is some water. Are you sure you're OK?" "Yes, Angie. This is so embarrassing. One of my closest cousins was very ill, terminal, and now he is miraculously in remission. I suppose I over-reacted. Sorry." Angie smiled, the kind of smile on a smart person's face that says *OK, for now, but I don't really buy that one*. "That's really great news. Call me if you need anything else."

John, in a barely audible whisper, took another ten minutes to fill Katie in on the major details about Germany and the process of debriefing. He told Katie,

"I'm flying to Germany in the morning. I won't be able to contact you or anyone else with regard to the 'Catcher'." Katie made a face. John continued. "I didn't come up with that code name. I'll call you; you'll know all is OK by my comments." Katie took the senator's hand in hers, "You mean like, 'The flowers are beautiful this time of year?' It's so *secret agent*. I don't think I'll be able to breathe until he's home." "No expectation for a time line, Katie. There is still a bigger issue that he may be involved in and we need to make certain he hasn't been compromised." Katie abruptly let go of John's hand. "You know Jack! You all know he could never be broken!" Her strong vocals, even in a whisper, made her voice sound scary. Senator White stood up and extended his arms for a hug. He held Katie tight and whispered, "You and I both know Jack is solid. He needs to convince everyone else. Jack is coming home, Katie. Be patient. Be ecstatically happy; but keep it internalized for now. Tell no one. Not even the boys. No one! Discussing things even with those with proper clearance can lead to bad consequences." Katie still appeared to be in disbelief. John took hold of her hands, "I'll see you around 8PM. I'll text you the restaurant information."

ADA Owens stood just inside her office doorway and watched as her dearest friend and closest confidant thanked Angie and headed for the elevators. Her heart pounded as if she had just run a marathon. Tears rolled down her cheek. Her emotions were all over the place. She wanted to scream out again in joy, but refrained from doing so, realizing that would not be wise.

Following the senator's advice, she settled back at her desk and began reading over some of her case files. She realized she was reading the same lines twice and three times. There was no way she was going to be able to think about anything but Jack's return.

"Angie, I'm taking an early lunch. I have something I need to take care of." Angie smiled, "Sure, Katie. Enjoy." "You want anything? A sandwich or some of that delicious gelato from the new bakery on Beverley?" Katie said it with a genuine smile that made Angie relax. "No, thanks. See you in a bit."

Katie stepped into the elevator with her phone in hand. "Hi, you at your hotel?" Her heart pounded, she wanted to share her joy with her close *friend*. "Something came up and dinner is not a possibility. What about lunch?" She thought he would be upset, but instead, he sounded excited. "Sure, your hotel's restaurant is perfect. I can walk there. See you in ten minutes."

I know Jason is here for me; but Jack is coming home. What can I tell him? Not the truth. Not yet anyway. He has heard "Jason, you are so sweet and such a dear friend. I'm just not ready yet." He will not understand. He will hate me.

Chapter 22

Jack once again found himself a prisoner *with slightly better accommodations*. He glanced over to his barracks style single bed and prayed for a solid night's sleep. The Three-hour layover at Camp Lemonnier afforded him little rest. He thought the flight to Germany would afford him time to calm his deep-seated anxiety. Instead, it left him with so many mixed and out of control emotions. Jack hoped that his request to a *higher authority* would be given serious consideration.

God, I know that I have apologized for each time I kneeled and prayed to Allah. I assumed you have an agreement to look out for each other's patrons. I imagined you both working a compromise to help keep me alive. For that great gift, I have thanked you both.

After a decent meal of roasted chicken breast and mashed potatoes and some warm tea, Jack dozed on and off, waking up every hour or so. The usual bad dreams haunted him and the mattress was too soft, causing his need for frequent position changes. Albeit, the accommodations were a bit drab and his bedding less than comfortable, they were far superior to his previous sleeping arrangements during the past eight months. In the morning, after a light breakfast of poached eggs on white toast and hash brown potatoes, the routine of examinations and probing questions continued unabated. Aside from the endless parade of MD's, neurologists and psychologists, Jack already had endured three interviews, labeled as part of his debriefing. The military reviewed his records and were familiar with his joint task force work with them. They were as respectful as could be expected. The FBI, on the other hand, treated Jack as if he were the enemy. They didn't view his past interactions with them favorably, and outwardly accused him of not being a team player. Their paranoia overrode anything good they might have read in his files about his dedicated and highly successful service to his country. The questions asked by them would be considered insulting and crude, but Jack understood that they had to push him hard. He would be the first one to toss the trust thing out the window if he were on the other side of the table. In the past few years, he'd seen beautiful people turn ugly. His most trusted associates suddenly betrayed him. After a pleasant lunch with one of the shrinks who thought a lunch date would help reveal Jack's inner soul, Jack returned to his somewhat shabby quarters for some quiet time. *Gee, that lunch visit was helpful. I guess it's good to talk about my inner demons with an impartial person. Those FBI guys are all over the place. So much like the many visits I had over*

the past few months. You know, "Good Cop, Bad Cop."
Only, there were never any, "good" cops.

No one visited him for hours. He had not seen Jane or Avi since they landed in Germany. His *combat* buddies' absence came as no surprise. After all, Avi was a foreign agent originally sent to work with another deep cover agent, Sanji, to obtain White House secrets for Israel. Sanji, a Presidential Secret Service agent, turned out to be a double agent himself. While spying for Israel, he also worked with an Al Qaeda terror group, spying on the White House for them as well. The new vice president and his wife were part of the terror group and their plot to infiltrate government at all levels. They arranged to have Jack arrested on fabricated charges. Sanji was supposed to escort him to a detention center to await interrogation. The original plan was for them to set the stage to look like Jack was trying to escape, ultimately ending in his death. In the end, they disclosed their true identities to Jack and brought him to a safe house so everyone would think he was dead.

Jane's story was much more complicated. A few words to describe her could be... former terrorist, assassin, evil seductress, and any other horrible monikers that would fit her to a tee. In fact, any good shrink would say she was a hard-core schizophrenic psychopath; albeit stunningly gorgeous and cunning. The one unnerving thing to be noted about Jane is that she is strikingly beautiful, damn sexy, and can pose as the most loving and caring person. Jane is definitely not schizophrenic; she is most assuredly capable of being psychopathic along with all the other deadly possibilities. Somewhere along their devastating relationship, Jane turned. Jack was certain the birth of her own twins, and the sinister attempt by her own people to take them from her, had a major role in her change of allegiance. In her defense, which most in Jack's world would never agree with, she never discerned any difference. From birth, like all the other "Twin" terrorists, Jane was raised to hate America and all it stood for. Deprived of any human nurturing, she was literally a homegrown terrorist. It took the first few years of living in the shadows of her children to start the metamorphosis toward humanity.

The click of the door lock echoed, indicating someone would be entering. Jack sat on his less than comfortable cot disguised as a bed. He leaned back against the wall and tried to appear relaxed. He assumed they were bringing him his dinner. With no clock, Jack relied on his stomach to indicate that it was dinnertime. Based on the grumbling noises emanating from Jack's mid-section, dinner was late. A marine sergeant entered.

"Sorry to disturb you, Mr. Owens. I will be escorting you to the executive dining room. You have a guest this evening." As they walked down the corridor, Jack noticed the clock on the wall. It was 1840. "Kind of late for dinner. Is this part of my integration back in to the civilized world?" The Marine kept his head pointed forward, "I wouldn't know, sir. Here we are, sir."

The dining room appeared to be set up to accommodate about thirty people, but there was only one person seated at one of the smaller picnic like tables. His back was to Jack, but Jack knew John White's physique and balding grey hair better than his own.

"John?" Jack's hesitation turned quickly to optimism as the visitor slowly and steadily stood up and turned to face Jack. "Oh, dear God! It is you!" They both raised their arms gesturing for that manly hug. With tears forming in his eyes, John exclaimed, "Son, you had us all in a state of misery these past months. I have to say that your predicament has sent the intelligence world tumbling upside down. It took the man at the top to get me a high enough clearance to visit you." John put his arms around Jack, taking in another hug. Before releasing his embrace, John whispered in Jack's ear, "I had to agree to our visit being recorded. They have ears on us."

The story Jack told, started with his first night home, and last night home with Katie and the boys. "The wine. It had to be the wine. We were drugged. I woke up back in that shit-hole of a desert." He described how the different groups passed him off to one another. He also told of his torture, not so much in detail; and of his resistance to them breaking him. "I've been through hell and back before all of this. There is no way anyone could break me. I think they resurrected an old plan to use me in some plot, but with no how or when. I think the last group of captors holding me had instructions to try one last time to break me for information, and then bury me deep beneath the sand. I overheard one of my guards boasting about it to another, during one hot-as-shit afternoon. I understood enough to get the unpleasant mental picture of my then, impending fate." John shook his head in dismay and compassion. "You have been through a lot, Jack." The senator whispered close to Jack's ear, "Tell them whatever they need to hear so you can come home. Just be careful not to give them any reason to hold you here." "I have nothing much to tell, John, except that of my starvation and torture. On the other hand, Avi picked up intelligence of something big planned for the states; something deadly." Jack stopped, as he noted John subtly signaling to stop talking. Jack understood, remembering John's quiet words, "They have ears on us." *No one is ever safe when there are ears listening in. Trust only those in your personal inner circle.* Jack heard John's words from years ago. They were the same words imbedded in his mind throughout his CIA training and career.

The senator looked up toward the canteen doors and said to the empty room aside from he and Jack, "We are starving; may we please have some dinner?

"Tell me about Katie and the boys; and Boston. Did you tell her I'm alive?" "Katie knows. I went to Boston and met with her to give her the news personally. As you can imagine, she was in a state of shock and then euphoria. She never gave up on you. I explained to her the covert nature of your emergence. She joined me for dinner later that night, actually, last night, to follow up. You won't be allowed to speak with her or anyone else until you return to the states." John sighed, "And, I'm sorry to say, we don't know when that will be. I probably won't be allowed access to you again either until then." Jack put his head between his hands, "I need to see my family. I will tell them what I can, related to my captivity in Yemen; whatever will get me home. But, I will not divulge any of the really important stuff. None of the information crammed in my head that will help fight these monsters. Not until I am home and with my family."

John departed shortly after dinner, but not before assuring Jack that, all would be worked out. He reminded Jack of how much his services were needed now, more than ever. Not more than five minutes passed, barely enough time for Jack to de-stress and sip his coffee, before a sergeant knocked on the canteen door and entered. "I'm here to escort you back to your quarters, Sir."

Chapter 23

"God damn it! The natives are restless in Boston. I'm heading over to see Mahoney. Maybe he can get the commissioner to take this serial killer problem more seriously." Mayor Ridgley was angry; at whom, he wasn't sure. Fortunately, the deputy mayor was an old schoolmate of Mahoney's. He called to give him the "heads up" that His Honor was en route to the DA's office. DA Mahoney summoned Katie to his office. They both waited for the grand entrance. Katie figured that the Boston office had little invested in their new senior ADA. She was the perfect fall gal. She was determined to deliver a different perspective. This tough lady was no longer going to allow anyone to step on her. Not even her new boss.

There was no "Hello" or any other form of greeting from the mayor as he stormed into DA Mahoney's office like a raging bull. He shouted, "I want to know what pressure you've been putting on Boston's finest. How many investigators are assigned to this case? The fine citizens of Boston are in hysterics. The wedding business is crashing all around us. I've received hundreds of calls from the music entertainment businesses, the photography studios, catering halls. Couples are canceling every day. What the hell are we going to tell the press?"

Katie lost focus as the mayor rambled on. She was thinking of Jack. Her mind played images of a battered, bloody man, thin and weak. These were real images, a replay of a previous, almost deadly reality of Jack's. She tried switching channels, now seeing the Jack Owens she remembered the last evening they were together. She could feel his touch and hear his voice tell her how much he missed her; how much he loved her. She had to focus on reality, but then her mind switched to a vision of Jason sitting alone in the restaurant that she had chosen, waiting patiently for her.

"ADA Owens!"

Katie snapped back to the present moment. "Mayor Ridgley, it is a pleasure to meet you, sir. DA Mahoney had me up all night reviewing the case. I also met with our lead investigator, Detective Lawrence, earlier this week. We are doing everything possible to assist the Boston PD in making a solid arrest; one that will stick. We will stop this monster." The mayor huffed, and then turned his attention to Katie's boss. "I like her. She has spunk. I have faith in her resilient determination. Make sure the press sees it as well, and sends the same message to the public.

We need to calm the masses." Leaving no option for additional discussion, Mayor Ridgley did an almost perfect military about-face and smartly marched out of the office.

"Wow." Katie found herself embarrassed at her one word remark. "Wow is an understatement. He can be a real pain, but the people get a charge out of him. They like his arrogant methods of communication." Mahoney sat down in his big cushy chair and motioned to Katie to sit in one of the chairs in front of his desk.

"You are aware, boss, that we have very little to go on at this time. Our only suspect, actually 'person of interest', is not a likely candidate for this. His only guilt is for a lack of self-control." Mahoney grinned, "You know how this is going to play out; you're the lucky face of the DA's office for this case." Katie's mind wandered a bit. *Yeah sure. Scapegoat is more like it.* "What do I tell them; the news media?" Her boss stood up. She did the same, his gesture was clear; the meeting was over. His firm, yet gentle hand on her elbow seemed a bit unethical, but had she been *one of the guys*, there would be no thought of impropriety. As the only female senior level ADA, Katie had to make some allowances; as long as lines were not crossed. He quietly told her, "Tell them as little as possible but enough to calm them down. Make sure you can meet the expectations they have for this office and our fine police department without making any promises that we can't keep." He released his grip on her, sending her off with his final words of encouragement.

"You got this, ADA Owens. You got this."

Katie's confusion over her boss's strange attitude must have shown. "Are you alright, Katie?" Angie tried to smile but her concern made it difficult for her to do so.

*****

Barely thirty minutes after she returned to her office, a barrage of reporters from CNN and several local stations packed the building's lobby. A frantic concierge asked Katie if she would come down and address their questions. She agreed to go down and meet with them. As soon as Katie exited the elevator, the reporters began shouting a barrage of questions at her.

"ADA Owens, Mayor Ridgley told us he had your office's assurances for a swift and thorough capture of this maniac killer. Would you care to make a statement elaborating on that?" Katie took a breath. "Of course."

"My office is working closely with Boston PD's finest to investigate and apprehend this vicious predator. Cases like this tend..."

Another reporter in the rear of the crowd interrupted her shouting loudly, "Public confidence in Boston's law enforcement is waning; are there any suspects or leads that you can share with the public?"

"Detectives are questioning several persons of interest. I have no other information that I can share with you at this time."

"What about the waiter, is it true that—"

"The waiter was an acquaintance of the second victim. He was a person of interest whom we hoped could give us information as to the timeline of the victim's alleged abduction. At this time we do not think this particular individual is directly responsible for this victim's disappearance."

Katie put up her hands. "That's all I have for now, except to say that we are devoting massive resources in our effort to solve this case quickly. The DA's office, along with our law enforcement agencies are determined to allocate any and all resources necessary to apprehend the person or persons responsible for these heinous acts."

Chapter 24

The jury sat quietly, focusing on the defendant and his lawyer. Early on in the home invasion trial, the suspect sat before them in his orange prison issued jumpsuit. Handcuffed during his two previous appearances, the jury perceived the accused as dangerous. The prosecution would now need to sway the twelve jurors, seven men and five women, in favor of a conviction. This would mean a possible ten-year sentence for the home invasion, followed by a minimum of fifteen years to life for each of the two rape victims. The sentences would run concurrently. Now, on this final judgment day, the young man of thirty-one, wearing his new suit, anxiously waited with his hands clasped in front of him. Fifteen minutes earlier, before they brought in the jurors, guards escorted the prisoner back into the courtroom and seated him in his designated spot. His feet, now shackled and out of sight from the jurors. His appearance, clean-shaven and well dressed, and with his hands absent of any restraints, promoted the illusion of his self-proclaimed innocence.

Throughout the two-week trial, the three victims gave detailed testimony of the assault by the accused. The wife described how "the monster" dragged her and her sixteen-year-old daughter into one of the upstairs bedrooms where he bound and gagged them. The male victim was beaten and tasered until he gave up the location of the family safe that contained cash and jewelry. As a husband and father, he only cared about his family's safety, so he gave this guy what he wanted. He pleaded for him to leave without harming his wife and daughter. Unfortunately, that would not be the case. The women endured repeated assaults while the man of the house lay bound and helpless.

As each of the victims took the stand and recounted the events of that day, the prosecution appeared to become frustrated with their testimony. There seemed to be some inconsistencies and confusion compared to what they had said in earlier interviews with police. This could leave a jury with "reasonable doubt," the basis for an acquittal. Katie had seen witness accounts change before and hoped the jury would understand that these women were tortured and humiliated. Very often, in cases like these, memories of actual events can get distorted. If she did her job right, the jurors would understand this and accept their earlier testimony as stated. ADA Owens had to turn their focus to the horrific events of that day. She had to convince all twelve of them, especially the men, that not only did the accused enter their home uninvited but also to the extent of physical and mental damage that he inflicted on the victims. DNA found at the scene would erase any reasonable doubt that this was their man.

The judge gently pounded his gavel and declared the completion of the testimony phase of the trial. "Counselor, are you ready for your closing arguments?" Katie methodically shuffled a few folders on the desk in front of her and then stood up facing the judge. "We are, your honor, thank you." The jurors had to take notice. ADA Owens was a beautiful and obviously intelligent woman with a strong will for making her case. She glanced at the defendant and his lawyers. They too had to admire the woman standing in the spotlight. She wore her moderately short pencil skirt, the gray one, and a silky white blouse. She complimented her outfit with a blazer that fell just below the bottom of the skirt. It was Jack's favorite outfit. He once told her that she wore the same type of outfit the day he admitted to himself that he was in love with her. Her intention to draw the jury's focus onto her seemed to be working. Now she had to add some smooth verbiage to get her conviction.

In the last row of the courtroom, one spectator looked on with unabashed admiration. The heavily bearded man wearing dark sunglasses and a backward facing baseball cap leaned forward in his seat. He asked the woman seated in front of him, "She is damn good, don't you think?" He figured by the brush off that she was there for the defendant. Jack considered that perhaps his battered appearance projected him as a homeless person. *Darn snobs!*

The defense made their last pitch to persuade the jurors of the defendant's sincere regrets for the home invasion. They held to the defendant's sworn testimony that he never physically assaulted the women even though forensic evidence proved otherwise. Katie was certain that his admission to being in the home would ultimately lead the jurors to accept his guilt on the more serious charges of assault and rape. Deliberation only took two hours. ADA Katie Claire Owens won her first case in Boston. The defendant received two concurrent twenty-five to life sentences for the assaults, plus the maximum of 15 years for the violent home invasion.

The media hounds crowded around Katie and her team. They shouted countless questions and asked about previous cases she had headlined while in New York. Before the trial had begun, Katie spent hours preparing for this moment. She smiled a lot, and gave short, professional responses. One reporter blurted out, "Can you give us an update on the Boston Wedding Serial

Killer?" Katie put her up hands for everyone to calm down. "All I can tell you is that we have every possible resource available to us; local and state police, FBI, my office, all are working to apprehend and put away this maniac. Thank you all for your astute and professional coverage of these cases." Another reporter yelled out, "That is the same thing you said last week. Have you all hit a stone wall?" Katie smiled, "Thank you, everyone."

Television viewers watched the early evening news, some to catch up on the events of the day, some to get a weather update. Many caught the end of the news while waiting for their favorite TV game show, Jeopardy, to air. One viewer in particular, paid close attention to the day's recap of the murder trial. He thought, *how lovely she is*. He opened his laptop and searched for everything about ADA Katie Owens. He found a wealth of information. *"Hmm, I see your husband took off on you. Perhaps you need someone to relieve some of the sexual frustration loneliness can stir up."* He looked across the small, dimly lit room into an old style mirror mounted above his hand-me-down dresser. One of the drawers stuck out further than the others; distracting him. This angered him. He glimpsed at himself in the mirror again. A dark and eerie shadow of a man grinned back. The image of that person in the mirror lived in another dimension. *I can be here and*

I can be in there. He took comfort seeing himself as if there were two of him, making his transgression into darkness easier. This obsession with himself made him hungry for more power, more violence; more control.

Katie looked around hoping to see him. The car she hired was parked at the curb nearby; the driver leaning on the front fender smoking a cigarette. Her heart pounded heavily in anticipation. Senator White had called her last night to tell her the good news of Jack's impending release, and reinstatement with the Agency. He assured Katie that Jack would be on a plane headed home, *very soon*. John could not give her a specific day or even a week for when Jack would arrive in Boston. John further explained of the tight security measures and covert nature of his return to the states. He told her that Jack was already *being Jack* and negotiating the terms of his reinstatement. *That's my Jack*. She took one last look before walking toward her car.

"Excuse me, ADA Owens. Would you be so kind as to grant me a brief interview?" The thin face, scruffy beard, and dark glasses threw her off for only a second. Then her heart seemed to stop and her head began to spin as tears rolled down her cheeks. She reached toward him to touch his face; to see if it was really him. He stepped back, "Not here. Walk with me." Jack pointed to a news van parked about three hundred feet down the block. They spoke not a word until they stood alongside the van. Katie's expression said, "Really? Cloak and dagger?" Jack pulled open the side door, and they got in. Katie noticed the two "Men in Black" wearing the traditional dark shades seated in the front of the vehicle. The agent sitting on the passenger side nodded as he slid the opaque privacy panel closed. Jack removed the baseball cap and glasses. The moment seemed so surreal, even though Katie should have been used to the *cloak and dagger* crap by now.

"Hey, you."

Katie said nothing. She sat frozen, staring at him; at his emaciated face. She drew in air, realizing she had stopped breathing. She feared she might faint. Jack had tears forming as he told her, "I am so sorry for what I put you and the kids through. I am so sorry for all of it."

"Shut up, Jack! SHUT THE FUCK UP!

Don't you *dare* apologize; not to me, not to your children." Katie still had not moved a muscle. She drew another deep breath and exhaled slowly. Her lips quivered as she spoke, "I was so confused at first. I didn't know who to trust. Then I hated you for lying to me about our new beginning, and you staying in the open. You promised me there would be no more undercover assignments. I hated all of them for lying for you. But, as the months, that seemed like years, went by, I knew it was something else. You never let so much time pass without getting some sort of message to me. Everyone said you were dead. Those who didn't know you, encouraged me to move on. I never gave up on you, Jack. I knew you would find a way to get home to us." Jack wiped the steady stream of tears flowing down his cheeks with his sleeve, and reached out to his wife.

"You can come closer. Amazingly, I still have all my teeth. I even brushed and gargled, this being a special occasion and all."

"Damn you, Jack!" Katie lunged into his arms locking her lips to his.

Part 2

JACK IS BACK

Wayne Lasner

Chapter 25

"Last call!"

The young couple stood up from their dinner table. The mom took hold of her little boy's hand, "Come on Charlie, it's time to go home. Say bye-bye to Mr. Pete." The husband placed two twenties and a loonie on the table. "Thanks, Pete. You've got the best Shepherd's pie in all of Canada." Pete waved his good night salute and ambled his way to the other end of the bar. "OK, Amos. In case your ears are soused too, last call for you means drink up and get out." The thin man with a scraggly beard slowly turned toward the barman that had been attending to his beverage needs for nearly ten years, and frowned. "But Pete, it's only 9:30!" He protested.

"Sorry, my friend. New rules set by the wife. I'm a family man now. We're only open late, Friday and Saturday nights."

Both men turned their attention to the gal coming through the pub's entrance. "That's right, Amos. You heard the man. Lights out in ten. You need a ride back to wherever it is you're staying these days?" Jane pulled off her knitted cap, letting her shiny reddish blond hair flow down over her shoulders. With every move, Jane seemed to be in stealth mode. She could enter a room full of people and take all of their clothes and they would never even notice her. But, if she wanted to be noticed, *eh*; noticed would be an understatement. Amos turned to face Pete. "She is a lovely sight, Pete. But, I hate when she does that." Pete winked, even though he had no idea to what his poor mate was referring to. Then, as if Amos' batteries suddenly died, he folded his arms on the bar and slowly laid his head down.

"Hey, luv. I'm home." She adored the way Pete still smiled when she entered a room. It was the same smile in the morning when they awoke, as it was when she saw him after an alternating shift at the bar. And, as it was when she returned after being away for weeks at a time. He made her feel special every minute of the day. She walked over to Amos first and rubbed his back gently. "Time to go home, old friend." Amos waved her off as he stood, almost stumbling. "*Eh*. See ya tomorrow, Pete, and bossy lady." Pete said, "You betcha, my friend." Jane escorted Amos to the door, locking up after he exited. She turned to "Smiling Pete," as she had nicknamed him, to find his arms outstretched, waiting for her. Envision a female cheetah in the wild lunging at its prey. Jane all but flew into Pete's arms, her killer grip embracing him.

"I missed you so much!"
"I missed you so much more!"

Fifteen minutes later, Jane fastened the last button on Pete's shirt, "There ya go. Like I was never here." She briefly filled Pete in as much as she needed to in order for him to relax. She needed him to trust her judgment and have faith in her abilities. He knew she went abroad to investigate a far-fetched story about Jack being sighted. Jane did not detail where she was going. She also did not divulge the results of her trip. Pete knew not to ask. Jane would tell him when and what she could. They vowed to never have secrets unless it involved her association with Jack and all that goes along with that relationship. "Let's go home, mistress." "Who's with the kids?" "They're with Ron and Marne, at their place. I'm supposed to pick them up by ten." Jane looked at her phone to check the time. "That gives us another fifteen minutes." She grinned, grabbed Pete's hand, and pulled him into the back office.

*****

The undercover news van pulled up at a small motel just outside of the Boston city limits. Jack tapped on the partition, which immediately slid open. "Give me two hours. Go get something to eat." "Sorry boss, but we

173

have orders not to lose sight of you." "Just two hours guys. Please." He pleaded. They looked at each other shrugging their shoulders. "OK. Two hours." Here. The driver handed Jack a solid white digital key card with no markings on it. "Room 222. I'll be knocking on the door in exactly 2 hours, not a minute longer." Jack replied, "Gotcha, boss. Thanks."

As Jack and Katie entered the room, Katie remarked, "Are you renting this by the hour?" She made a face showing her disgust for its lack of ambiance or anything else. Jack smirked, "Give me ten to shower."

Katie waited patiently. Her heart had not found its normal rhythm yet. Finally, the bathroom door opened and a huge plume of steam rushed out. Jack had shaved and trimmed his beard. There he stood, with only a towel around his waist. Katie looked at him, starting at his feet and gazing slowly upward until their eyes met. Jack spoke first. "Most of me is intact. At least the important parts." He looked at his wife sitting on the bed, tears again rolling down her cheeks. "You're still dressed?" Katie stood and walked over to him. She touched his chest.

"They starved you…"
"Yes."

She wanted to ask more questions, but her mind, frazzled and still adjusting to the present situation of Jack's return, made it difficult to form her thoughts into logical sentences.

Jack reached for his pants. "It's OK. We need to give ourselves some time to adjust. This whole crappy mess; the past eight months, has been as difficult for you as for me. It was presumptuous of me to think we could just... just resume our lives again."

"I'm so sorry, Jack."

Jack took his wife's hand and led her to the bed. "Please, just let me hold you." As they lay together, Jack told Katie how much he missed her and the boys. He told her that knowing they were OK at home was all he had to keep him going. "I was determined to return to you. I dreamed of you every day. When bad things happened to me, I tuned them out and instead imagined holding you in my arms. You were the reason for my survival."

As they lay holding each other, Katie's mind became flooded with questions. She stroked his hair gently, noting that it had thinned out considerably. She tried organizing the most logical ones to ask. The ones Jack might be able to answer. "When will I see you again? When can the boys see you? Can I tell them that their daddy is OK?" Jack ran his fingers through her perfectly groomed, silky hair. If he could, he would lay there as they were, for eternity. "I don't have an answer to either. The less anyone knows the safer you and the boys will be. I promise to keep in touch in some way. It may be a few days or weeks. Jane will be working with me. We have to bust this conspiracy wide open once and for all. Can you wait for me?" "After all we have been through... you better get this done quickly." Jack took her in his arms again and kissed her gently, then harder. This time she returned his passion. "I promise you, Katie Claire Owens, when this is done, so am I. I'll retire for real. Not even an office job."

Jack walked Katie back to the undercover news van. He noted the black SUV parked across the way; no doubt part of his twenty–four hour protection team. The driver made sure he had Jack's attention and motioned to the Black SUV. "We'll take your wife back to her office. The other team will escort you back to your secured residence." *Funny how secret agent Jack Owens needs a protection team.* "What bullshit!" He looked across the way. "Sorry guys; nothing personal."

*****

"The twins really missed you, Jane. I really missed you. How could you leave us again so soon?" Jane saw this coming. "Look, Pete. You know just about every horrible thing about me." Pete put his finger to her lips stopping her attempt to make an excuse for leaving again. "You're not that person anymore. Everyone has a good and a bad side to them. You found your good side and allowed it to become a dominant force. You are a wonderful mother and an incredible wife. You do not owe the Yanks anything more than you have already given." "But I do, my love. I owe more than I can ever repay. I owe Jack for trusting me even after all the atrocious things I did to him."

"But, Jane."

"I promise you, Pete. This is going to be the last of it. We will expose and eradicate this deadly conspiracy, and only then, will I come home and never leave you and the kids again. I promise."

Pete held Jani and Mikeal, one arm around each of them, reassuring them that their mother would return home soon. "You're going to miss your mom, eh?" The kids looked on silently, as Jane got into a cab. Pete took their hands and led them back into the cabin. For a moment, his mind played back images from earlier in the year when the judge finalized the adoption papers. He wasn't sure how Jane would react, given her sordid past and lack of family experiences. To his surprise, she was ecstatic over his suggestion to be legally declared the children's dad.

Jane wiped away tears as her car approached Pearson International. She needed some of the old Jane if she wanted to get the job done.

"As our hearts heal from the painful loss of a loved one, our minds gradually transition from the haunting memories of the sad and painful events leading up to that loss and we start to remember the happy, more significant moments shared with them.

It is then, that our tears turn to smiles."

Chapter 26

It had been more than six years since William's tragic death. He was the best friend Jack had ever known. Unlike Jack's extraverted, and somewhat conceited personality, William would always be remembered by those *not in the know*, as the calm, cool one. William, much like his father in his day, displayed impressive intelligence and irrepressible debating skills, making him everyone's choice for a successful run in politics. Jack first met his best friend when they were small children playing on a South Carolina beach. William's parents, John and Rebecca, quickly became friends with Jack's parents. Both families made it a tradition to vacation together each summer for many more years. The boys eventually ended up roommates at Emory's Atlanta campus. The two boys both had competitive personalities and played the challenge game against each other since early on in their friendship. Their bond so strong that neither took offense at losing to the other. They shared just about everything with each other, but still maintained their own personalities and respected boundaries.

Like most relationships, strong friendships can endure most anything. The true test came about in their senior year at Emory. Jack had already been indoctrinated into the CIA program, which would start him in training immediately after graduation. This would be the only secret he kept from his best friend. William had already met the love of his life, Katie Claire. Katie of course being the one thing not shared, that Jack found difficult to adjust to. Years after William's death, the randomness of life and a series of unfortunate events would later reunite Jack and Katie, allowing him to recognize his true affection for her.

A few months before their college graduation, Jane entered the picture with a mission to draw William into her world. A more devious plan involved breaking him away from his friends and family and causing friction and a breakup with Katie. Jane's mission was to estrange him from those who knew him best. The seductress would open the door for William's replacement by his terrorist groomed, believed dead at birth, twin brother, Carlton.

Jack hated William for his betrayal of their friendship. He hated what he did to Katie. It wasn't until that fateful night he ran into William, who was actually Carlton, that he realized something was different about his former friend. After years of hate and anguish, Jack now remembered William back in the day, as his best friend. He could again dream of the good times as children, playing on that South Carolina beach. He played images over and over again of the first time they both met Katie Claire. William's huge, infectious smile re-imprinted itself back in Jack's mind's eye.

Jack Owens, *desk bound CIA Analyst*, was abruptly thrust into the world of international espionage. This would be the beginning of his efforts to save the western world's destruction by foreign enemies, from within our borders.

After his arrest, Carlton could not show remorse for what happened to his twin brother, William. That was one of the many emotions his groomers prevented him from experiencing. He died sometime later in an undisclosed military prison, from "undisclosed causes."

Using the utmost discretion, Jack would continue to build a team of covert agents and military specialists, along with Senator John White, who was both William and Carlton's dad. Together they sought out and obliterated major drug rings that helped to fund these diabolical plots and eventually battling the infiltration of these covert Twin terrorists. All of which lead to an explosive ending at the highest levels of government.

They thought they had won the battle. They thought America was finally safe. Jack's captivity in Yemen and long endurance reunited him with his allies

Avi and Jane.   Avi's unrelated mission uncovered information that the war of "The Twin" was still on.

Chapter 27

"You seem to be in much better spirits today, ADA Owens." Katie smiled at her junior intern. Ellen smiled back. "I mean, well, this is so nice. Thank you for inviting me to lunch." Katie's distraction went unnoticed; she wondered what Jack was doing. She missed him so much; but now, things were different. She had seen him and touched him. He was alive and well considering all that he had gone through. The dangers he would face going forward, she could deal with. She had been living that hell for years before his disappearance. That was their lives together. "Oh, I'm so glad you said yes. This is nice. You can drop the formalities and call me Katie when we are out socially." Her intern giggled softly. "Thank you, ADA - Katie." The waitress casually strolled over to their table. Her tall appearance and frumpy red hair made Katie imagine one of those food servers from the old fifties sitcoms she watched as a kid. Her nametag said "Agnes." Even Ellen seemed to notice and tried to hide her grin. By her facial expression, Agnes appeared to be less than overjoyed with her job. "Hello, ladies. What can I get for you today?" As Katie took one more scan of the menu, she observed a somewhat shady guy in dark sunglasses and a knit hat seated a few tables in front of her. She was sure he was looking at her. *Maybe he's just a creepy guy*. Katie turned her attention back to the waitress but as soon as she started to speak, Agnes turned and walked over to the next table to toss a straw onto the table where an elderly man was seated with a large vanilla milk shake in front of him. Obviously, with no sense of urgency, Agnes did an about-face and took the three steps back to Katie and Ellen's table. Katie continued as if the waitress had never walked away. "I'll have the tuna with bacon and tomato on lightly toasted rye, and an iced coffee. Thank you." She looked at the menu one last time out of habit confirming her choice to herself before handing the menu back to the waitress. She glanced over to see if the *perv* was still ogling her, just in time to see his back as he left the cafe. *I'm being paranoid, that's all*. At first, alarm bells from the past rang out. After all, and more than once, one of her husband's dangerous adversaries had kidnapped or assaulted her. In at least one situation, her abductor stalked her while she and her family vacationed at the beach on Long Island. She ignored it then, and paid the price later. Then she considered the possibility that *Jack is getting involved in some deep shit. He most probably has one of his agents keeping an eye on me. They all have such big egos. He probably spooked himself, believing that I caught him*. Katie asked her intern, "So, Ellen, what's your plan after graduation?" Ellen giggled as she proceeded to dominate the conversation with her bubbly personality. Katie liked Ellen and felt comfortable having her around.

The rest of the day moved along quickly as ADA Owens followed up with her law enforcement associates assigned to work on the serial killer case. Unfortunately, they had little more to report. Katie's *major* case was going nowhere; except cold.

****

He recorded all the major news broadcasts including CNN, whose reporter just finished a profile on Boston's newest prosecutor. The killer searched through a few of the recorded networks looking for his next mark before replaying the CNN one. This next one would be a major milestone for him. His mind raced with determination. He began to rant to himself; again.

"How could it have taken me so long to realize that you're the one that I've been waiting for? The others were simply to pass the time. I'm coming for you ADA Owens. You are new and alone in this big city. I will be your special friend. I will show you affection; and discipline. You will experience pain in a way that will make you crave more of it. I will have you begging for more." He calmed himself during a brief moment's pause from his delusions.

Suddenly, he became agitated again, asking and answering himself as he moved back and forth across the room in a tirade

"So, you want to find me and restrain me?"

"No! I'll decide how this will play out."

"I'll find you first. I will show you that going to hell can be erotic. You want to know me? Well, you will. Only I can satisfy you in a way that God meant it to be. God created men like me to show women like you, true love." He paced the room a few more times before continuing his shouting rant.

"It is man who has perverted society with his warped rules of acceptability."

"You will know me as God wants all woman to know a man. To hell with sweet virginity. I will set you free."

Alan Mayfield clicked the remote, silencing the television.

"I will set you free*!" I will set you free...*

His mind continued the rant in silence. *But first, you have to really want me. You have to eat, drink and sleep thinking of me. I need to allow you to get a little closer to keep your attention focused.* Alan clicked on the TV again and replayed the 6PM broadcast. Again, speaking aloud as if she were standing in front of him in his lonely room,

"You have beautiful eyes, ADA Owens; Katie. I suppose if we are going to be intimate, we should be on a first name basis."

Alan Mayfield sat on the edge of his one, wobbly kitchen chair with his feet stretched in front of him, and his head down. If someone snapped a picture of him in that moment, they would surely feel sorry for what appeared to be an extremely lonely man in deep thought. If they knew what evil craziness ran through his head, they would have a much different impression of him.

With his eyes now closed, he let his mind replay the events of his afternoon. He had not planned his day around ADA Owens. He was walking down Water Street when she passed right in front of him. It was the way the sunlight reflected off her lovely hair that caught his attention. *She didn't even notice me.* He looked on as she met up with another lovely young woman. Both were dressed in skirts and wearing long jackets. Alan followed them to a café on Washington. He sat in a booth near the entrance and quietly observed as the two women talked and perused their lunch menus. The waitress startled him when she asked if he would like to order lunch. In a monotone voice he told her, "Only coffee for now. Thank you." ADA Owens had his full attention. Suddenly, she looked up; right at him. He could tell from the way her expression changed that she caught him staring at her. He thought, *maybe not*. *Wait!* Now, he was sure. She made two subtle and quick attempts to look in his direction again. *Time to go*! He considered his next move as he waited across the street from the café. Alan was certain she had recognized him but then again, maybe not. He was unshaven and wore sunglasses and a hat. If she did, the feisty ADA would have confronted him. The women walked out of the food establishment forty minutes later. They shook hands as he heard Katie tell the other younger woman, "See you tomorrow, Ellen." "See you tomorrow, Katie. And, thanks again for lunch." Uncontrollable tremors made him shake. He almost lost his balance. He leaned sideways against the warm stone frontage of the building to steady himself. Alan Mayfield was a sadistically frustrated sex addict in need of a fix, much in the same way as a drug or alcohol starved addict. ADA Katie Owens was not ready for him; not yet.

Chapter 28

Deep below the earth's surface, security teams activated protocols in preparation for a highly classified meeting. Careful technological planning afforded the rather large *"War Room" to be outfitted with all the glitz and tech one would expect to see in the movies. The* original team from the "Twin Project" gathered together, comparing past notes and compiling a revised risk assessment. Jack had never been in this part of the Pentagon, which was two levels below where he entered the building. One of his two military escorts, apparently the more senior officer, used retinal recognition and push button pad codes at each access point. Sub-level 2 had several maze-like corridors that interconnected to each other at several points. Jack mumbled to himself, "This is the land of confusion." He started to hum the song by the musical band Genesis. The guards gave him a look, and he stopped humming. "Sorry, boys. Nerves got me a bit on edge. "Each person, including the guards, took turns standing in a booth for a full body scan, much like the TSA systems at major airports. Wristwatches, cell phones, anything electronic had to be removed and placed in a locker. Jack asked, "What locker number is that? Do I get a key? A receipt?" The stone-faced security officer ignored Jack's sarcasm. Jack looked around at the consistent lack of patterns. The non-distinct monotone rough grey walls reminded him of a Federal prison and a strong sensation of isolation. Jack followed his escorts another fifty yards down the corridor. He continued his analysis of the underground cave. "How far down are we?" He didn't expect an answer. Judging by his gut, Jack decided to go with the walls being made up of concrete and steel. And, at least three feet thick. He looked up; the cavernous ceilings had to be at least twenty-five feet high. He figured this level was around a hundred feet underground.

"Follow me, Sir."

Jack held off on the jokes and fell in line, one officer in front and one behind him. Another set of heavy doors slid open. Using a credit card like device to get the password of the moment, the lead officer entered a series of digits and, like magic, the massive doors parted. To Jack's amazement, they opened up to reveal a rather nicely done, heavily tech oriented conference room. Definitely one of the largest he had ever seen.

"Hello, my boy." Senator White shook Jack's hand followed by a brief and manly embrace. "Hey, John. It's so good to see you back on the home turf." Senator White asked Jack why he looked so frazzled. Jack laughed. "I have to say, my traveling accommodations were simpler over there than it was to get to this conference room." He paused before adding, "But, I'm very happy to be here and not there. I wish it was for more pleasant business." Jack acknowledged the others in the room, at least those he knew, with hugs and handshakes. He introduced himself to the few others he was not acquainted with yet. General Armstrong introduced them as part of his special-forces team. Jack was glad to see his old boss from North Carolina, Kevin Sorenson, and his current boss from New York, Martin Shaw. Jack gave his associate, Donald Graham a bear hug. Donald whispered, "I'm so glad you're safe, partner." Jack was not sure what his current status was or who he reported to or if Donald and he were still working together. Jack knew he had to let the minutia sit for a while. They were all here now, and the matter at hand is all that anyone would be concerned with for now.

Jack jumped at the brash sound, as the light above the massive entry doors flashed and began to open. John patted Jack's back and whispered, "Nerves will be on edge for a while. It'll get easier." Another guard entered, followed by still another, "Sight for sore eyes." Marcia walked quickly toward her dear friend, associate, and confidant; tears rolled down her cheeks. "I prayed every night, and finally God has answered my prayers." She kissed Jack several times, trying to reach every bit of his face, and then hugged him again. Jack held her hands and said, "I have to be abducted and tortured more often." Marcia pushed him away. "Hello, everyone." She wiped one last tear with her sleeve before whispering in Jack's ear, "Lucky for you they took my Glock at the first security point." Jack grinned. "Mine too." He rolled his eyes. *OK, the truth is, they still haven't seen me as fit to carry a weapon.* These highly capable people, all of whom he considered his special extended family, felt like strangers to him. His eight-month absence left him with questionable guilt as to whether or not he belonged in this room.

General Armstrong took the lead, first by welcoming everyone with a smile; then he went all business. "The first thing I need to tell you all, is that Agent Owens', Jack's reemergence, was meant to be kept in confidence of this team. Only a few other top level personnel vital to this operation have also been given security clearance. Unfortunately," the general glanced at Jack, "a White House press staffer was on assignment in Germany and somehow saw him, or got tipped off. The fool made an unsecure call to his office, which WikiLeaks picked up. Either way, the 'Cat is out of the bag' on that one." He looked at Jack, "You will need to be very vigilant." Jack shrugged his shoulders, "I guess so. Can I get the name of this moron?" He didn't expect a response and got none. *Better not knowing, I'd have to cut off his or her fingers.* Jack had no doubt the news of his return would get out as soon as he showed his face around town anyway. The cloak and dagger charade was well worn out. The general suggested that Jack give a short account of his ordeal. If for a lack of a better reason, he stated, "To address the *600 pound* elephant in the room."

For the next two hours, they discussed all of the risks and vulnerabilities of the operation. By 2PM, color-coded data filled three large white boards. During lunch break, Jack, Kevin Sorenson, Donald and Jack's current boss, Martin Shaw reminisced about the past few years and the tragic events that unfolded during that period. Senator White had just finished speaking with the general; they were huddled in a corner away from the rest of the group. Jack got up and walked over to him. "Hey, John. I wanted to thank you for everything you did to help bring me home. And, for looking after my family." John put his arm around Jack. "You are all my family. Mine and Rebecca's." Jack asked, "Are you going to be alright?" "What do you mean, Jack?" Jack had a sad face. "This is bound to roll back to William and Carlton's involvement."

"Yes, Jack. It will undoubtedly be difficult for me; and you as well. I have always considered you like a son, much the same as you and William were brothers. It will be difficult but we will avenge them again; and again." Jack asked, "What about Katie and the boys? Do you think they are in any danger?" Senator White scratched his head. "I can tell you what you want to hear, but you know the truth is that they certainly could be. The media numb-nut outing you added to the risk. At the very least, they are in no more danger than they were after last year's resounding victory against the terror group. We all had a false sense of relief from that. Perhaps Boston will offer a bit more anonymity for them." "Sure, John. Except that after the attacks at the Boston marathon race last year, I have to believe everyone is vulnerable." John quietly said, "Perhaps I can get coverage for them." Jack put up his hands, "Absolutely not. Katie would never go for it. She would make a case that security would only bring undue attention to them and it would disrupt her ability to do her job. And truthfully, I'd have to agree with her." Jack touched John's arm affectionately. "But, thank you."

The lunch break was over. No one was allowed to leave the conference room except for personal needs; and only if accompanied by a security escort. External calls were not allowed either. General Armstrong continued, finishing his detailed report on the situation. He addressed Jack formally as Agent Owens. "Since all roads seem to lead back to Afghanistan, that is where we hope to gain the best intel. Since Agent Owens' efforts were so successful last year," Jack thought, *and the years before*. "And other earlier trips abroad, I'm thinking 'third time's, a charm'. Jack, could you please give us your thoughts on this idea?" Before Jack could utter a word, John White sprung to his feet; his face appeared tense. "For God's sake, Armstrong! He only returned last week from eight months of torturous captivity. Why would he even consider going anywhere near that region again?" Jack now stood, instantly drawing all participants' direct attention. "Actually, John, I agree with the general. I always believed in FILO, like the accounting term." His colleagues looked confused. "First in, last out. I applied it to my quest to finish this thing, so it's my new 'Jackism'. I started this thing, I want to finish it." He looked at the general. "But I need to do it my way, and with a team of my own choosing." "Listen here, Owens!" "No, General. My way. My people. Furthermore, Jane is essential and must be cleared for all future meetings. I understand her past negates privileges here. We will find a secure, less sensitive meeting place in the future." General Armstrong stood silently for a moment; his face beet red. He leaned over to one of his staff and whispered something to him.

He glanced in Senator White's direction to receive his nod of agreement. Begrudgingly, he gave in; mentioning that presidential approval for all of this would be needed. Jack added to his demands, "I'll need a week to take care of personal business and to work out the game plan with my team. You will have my report and plan of action one week from today." General Armstrong agreed and told the group, "Barring no *red tape* obstacles, we'll reconvene next Friday; location to be announced by secure messaging. Thank you all; and remember, this project is truly top secret. Lives hang in the balance."

Chapter 29

"Down girl! Ok, ok; easy." Jack squatted as he extended his arms in a welcoming gesture. Lacy's tail wagged at supersonic speed, showing her excitement. Her paws held fast to her human daddy's shoulders as she sniffed and licked his face. Jack wasn't sure if she would remember him after almost nine months. The dog's memory surely was good. She continued to lick Jack's face for another minute and then released him, settling for one of her rawhide bones instead. The cat's remembrance seemed keen as well, but he obviously held a grudge. "Hey, buddy. How's my Sir Oliver Jones doing?" Oliver sat with his back pressed tightly into the corner of the room. His covert stance allowed him a sense of security while he evaluated his human's reemergence into *their* new home. Jack whistled "Dixie" knowing the cat could not resist. Oliver tilted his head and meowed a few times before finally giving in. His little feet danced as he ran towards his best human buddy. "That's my boy." Jack rubbed the cat's head. He smiled as it's purring made him feel a little more welcome in this strange place that Katie and the boys called home.

The awkwardness of letting himself into *their* home made Jack uncomfortable. He did not have a key, so he used his spy tools to pick the lock. He'd have to speak with Katie about the lack of security. The apartment was tiny compared to their big Dix Hills home on Long Island. Jack walked around, picking up a picture frame here and there. He liked the shot of him and Katie in Washington last year. *God, she's beautiful*. Another picture sat on the buffet table of the four of them in Montauk. The boys kneeled in front. Katie and Rosa, their nanny, stood behind; all were smiling and waving. The picture reminded him of the good times they shared that year. He smiled even though his mind's eye tried to re-play images of not so pleasant events from back then.

Oliver charged past Jack, making crazy meowing sounds, and finally quieted down as he settled back into his corner. Lacy growled softly, as if she was not sure of why she had concerns. Instinctively, Jack reached for his firearm. The doorknob twisted back and forth. Katie had no idea that Jack would be showing up, and he was sure she had to pick the boys up from after school. She would not be home for at least another hour. The door swung open. All Jack saw at first was a pink sneaker emerge as he started to draw his weapon.

"Jesús Cristos! Mr. Jack! You want to give me a heart attack?"

Jack shouted, "Rosa, what are you doing here? How did you get in?" Rosa tilted her head; Jack thought, *just like the cat.* "I used the key. Miss Katie told me she keeps it on the top of the door frame." *Ah, another security lapse.* "I see your face, Mr. Jack. The building maintenance crew has keys to all the apartments, anyway. Anyone could get into the apartment, if they wanted." Rosa put her package down along with the cane she used to push the door open. She petted Lacy who waited patiently for some acknowledgment. Then she stared at Jack.

"You scared us all, Mr. Jack. We thought you were...."

"Dead?"

"Jes. Does she know you are here, and OK?"

"Jes. She does. Well, not here, here. We saw each other earlier in the week. I haven't been to this apartment until a few minutes before you arrived.

"Are you still making fun of my accent? You didn't pay me enough to take care of *three* children. You're still a child!"

Jack and Rosa bumped heads often during her tenure with his family, but they always had a special fondness and utmost respect for each other. "I love you, Rosa. I'm so glad you're here. She really is going to need you now, more than ever."

Tears rolled down Rosa's cheek as she reached out her arms. Jack embraced her until the dog pushed in between them. Rosa asked, "Do the boys know?" "Yes. Katie told them I was back from my special mission. Although, she and the boys have no idea that today is the day that I would come to see them. My situation is sort of day to day." Rosa took Jack's hand. "But now you are home and they will be OK." Jack put his other hand on top of hers. "Actually, your being here is a 'Godsend'. I am shipping out of the country for a few weeks on company business." Rosa pulled her hand from his. "You made a promise to your wife that you already broke. You cannot do that to your family again!" Jack knew she was right, but also could not explain in detail why he had to go. "Katie understands the situation. Please, let's not discuss this any further." Rosa turned and picked up her package. She headed to the kitchen in silence.

Thirty minutes later, the dog's tail started wagging and the doorknob started twisting again. This time, Jack sat on the sofa patiently awaiting his family to enter. His heart pounded with anticipation.

At first, Katie gave a little squeak, then a huge smile spread across her face. Ryan and Kyle stood just inside the doorway, ignoring Lacy as she tried to jump on them. The dog crouched down on all fours, and barked.

After staring at their dad, obviously confused and unsure how they should react, Katie told them, "Well, what are you waiting for? Give your dad hugs and kisses." That was all they needed to break the ice. For ten minutes, Jack kissed and hugged his boys. They asked so many questions that could not be *truthfully* answered.

"OK, boys. Time for bed." Ryan's eyes were slits, fighting to remain open. Kyle latched onto Jack, his arms locked around his neck. He whispered into his dad's ear, "Let's go to bed, daddy."

"OK!" Jack tossed Kyle airborne, the little man's legs flew out but his arms remained locked around Jack's neck. "Yowser. That didn't go as planned. You have become quite the strong little man." Kyle giggled, and hugged even tighter. Jack held Kyle with one hand while reaching his hand out for Ryan, who reluctantly took hold of it. The three of them marched off to their room, with Katie in tow. "Here are your sleeping bags, boys. Right to sleep and no horsing around. Don't wake Rosa in the morning."

"Silly Mommy!" Both boys chanted in unison. "Rosa is always up before us." Katie smiled, "Well, you both just mind your manners. She is our guest, helping out for a few weeks."

In unison again, "OK, Mommy!"

Jack gave them each lots of kisses and Katie gave them each a final tuck and the ritual "Love you; love you more. Sleep tight and don't let the bed bugs bite." Ryan giggled, "Silly Mommy." Kyle searched for any creepy crawlers. He tried to hide his concerns from his dad.

Katie and Rosa sipped some wine, Jack abstained. Somehow, he lost his taste for the fermented grape beverage. The three of them reminisced over old times; the good ones. After an hour, Rosa yawned, "Long day. Good night, you two."

Katie's odd shyness made her seem like a schoolgirl about to invite her first boyfriend into her bedroom. Jack took her hand as they entered the room. "I can sleep on the couch tonight. It's OK. We can take this slow." Katie kicked off her heels and laid down on the bed, gesturing for Jack to join her. She remained fully clothed, he followed suit. She said, "Can you hold me? We can talk for a while." Jack squeezed her hand. "The other day, I didn't mean to push you..." "We both needed that moment, Jack. Now we need to set a pace for moving on. You have business to attend to, and I completely understand that you have to do this. But, I can't go through this again. The boys just got you back." Jack felt his stomach churn. This was the type of conversation they had when she asked him to move out last year. He was back home with his family for one day when all this happened to them again. *She was right!* "Maybe this was a mistake. I should have stayed in-country and finished this business, then came home with a clean slate. I was selfish."

"You stupid ass! I was just as selfish. That would have been easier on both of us; all of us. But, if you had asked me, I would have told you to get home as fast as possible, anyway. I just can't bear the thought of losing you again."

Katie's back was to him but Jack could tell she was crying. "I will not let that happen again. Payback is coming to them. It will be swift and thorough. They could not break me then, or ever. I will destroy them." He whispered, "Jack is back." He held his wife close. They both fell asleep quickly.

Jack awoke to the unmistakable aroma of bacon and it was like heaven to his senses. As he sat up, he noticed a freshly pressed set of slacks and a shirt were hanging on the closet doorknob. *Wow. She moved my things. She knew I would come back to her.*

"Good morning!"

"Daddy!" The boys tackled Jack. The dog sat up and barked, joining in with the twins' excitement. Oliver Jones marched back and forth in front of Lacy, rubbing against her fur with each pass. The dog grunted, shook her head and sneezed.

Jack kissed Katie and whispered, "I love you more today than yesterday, and each day before that." He took her hand and brushed his freshly pressed shirt with it. "Thank you." After breakfast Jack told his boys, "I'll see you guys in few a weeks, and we'll plan a vacation to Disney World; OK?" They jumped up and down, showing their continued excitement. He saw both Katie and Rosa's shocked faces. "Whoa, girls." He took Katie's hand, "If I stay a few days it will be harder on both of us when I have to leave. Let's drive the boys to school. You can drop me off at the train station. I'll meet my team in Washington and get this business taken care of. John will know where I am at all times. He will keep you updated." Katie asked, trying not to tear up, "Why not fly?" She realized the answer before the words left her mouth. She said, "Oh, my." Flying would lack anonymity and for Jack's safety, the fewer records of his travels, the better. Jack glanced at Rosa, hoping for a sign of approval. She smiled. *That's an encouraging sign.* "Don't worry, Mister Jack; I'll stay until you return. You better be quick though because I miss my grandbabies." Jack hugged Rosa. He held her for almost a full minute until she pushed him away... "Enough of that; get out of here."

With a cup of hot coffee in one hand and a small duffle bag gripped in the other, Jack entered the Amtrak terminal at Back Bay Station. "Rush hour" upheld its reputation for large crowds and big noise. Jack took it all in. This was his country and these were his people. He waited for his train to D.C. feeling rejuvenated and confident. His anger finally waned, allowing for clearer thought.

Jack is back!

Chapter 30

Most humans are creatures of habit. They rarely deviate from their normal routine. In some way, this practice provides them with a false sense of security. Ellen worked for the DA's office part time each day. Then, she headed home to her modest apartment to eat lunch and to walk her new puppy. Alan watched her the previous day and thought, *they are so cute together,* as the fluffy pooch tried to control the direction of their walk. She impressed him with her soft but firm command for the pooch to walk with her. He thought, *that's good; she'll be a fighter. Fighters always experience a heightened sexual response.* After the dog was brought upstairs, the young woman headed out again. The killer tried following, but lost sight of her in the crowds of people rushing to their destinations. The fact that she attended evening classes made no difference to his planned schedule for her.

Friday was Ellen's favorite day. She did not have any classes on Fridays. "Hi, Fluffy Muffy." She picked up the "Yorkie-Doodle" and gave it lots of kisses before putting it back down on the floor. The dog ran a few circles around her owner before sitting next to the tiny kitchen table with her tail wagging. "Oh. You're ready for lunch are you? You're so damn cute! OK. Lunch first, and then we'll go for a nice long walk."

Fluffy Muffy started barking just at the same time as Ellen heard the knock on the door. She wiped her hands with a kitchen towel and briskly walked to her apartment door. "Yes, what is it?" "Sorry to disturb you, miss, but we have reports of a gas leak. We may have to evacuate the building. Can I please check your apartment?" "Everything is fine here. There is no smell of gas." "The landlord, Ellman and Fitzgerald, sent me. Please, miss. I'll be fired if I don't inspect each apartment. I have keys for the apartments where no one is home. Obviously, you are; so I can't let myself in. Please miss. You can call them to verify. I'll wait."

Ellen walked over to the kitchen table to retrieve her cellphone. She scrolled through her contacts, unable to find the landlord's number. "Oh, c'mon! Stupid phone! Where the heck is the number?" Outside, she heard the utility guy talking to some neighbors. "Yes, ma'am. Everything is alright. I'll be in shortly to inspect your apartment. No need to worry. It's just routine because we had a complaint." Ellen heard another neighbor down the hall thanking him. "Are you sure my apartment is safe?" She said to herself, "Oh, for Pete's sake."

Ellen opened her door. "Please be quick." She pointed to her little dog who was still whimpering. "She needs her walk." The maintenance man smiled, "Hi, cute puppy." The dog growled, showing her teeth. Ellen softly scolded, "Bad girl. So sorry. I have no idea why she is behaving like this." "Not a problem, miss. I'll be done momentarily."

Ellen knelt down to calm her dog while asking, "Don't you use some kind of sensor device to sniff for gas?" The dog yelped as her best friend fell to the floor. The last thing Ellen remembered when she awoke was a firm hand covering her mouth followed by a sharp stinging in the back of her neck.

"Wonderful. You're awake. You slept longer than I anticipated. I had to control myself; be patient. I suppose, well, imagine this, a lion in the bush waiting for his prey. Imagine the gnawing hunger until he pounces on the unsuspecting animal. Oh, the glorious satisfaction of triumph. Oh how it is, the passion that lies in the belly of the beast." The words were clear, she knew what he was saying, but understood nothing. His breath on her cheek burned like acid. He whispered in a childlike voice, "I am going to do things to you that will excite every part of your being." As she began to regain consciousness, Ellen struggled to clear the fog in her head. Pieces of the last moments in her apartment started to come back to her.

She had let a stranger into her apartment. The man from the utility company, then a sharp stinging sensation in the nape of her neck. She imagined the echo of her little dog Muffin, barking. With her brain still addled from the effects of the drug injected into her, panic and confusion reigned. She tried to scream, but was stifled by a gag securely tied to her mouth. Her eyes saw only the blackest ebony of darkness as she realized she was also blindfolded. Attempts to move either arm or leg were met with the sickening realization that she was laying naked, with her legs spread apart. Each of her limbs were secured to a bedpost with a length of clothesline that bit into her flesh with every movement. She was completely vulnerable. *The lion's prey*. He started down below using his tongue. The more she twisted and fought, the more aggressive he became. The sensation of his physical *anything* touching her made her skin crawl. As Alan made his way closer to his victim's face, he stopped for a moment, still holding her in position. He entered her firmly and stilled inside her. "I'm going to take off the blindfold. Do-not-move!" He removed the blindfold. She did as he instructed, remaining motionless. His face was hard and determined. She now knew for sure that death was on her doorstep. She could identify her attacker. He saw her face and understood that she understood her fate. This was his moment. With each of his "dates," this would be the highlight of his time with them. Yet, ADA Katie Owens was all he could focus on. His inability to give this woman what he imagined she needed, frustrated him. He pulled out of her quickly. "I'm sorry, but there is someone else on my mind tonight. We can't do this anymore." Her eyes pleaded for compassion.

He could do that, for her.

Chapter 31

The level of threats around the world seem to increase on a daily basis. Last week, an Isis sympathizer used his SUV as a lethal weapon, mowing down more than a dozen tourists in Paris. On that same day, less than three hundred miles away, a London train hit a sabotaged section of track and derailed, killing six people and injuring dozens. An Isis faction out of Turkey declared it as their victory. Two days later, a concert hall in London fell under siege by a lone gunman claiming allegiance to Isis. A raid on his home uncovered various items used to make pipe bombs and literature printed off the web on how to make it all work. The apparent end goal was to cause maximum damage to life and property. His family denied knowing anything of the now dead terrorist's intentions. His own father was on a "No Fly" list due to affiliations with terror groups back in Afghanistan. *But, he swore he knew nothing of his son's intentions.*

N.Y.P.D SWAT teams thwarted a planned attack after finding a lethal I.E.D hidden in a backpack at Penn Station. Surveillance video lead them to another "No Fly" person of interest. A search of this terrorist's home lead to the seizure of several automatic weapons, pipes, fuses, boxes of tiny ball bearings and gunpowder. In this case, anti-terror snipers shot a young woman from Libya as she attempted to ambush first responders entering her apartment.

Who would ever suspect twenty-six-year-old Roya Abasi of being a terrorist? American born, blond hair and blue eyes. If not for her smooth cocoa skin coloring, she would pass for a California *valley girl*. Twenty-seven years earlier, her mother, here on a tourist visa, had made a mistake of infidelity that resulted in an unwanted pregnancy. A mistake that could ultimately end in her beheading back home, and quite possibly here in the States, should her husband have found out. Her husband, still in Syria, had difficulties getting his visa approved. It would be eighteen months more before his approval would come through. She delivered the child and left the newborn with a neighbor while she went for a doctor visit. She never returned.

After sixteen years and three foster families, Roya needed to find her identity and a purpose in her life. She started frequenting a local mosque where the Imam profiled her as a troubled teen with little or no family ties. He eventually arranged her recruitment by a local Isis cell. Three years later, Roya Abasi, an expert in martial arts and hand-to-hand combat using various weapons, emerged as another beautiful but deadly assassin.

****

With her purple backpack already stuffed, Roya tightly rolled her jeans around the plastic dagger. She secured it in the stiff fabric, exactly as she did earlier for the small .25 caliber plastic firearm, and hard Teflon coated plastic ammunition. As long as she stayed clear of police and military dogs, trained to sniff for bombs, she would be fine. Even the airport scanner would be unlikely to pick out these images. Unless of course, they were specifically looking for something and did a deep scan with a keen set of eyes on the monitor.

Her instructions were clear and precise. Find the man in the picture and kill him. Use whatever means necessary, and leave no witnesses. Roya held one of the 4x6 pictures given to her at eye level, allowing the image to burn itself into her memory. On the other side, written in tiny print, was "Last known residence: Dix Hills, New York." It also listed Jack's family members and key known associates. One name stuck out. She remembered her Imam describing the traitor. She played back the image of a beautiful reddish blond haired woman with fair skin. "She is beautiful, and deadly, just like you." Her Imam's angry expression unnerved her. "She betrayed Allah. She betrayed all of us who believe in jihad. Beware of her cunning and treachery. She will be your greatest enemy should she again be aligned with the infidels." He also emphasized how pleased he would be if Roya brought Jane Austin's head in a bag to him. She looked at the other two pictures, one of Jack Owens' wife Katie, and one of all of them as a family. Roya focused on the family picture. It made her smile for a moment. She envisioned herself standing there with them as part of their family. "This is all fake family crap. It's not real." She crumbled up the family picture and tossed it in the trash can. She looked at the picture of Katie Claire Owens, also labeled "NYC ADA." She thought, *you'll look so pretty in black as you mourn your infidel husband*. After one more quick glance at each picture, Roya destroyed them as well.

I'm coming for you Jack Owens. I'm coming for you.

Chapter 32

The more than thirty FBI and police Investigators assigned to the serial killer case worked tediously long hours. Panicked residents of the greater Boston area and its suburbs continuously put pressure on their elected officials to put additional manpower behind their efforts. All the intelligence of the day, each day, ended up on Katie's desk for her to review.

"Knock, knock." The DA's lead investigator, Detective Nick Lawrence, let himself into Katie's office. "Hi, Nick. I guess knocking for real and waiting for an invitation is beyond your etiquette boundaries." "Sorry, ADA Owens. Angie was not at her desk. She must be taking a..." Katie put up her hands in protest. "Stop right there. Do not be inappropriate in my office. Please control yourself."

"What? Oh. Sorry. I get that way when I'm excited with news."

"Give it to me, detective."

"OK. So. A rookie, barely six months on the job is looking to earn his first gold star, and probably some overtime as well. Anyway, he is running data for matches based on local arrests or persons of interest in any related violent sex crimes. He gets a hit; one Alan Mayfield. This person of interest is at least six-one, around two hundred-ten, light skin African American." The detective handed Katie a Department of Corrections photograph of Alan Mayfield as he continued. "He had a record for sexual misconduct in the Marines, resulting in a dishonorable discharge after only nine months. He has two priors for stalking; one in Maine three years ago. The witness in that case was a no-show for the first day of the trial. The prosecutor had no choice but to drop the charges. The creep got a lucky break. The second time around, only as recently as last year here in Boston, the witness described him before passing, but never actually identified him in person." Katie didn't let herself get too excited. She was well aware that these "persons of interest" usually never pan out. She supposed, *but he sure seems like he could be good for these serial killings*. Katie asked, "Are you going to have him picked up?" She noticed his face scrunch as he replied, "We would, but he's in the wind. He has moved several times with no forwarding address. His last place of employment was at Al's Trucking, located in the Back Bay area. One of my guys spoke with them, but we hit a brick wall there too." Katie asked, "What did he do there? Driver?" "Actually, he was their bookkeeper." Katie grinned.

"So, he's no dummy."

"I guess not."

"Knock, knock." Angie poked her head in. "Can I interrupt?" Katie remarked, "What? Are you two the Bobbsey Twins?" Nick laughed, "I'm Pete, and she's Repeat."

"What is it, Angie? I need to get Nick on his way before he gets completely out-of-hand." "There's a Mr. Mayfield here to see you. He said you were looking for him." Katie sat up straight. "Alan Mayfield?" Angie said, "Yes, I think so." Katie glanced at Nick then back to Angie. "Give us five minutes and then send him in."

She looked worried and asked her detective, "Why here? Why me? I didn't inquire about him." Nick shrugged his shoulders, "You are the 'face of the case'. The news media had you on every channel the other day. We said he's smart. This guy is taking control already by coming to us." "Hold on, we can't be sure this is our guy. Right now he's just a person of interest." Nick sneered, "Interesting, indeed."

The first tap of Angie's methodical knock startled Katie. "ADA Owens, this is Alan Mayfield." Katie noticed

Angie's bewildered expression as she closed the door behind her.

"Mr. Mayfield, thank you for voluntarily walking yourself into my office. How did you know we were looking for you?" Katie kept her focus on Alan Mayfield. Her eyes remained locked on his. Katie noted his strong physique. He stood tall and was very handsome. The aura of her intensity made Nick's palms sweat. He thought, *she may be nervous, but no one would ever know it*.

"I find it interesting, ADA Owens, that you would have to inquire why I'm here. I stopped in to my previous employer to pick up my last paycheck. They mentioned that your investigators were asking about me." Nick grinned, "That would be me." Alan Mayfield disregarded Detective Lawrence and continued. "I figured it best I come directly to you, to find out what it is you want with me. After all, I wouldn't want some promotion seeking detective jumping the gun and mistakenly shooting me or something like that." He glanced at Nick and then directly back to Katie.

"Absolutely stunning."

"Excuse me, Mr. Mayfield?"

"Your wedding band. It is stunning."

Katie let down her guard and reacted when she should have remained pokerfaced. This guy was definitely taunting her. She nodded to her detective; she needed a rescue moment.

"Again, thank you for coming in. Saved my people some legwork. Can you tell me where you were the Saturday night before last?" Alan pondered his response as he paused before answering.

"Hmm. I'm fairly certain that I was at home enjoying several cocktails."

Nick asked, "Was anyone with you that can corroborate your whereabouts that evening?" "Why would I need to do that? I already told you where I was and what I was doing. If I gave you a name, don't you think it would be for someone who would corroborate what I'm telling you? Can't you *Dicks* come up with a better questioning strategy?" Katie could tell that Detective Lawrence was clearly having a hard time keeping his temper in check. She was sure that if Alan Mayfield used "Dick" one more time in a descriptive sense, Nick might punch him out.

The back and forth lasted for over an hour. Katie had this eerie feeling she had seen this guy before. Her mind replayed images of places she had been recently trying to place him there. Then her mind flashed a vision of him with a beard and a hat staring at her and Ellen the day they had lunch together. *Gotcha*!

"Shit!" She said it half to herself, and loud enough for the other two in the room to take notice.

Both Detective Lawrence and Mayfield stopped their back-and-forth verbal sparring and turned their attention to her. Katie's mouth was open in shock over her realization. She felt rage rising like a volcano about to erupt. "It was *you* in the cafe the other day. You were staring at me." Alan abruptly stood up. His chair flew backward and toppled over. Katie flinched backward, immediately regretting it. She knew better than to allow a suspect to see fear or hesitation, no matter how intense it might be at that moment. Nick's subtle "knee-jerk" reaction to place his hand closer to his firearm caught her attention as well, adding to her split second reaction. She hoped this creepy guy didn't notice.

"Am I under arrest?"

Mayfield's grin was unsettling. Nick shook his head.

"I didn't think so. Then, we're done here."

He looked at Katie, his eyes showing a barely controlled rage. "I hope to see you again soon; under better circumstances. Perhaps a more *controlled* environment."

221

Nick and Katie both watched, speechless, as their unexpected guest marched out of the office; never looking back. Katie finally took a breath.

"It's him, Nick. He's been stalking me." Nick said, "I'll have my guys pull more camera footage and run facial recognition for this creep. We'll find something to tie him into all this. In the meantime, you need to be careful. Don't go anywhere alone." "I can't have a babysitter for you twenty-four, seven." "You need to order in or make sure you go with people. Take your intern on errands with you." Katie picked up her phone. "Angie, did Ellen arrive yet? Today is her day to work, isn't it? OK; Thanks." Nick asked, "What?" "Ellen is forty minutes late. She's never been late before."

Katie tried to hide her agitation. She needed Jack, but he was off on his mission to save the world.

But, what about saving Katie?

Chapter 33

The special OPS team of three arrived at Andrews Air Force Base exactly on time per General Armstrong's explicit orders. Jack checked his old but functional chronograph wristwatch, which he trusted was still very accurate. The fancy new one that Katie had given him two years ago disappeared during his abduction eight months ago. It was over a month into his captivity and during a short rest period that Jack remembered the watch was on his wrist the night of his abduction. He played back the quiet family celebration of his birthday. In his mind, the boys were excited as they handed their dad the beautifully gift-wrapped box. He visualized Katie's big smile as she told him, "Go ahead, Jack, open it!" *Bastards!* His desert nightmare was over; he had to get a grip on reality. Jack looked up from his vintage timepiece, "7PM, as instructed. Where's the marching band and pretty high school cheerleaders with the short blue skirts?" He glanced over at Donald for acknowledgment of his attempted "funny." Donald appeared a bit uncomfortable. In fact, he looked like he wanted to turn and run in the other direction, away from the airfield.

"First trip abroad, Don?"

"First time voluntarily heading into the Gates of Hell."

Jack smirked and came back with, "Gates of Hell, for sure. But, I don't remember you volunteering. Now, take Jane for instance; she is raring to go. For her, it's like going *home*." Jane whipped back her hair; *God, she still had it*. "I guess it's the same for you, Jack. After all, you spent some quality time 'in country' just recently." Don put his hands in the air, "Are you both going to bicker the whole trip?" Jack mumbled something that Don could not hear clearly. "What? What, Jack?" Jane, in a somewhat nasty voice said, "He said, 'Probably not! Cause we'll be killed soon after we arrive.' But, don't listen to his pessimism." She pulled her hair out from in front of her eyes and smiled. Donald found little comfort in her words or soft facial expression. He knew her as "Jane the terrorist," and still had misgivings about trusting her. *She'll be back in her own environment even if it's Afghanistan instead of Yemen. Who knows what demons will rise up inside her...* Where they were going, Taliban control was prominent. The Taliban, Isis factions, and Al Qaeda each had differing methods for how they achieved the desired result. It was the end result tied to the kindred hatred of the West that made movement in those territories so dangerous.

"Hello, team!" The two soldiers who had been sitting on a bench some distance from Jack and his team jumped to attention. The general's assertive greeting shocked Donald as well. He jumped to attention, and then relaxed before turning away from the group to puke, due to his nerves. Armstrong gave a hearty laugh. "First time?" Jack and Jane both nodded. The general added, "OK. Get it all out; no time for that nonsense once you're 'in country'. Let's get your bird in the air."

Apparently, the first leg of the trip would be via military transport to Germany. Jack thought to himself, *God how I missed my friends there. NOT!* In Germany, the plan was for the team to transfer to another smaller and less conspicuous transport headed for Ethiopia. The last leg of the outbound trip was Afghanistan. The exact drop zone was unknown. Jack would leave it in the hands of General Armstrong who would take care of all the last minute details as needed. In some ways, this was like déjà vu of two years ago when he and Jane took this very same journey, for a very similar purpose. It went as planned then, so all should be good this time around as well. He just had to keep his people safe and get the information needed to expose those who infiltrated the U.S. governmental agencies.

A fairly new aircraft, the Boeing KC-46 Pegasus was capable of reaching airspeeds up to Mach .86, or about 570 mph and distances greater than the team's end-point. Unfortunately, it was also too large and noisy to fly into Kandahar and would likely draw unwanted attention. The plane into Afghanistan would need to be a much smaller, less obvious aircraft. The planned two-hour layover in Ethiopia left time for a final review of the strategy with local agency officials and emergency ex-fil teams; should they be needed. Jack knew the drill. The local agency, his agency, would remind the teams of the same crap as they did before each mission. "Should you be caught operating in a foreign and hostile country, the American government will disavow any knowledge of any such operation." Put in plain English, "You will be on your own." Jack was well aware of what *"on your own"* meant. He had eight months to make peace with it. He would be damned if that would happen to him or any member of his team.

Thanks to strong tailwinds, in just over eight hours they were on the ground in Ethiopia. Jane released her safety harness. Jack asked, "Where are you headed in such a rush?" Jane whipped her hair back, "Same place as last time. 'A girl has to do, what a girl has to do.' You remember; don't you, Jack? Last time you accompanied me." Then like magic, she disappeared off the plane. Don gave Jack the "Stink Eye." "I'm not even going to ask." Jack replied, "Good!"

Jack, Donald, and Jane, as well as the two soldiers assigned to them, enjoyed a hot meal and the strongest spiced tea Jack had ever tasted. Don made a face. Jane laughed, "Oh, come on Donald, '*man up*'. The caffeine will keep you alert. It might actually help save your life." Jack figured it was a good time to end Jane's browbeating of Don. "I guess it's time." Jack nodded to the security guys and winked at his team of two. "You good, Don?" Don gave his thumbs up.

They boarded the smaller Antonov An-12 plane code named "Cub". "Ok, a Russian four engine turbo-prop should fit right in." Jack smiled with his approval. Don asked, "What's so wonderful about this flying boat?" Jane patted Don on the back. "Even I know this one. Corporations use these all over Africa for small cargo transports." Jack added, "And, for drugs and gun smuggling as well." Don smirked. "That's just great! I suppose we'll fit right in as spies on a mission." Jane whispered in Jack's ear, "You're usually the one with the smart mouth. I know, because I almost put you down for it a few times back then. This one," she glanced toward Don, who caught her worried look, "He could get us killed." Jack turned to Don, "Actually, Don; you make a good point with your sarcasm. It's common for both legitimate and less than legal opportunists to use this aircraft; we *will* fit right in. It would have been incredibly bad luck for us to be singled out and interrogated." Don grinned and glanced over toward Jane, to check her reaction to what Jack said. She was preoccupied with packing her rather large backpack. Don asked, "Would have been? Is she planning for a longer trek than we originally discussed?" "Um, no. That's her backpack over there. We seem to have hit a bit of a hitch in our travel plans. Ground forces, unfriendly troops, are swarming the major roads from Kabul, north and south." "So, there's no safe place to land?" Don refocused on Jane and her packing of another large pack. He sat down with his hand holding his head. "Shit, shit, shit! And the 'terrorist' is packing our lives in those chutes?" Jane, with her back to her two partners exclaimed, "I can hear you." Jack nodded, "Ex-terrorist. She is an ally now, and I trust her with my life." Don shook his head. "And mine too? I'm not sure I can do this." The plane started to taxi down the runway. Jack leaned in and quietly said, "You did this in basic training. It's like riding a bicycle. Think of the cool stories you can tell when we get home." Don caught Jane looking his way and then trying to hide it. Jack continued. "If you want, we can go tandem." Don was embarrassed. He had trained and made two obviously successful jumps. "No. I got this. When was the last time you made a jump?" Jack though for a second, trying to come up with a witty retort. "Actually, not since the farm. How about you, Jane?" Jane tossed the heavy pack to Jack who passed it to Don. As he caught his, Jane shrugged her shoulders. "Never. Back in Yemen, they trained us to pack, and showed us videos of how to land and what to do if the chute failed to open. Seems like a no brainer. Land on your feet and roll into the fall." Don looked freaked out. He abruptly commented, "Did they show you how to rig the explosives so they don't blow before you drop on your target?" Jane said without looking up, "You should recheck you pack before the jump." She looked up and directly at Don, "Oh, forgive me. You have no idea what is correctly packed and what is not." "Enough!" Jack was red-faced. "Both of you cut it out! Don, that was uncalled for." Don put up his hands, "Whatever."

With its four powerful engines screaming, the AN12 raced down the runway, then suddenly shot straight for the sky. The parachute packs appeared to float as gravity took a momentary leave of absence. They then bounced, and rolled behind their owners, Don's being ripped out of his hands. The Cub made a steep and forceful ascent. The Ethiopian runway rapidly disappearing like a camera's zoom lens going from five-hundred millimeters out to fifty.

"Shit, shit, shit!" *God, I hope you're watching over us*.

Chapter 34

For the better part of the six-hour flight, the trio said little to each other. The two backup pilots and the security officers sat and talked among themselves with little regard for Jack and his team. The loud and abrasive klaxon sound of the ten-minute warning alert made them all jump. "That would be for us. The rest of them will stay on the plane and land in Kandahar. They will appear as any other American team that arrives several times each month." Jack took hold of Don's arm. "You good?" Don showed his thumbs up, but he looked frightened. His concerns were well warranted. Surviving the jump was one thing. Averting rebels on the ground or Taliban or Isis troops was another. Skill would take a backseat to luck until they secured the ground perimeter ensuring there were no hostiles waiting for them.

"OK, it's 8:30PM Ethiopian time; set your watches. It's dark out there so we are dropping down in stealth mode. Do not activate the flashing UV beacon until you are on the ground. Once we all do that, only we will be able to find each other. Your goggles are fitted with special filters to see the otherwise invisible UV LED. The pilots assured me we will be over an open field of farm crops. There are no significant winds affecting drift so we should stay on course. The crops should provide a soft landing and some useful cover." Jack smiled as he took Jane's hand; its warmth had a calming effect. Her cold-bloodedness and wretched past, now just a story to never tell. She returned the smile. Jack quietly expressed his appreciation. "Thank you, Jane; for everything."

One of the military guys announced, "The pilot says it's now or never." He checked his portable scanner and advised the team, "Infrared shows clear, no bodies or other movement, we are at too high of an altitude for an accurate reading, so no guarantees. Good luck!" The soldier gave a soft salute and added, "See you on the other side..." He opened the small hatch; the howling wind sounded ominous. Jack looked at his team, making sure they had their automatic weapons in a ready state should there be hostiles on the ground. Jack jumped first. Don displayed some hesitation. Jane jiggled his line to make sure the Automatic Activation Device would open his chute automatically at the correct altitude from the ground. She gave him the thumbs up sign, but Don didn't move, so she assisted his jump by pushing him out of the plane. She waited five seconds and followed.

Jack's adrenaline flowed like a river of jet fuel on fire. They had a mission to complete of the utmost importance, but he knew part of this mission, for him, was payback. Jane needed the excitement. She spent the earlier part of her life numb to humanity. Only in the past two years did she start to recognize her need for human emotional interaction. Jane learned how to care for someone other than herself. Most importantly, she found out how to love, and be loved. She owed Jack more than she could ever repay. Jane would all but give her life for him. As she floated downward into darkness, her parachute now open, she wondered if she would be giving up her life as well, this time. Don, on the other hand, thanked God several times for his chute magically opening. For the fifteen or so seconds of free fall, he thought he would surely pass out. The cool, almost cold air temperature, and the darkness that masked the impending ground contact, saved him.

The trio each fell to earth within a few seconds of each other. Jack landed first in the soft bed of vegetation. As he freed himself from his chute and pushed his way free of the soft flowers, he realized they had landed in a giant poppy field. He immediately proceeded to secure the area. He flipped his night-vision glasses on and panned the area in a 360-degree sweep, his semi-automatic in ready mode. As soon as he confirmed they were alone out there, he activated the UV signal. Within a few seconds, he saw the soft glow of the two others.

They were all safely on the ground. Jane helped Don release his chute before a wind gust caught it and dragged him off to another part of the desert. She put her arm around his shoulders. "That was awesome; don't you think?" In the dim light, she noticed some color coming back to his stressed out face. "Dude, you were awesome!" She gave him a little "Sexy Jane" hug and tapped his nose as if he were a little boy in need of a compliment. "You'll be a changed man by the time we get home. That's when you'll know how cool you are. This is the mission of a lifetime." She turned to Jack. "We all good?" Jack replied, "As good as good can be, given the conditions." Don mumbled, "Sure, like sitting ducks in an open field. The drug lord whose field of heroin we just landed in is probably loading a portable rocket launcher" "What's that, Donny boy?" Jack laughed as he asked. "Nothing, Jack. Are we moving on, or what?" Jack cleared his throat, "Besides, they would never launch at us while we're in the middle of the crops. These puppies would ignite and burn in a flash." Jane added, "For sure. They would wait until we clear the farm area, then launch a strike."

Jack patted Don on the back, "Ok. Long guns at ready. Let's get moving."

Nightfall brought with it dryer air and a brisk breeze. The somewhat smooth and sandy terrain quickly transformed into rough, and rocky. "Careful. We don't need any twisted ankles." As Jack advised his comrades, Don raised his fist signaling an "all stop" and "silence." He pointed to his right; two o'clock. Jack and Jane both readied their weapons. Now they all heard the steps. Sand and stone crunching beneath boots. It sounded like three or four bodies heading toward them. Jack signaled Don to take cover just behind them where a small cluster of rock formations created a wall-like barrier. The next sound was crystal clear; the unknown visitors readying their weapons. Without warning, Jane shoved Jack hard, pushing him down a small ravine. He landed in some thick bushes with Jane on top of him. Whatever species of bush it was, the sensation of needles piercing his back sent pain throughout his body. The dampness that followed confirmed his fear of blood oozing from his shoulders to his butt. Jack whimpered, "Ouch. Crap!" Jane's face was literally pressed against his. Even now in the predicament they were facing, he felt her soft skin against his. "Shush, Jack! Oh my..." The reprimand for quiet was expected. The embarrassment of her noticing his reaction to her, being on top of him; awkward. Jane whispered, "Just like old times." "I have no idea what you're referring to." Jack ran all sorts of things in his mind but none brought back memories of anything of a sexually physical nature between them. His mind at the moment blocked out those seductive moments back then when her leaders tasked her with ending his life. Jane lifted her face off his. Her lips now millimeters from his. "Our last trip to this shit-hole. Camping out here on this very same terrain." Jack gave no response. Jane made a disappointed face. "Really, Jack?" It had been quiet for a while but suddenly there were more footsteps. Before Jack could ready his weapon, he heard the crisp snap of what he assumed to be large caliber ammunition being loaded into a weapon chamber. "Really? This is what you two are up to while I was up there securing our well-being. Why don't you two get a room?" Jane jumped up and brushed off her camos. Jack sat up, his eyes trained on Don. "One of us could have easily shot you. Or worse," he glanced at Jane who was smiling, "Or sliced open your throat. It's her specialty." "*Was*, my specialty." Jack stood and started brushing himself off. The stinging pain he suffered from the fall showed in his face. "Don, did you see who they were?" Don shook his head. "Negative. It was too dark. They spoke some form of Arabic though."

"Thanks, Don."

"No problem, Jack." Don whispered, "Does Katie know about your intimately close working relationship with Miss Terrorist?"

"I can hear you, Don!"

Jack shoved Don. "Ouch, damn it. Let's get moving." Jane handed Jack his backpack. "I found this over there. Good thing our mystery guests didn't find it." She paused a second, "Crap, Jack. Your back is all bloody." His shirt had red polka dots all over the back.

Jane used antiseptic from her First Aid kit to clean Jack's wounds. "Looks superficial. You'll live, my friend. Don and I can take turns with you to carry your pack. There's no way you're hanging that on your back." "I'll be fine, thanks. Jack swung his backpack behind him and pulled it onto his shoulders. It hurt but he would not let on just how much.

"Who's got the GPS?"

Chapter 35

The last time Jane and Jack ventured through the Afghan desert, they did so undercover, posing as drug smugglers working to fund Al Qaeda. Jane posed as the terrorist seductress who lured Jack, the American, into helping her. This trip, there was no cover. No one expected them. They had to hope God kept a watchful eye out for them and that Allah was busy somewhere else. It was just the two of them back then, along with a good deal of mistrust. This time, no explanation would save the trio should they encounter any of the many possible enemy factions roaming the desert terrain.

Don appeared a bit fatigued as he haphazardly asked, "What if we run into Ministry Police out patrolling?" Jane glanced at Jack, "I got this." Jack tilted his head, silently communicating to her to *take it easy on the poor guy*. She turned to Don, who was breathing heavily as he flanked to her left, "Are you OK? Do you need a moment…?" His expressionless face conveyed his disregard for her concern so she simply answered his question. "We will be charged as spies and shot in a public execution." Jack added, "Don't sweat the little things,

Don; this is primarily Taliban country. The police are corrupt but can be reasonable, for a fee."

Sunrise began to brighten the desert sky. The frigid night quickly gave way to a welcome but bittersweet warming of the air. Jack and Jane both knew that within the hour, the comfortable transition would turn into unrelenting heat. Jack worried about Don's inexperience and potential lack of adaptability to the extreme desert conditions. The week before this trip, Don approached Jack and asked to be part of the team. After all, he had been an integral part of the home based operations during the previous year's adventure. He almost demanded to be part of the covert operation with them. At first, Jack made excuses knowing that Don had limited experience in field operations outside the United States and Europe. Don did make a convincing argument for his powerful analytic abilities and sharpshooter skills. He received a Distinguished Marksman badge while in the Marines and completed a survivalist course in the Mojave Desert with a score of ninety-six percent. That was nine years ago; Jack hoped those skills had not been forgotten.

By 9AM, they had climbed the rocky terrain to about fourteen hundred feet. The sun was brutal. Jane stopped and threw down her backpack. She pulled off her hooded long sleeve shirt exposing her slender but well-toned arms. The men followed suit. Jack noted her tight fitting short sleeve undershirt, "You better keep some covering ready in case we run into any locals." Jane nodded, acknowledging Jack's concern. Don remarked, "How the hell do the woman here wear those heavy black garbs in this heat?" Jane smirked, "Those 'garbs' are called Abaya." He asked, "You ever have to wear one?" Jane grabbed her pack and slung it over one shoulder. She drew her pistol, Don got nervous; she blew desert dust off it and holstered it. "Only during prayers, Don. My grooming taught me to appear American but think like a local. No one in the camp I was brought up in wore those, except as I said, during prayers; and, only the females." Don was relieved that Jane actually replied to him in a civil, non-sarcastic or demeaning way.

Three hours later, they arrived at their destination. "OK, Jane. This looks like the right place. I remember these boulders. We hid behind them last time." "Yes, Jack. I think you're right. Last time, Hakim was expecting us. He may not be so accommodating this time since there is no pot of gold dangling for him on the other side of the American rainbow." She looked at Don. "Do not speak. Not one single word. I do all the talking until we are either welcomed or fighting for our lives." Don nodded his understanding. Jane placed her pistol on a flat rock ledge hidden well in the cluster of stone. Jack and Don did the same. They all understood that any show of weapons would leave no room for discussion.

Déjà vu made its grand entrance, much like the previous time that Jack and Jane were in this situation. Easily, two dozen women and female children were working; more like slaving, to remove rocks and other natural debris. Apparently, they were clearing large areas, likely for more tent space. Jack wondered how many more wives Hakim had taken on since his last visit. Some were carrying water to the tents. Others removed waste containers. Jack pointed to one of them and quietly remarked, "I guess she's an older wife; he's bored with her." Don looked puzzled. "She can't be more than nineteen or twenty. How many wives does he have?" Jane said with an attitude, "Way more than he can handle. When you meet him, you should inquire. Perhaps ask how many he has beheaded this year." Jack laughed, "It's cheaper than divorce."

From behind, footsteps approached quickly along with the distinct snap of rifle actions being worked on multiple weapons.

"OK. Here we go. It's Showtime!"

Jane gave the stare of death to Jack; she looked unnerved. "Quiet, idiot." Don looked panicked and asked in a half whisper, "What's going on?"

"Shhh!" Jane admonished.

****

From thirty-five thousand feet above the blistering rock and sand, the "eyes in the sky" observed the movements below. The RQ-4 Global Hawk stealthily flew racetrack-patterns over the covert team. An alert senior analyst from Jack's intelligence unit exclaimed, "General, we have movement thirty degrees southwest of our ground team." General Armstrong asked. "How far out?" The CIA stationmaster answered, "Not far enough. Perhaps a klick or less. It appears they are in a position to engage." Armstrong shook his head. "We should have had eyes up earlier. Either way we only have two options." He exhaled, making a most dissatisfied sound. He noted the analyst's edgy hand movements. "Stand-down, son. You'd get our team killed as well as raise all sorts of issues down below. Our team can handle this. There will be no missiles going hot today."

****

Five heavily armed soldiers dressed in full white garb, their faces covered as well, took a firm stance with guns aimed at them. Jane immediately spoke without moving a muscle. She feared the cards were already stacked heavily against them. "sabaah al-khayr, atayna musalimin." She hoped her greeting of peace would calm some nerves. The one who seemed to be in charge stared at her bare arms and coldly asked, "mahw eamalik?" If Jane had even a few seconds more warning of their approach, she would have covered herself. She looked at Don, who was doing his best not to cry. She glanced around, looking for Jack, who somehow did a magic disappearing act. Amazingly, no one else seemed to notice either. She took a chance. "naseaa liltashawur mae Sultan Hakim." Don asked in a nervous whisper, "What are you saying?" Jane felt bad for him in his most likely last moments. "I told them, 'Good morning, we come in peace.' He replied 'what is your business?' I told him that we wanted to have a consultation with the Sultan Hakim." The idiots were arguing among themselves when the leader shouted, "jawasiasa! 'atlaq alnaar ealayhim!" Don's eyes asked the question without him having to move his lips. She said, "They think we are spies. They're going to shoot us." Don started to shake and shouted, "Not spies. American allies." "No, Don! Shut the fuck up!" Jane thought this might be the end of them. All five abruptly raised their weapons to a ready position; *seemingly, ready for the kill.*

"albanadiq 'asifal!" Jack came out from behind the militiamen holding his automatic M249 SAW and pressed it firmly into the leader's back. This impressive firearm needed no introduction. Used by NATO forces, these goons had to realize that he could take them all down before the blink of a camel's eye. He was sure his weapon clarified his intentions if they refused to comply with his demand to put their guns down.

"albanadiq 'asifal! ealaa rakbatayk." Jane collected the weapons and placed them far out of reach of their owners. The leader spoke. "You will all meet your infidel God very soon." Jack poked him in the back with the M249. "So, you speak English? Why didn't you say so and make things easier? We are allies of Sultan Hakim. We have taken great precaution to arrive without alarming other agents of the desert. Do you understand?" The leader nodded, but did not put on his happy face. His boss, the Sultan, would not appreciate finding out that a single American agent overpowered his elite guards. Jack envisioned his white veiled head as it rolled across the desert floor. "Will you agree to take us to Sultan Hakim?" The leader replied, "As you please." Jane knew that as a woman, unveiled, and speaking to them as she did, they were somewhat infuriated by her. "Let's get going." One of Hakim's soldiers asked, "And, our weapons?" Jane stepped in front of him, blocking his access to the rifles. Jack said, "You can come back for your weapons after we have our audience with Sultan Hakim." Jack gestured for the other soldiers to stand, and motioned for them to lead the way. Jane holstered her sidearm and put on her hooded shirt. Jack lowered his weapon. "We are all friends; yes?" The leader replied "Yes. as-salaam 'alaykum." Jack grinned at Don, who was now calming down knowing his group was in control. He replied back saying, and unto you, peace; in Arabic. "Wa-Alaikum-Salaam."

Jack looked up to the clear blue sky and smiled. He mumbled to himself, "I hope you guys had a good laugh at our expense." Jane gave him an admiring look as she gently touched his arm. "Well done, my friend."

The two-minute walk down to the compound went without further incident. As if he had telepathic abilities, the heavy white flaps parted and the great Sultan Hakim emerged from the huge tent. He displayed a sinister smile that quickly turned to a frown. It was clear he was angry. He loudly shouted at his men in Arabic. His soldiers curtseyed, turned and marched off like sad little puppies.

His intense stare made Jack uneasy. "I know you!" Then he focused on Jane. "And, I know you. How can one forget such a lovely desert flower? I see my men have insulted you. Please, come and sit with me for some of our fabulous coffee." The sultan said something in Arabic and in a flash one of the females approached with a shawl for Jane to cover herself. Jack, Jane and Don followed the sheik into the main area of the tent. There were many women roaming around doing chores of one type or another. Sitting in a chair, provocatively sipping tea, was a very attractive young girl of about fifteen. Most of the other woman were somewhat haggard looking. Perhaps they too were attractive in their younger years. The stress and hardships of living in the desert and the demands of their master likely wore them out.

"I'm hungry. Introduce me to our guests!" The young girl commanded. Don assumed she was the sultan's bratty daughter. Jack and Jane assumed otherwise. The sultan exclaimed, "Ah, this is Fatima. She thinks she is the boss of me; and she is always hungry." Hakim signaled to Don with his index finger to approach close. He whispered in Don's ear, but loud enough for all to catch his cynicism, "She's my nineteenth wife." He giggled like Dr. Evil, "She's a, how do you say? Ball buster? You know, spoiled like your American females." The sultan shrugged his shoulders and grinned slyly. "Ah, the things a master has to put up with; she is like a wild bunny in heat, when she accompanies me in bed." His laugh was sinister; his breath stunk like a dead and decaying camel.

They sat and had coffee, Hakim asked all sorts of questions, but paused as two gunshots rang out in the distance. Hakim looked at his uninvited guests. "Not to worry. Those majnun's will not cause you any trouble again." Don looked worried. The master again bellowed out a hearty laugh. "So, Mister Jack Owens, you promised never to cross paths with me again unless it was I visiting you in America. We spoke of the consequences." He glanced at Jane and smiled. "Did I mention how lovely you are? Perhaps you would like to take a bath in warm camel milk. It is very good for the sun damaged skin." He winked to an unimpressed Jane. Fatima subtly, but flirtatiously, tried to get Jack's attention. Her persistent glances in his direction were distracting, and made him feel uncomfortable. She seemed uninterested in her husband's business or his flirtatious remarks. She got more attention than any one female could possibly handle from a dirty old man. She also knew that his keen interest in her would wane, or end within a few months, when the next batch of captives arrived. Jack refocused his attention and asked, "Ok. Time is precious for all of us. Shall we get down to business?"

The desert version of Sponge Bob Square Pants' buddy, Patrick Star, rocked back and forth. "Of course, my friend." Jack supposed that he should try to control his warped imagination.

As his servants poured more hot coffee, Hakim brought his distinctively large nose close to the brim of his cup and took an exaggerated inhalation. "Many would consider drinking coffee instead of tea with honored guests to be blasphemous." He then boasted, "But not in this region! Is this coffee not the most delicious you have ever consumed? Yemeni grown Arabica coffee is considered the best in the world. I have it flown across the Persian Gulf; just for me." He paused for a second, as if in thought. "I suppose we have to thank the Ethiopian's for their contribution. The beans originally came from the Red Sea port of Mukha." The sultan paused again. Jack quickly took the floor before his host could continue, and expounded on the continuing terrorist threats to the Americas. It was clear to all that the evil forces threatening Jack's home posed different, but equally dangerous problems for the sultan. Much of Hakim's wealth and power depended on certain trade agreements with other factions that needed clear and safe passage through his tribal territories. In a discreet and calm voice, Jack explained the need for intelligence. The sultan listened and nodded but said nothing as Jack laid out the situation and his dire need for information. Hakim appeared distracted at times. Jane relented to local custom, and kept silent. In the eyes of the sultan, Jack Owens was her master. She had no independent autonomy in his land. Yet, her outspoken, and in his eyes, rude attitude, somehow intrigued him. The sultan always enjoyed a good challenge from his women. In the end, he always triumphed; even if it *killed* them.

"I'll tell you what, Mister Jack." Hakim leaned in close to Jack, speaking quietly so no others could hear. Jack had to endure his foul breath and try not to insult him by leaning back. "I have some very useful information for you. Will you agree for the same fee as last time, wired to the same account? I will give you two days, Mister Jack Owens, to complete the funds transfer. See how much I trust our friendship? Besides, if something should go wrong, AND I DON'T GET MY MONEY, no worries. A little birdie will tip off our mutual enemies, and they will find you instead." Jack looked insulted, "Hakim, trust is all we have, my friend. No worries. From the impressive growth of your encampment, it seems our previous arrangement worked out quite well for you. Fear not, this one will reap you equal benefits." Jack extended his hand. "One more thing, Mister Jack Owens. As friends, it is customary to offer something one holds dear." He looked at Jane as if he was undressing her with his eyes. She turned away to hide the killer instinct building up in her. Hakim continued. "You can pick any of the wives. Even that one. She is an insolent brat, but quite the little whore under the covers. I'm growing bored with her, anyway; and it appears she is taken with you." Jack took a breath and discretely gestured toward Jane. He quietly said to Hakim, "She is an assassin who has sex with her targets, then slits their throats. You will never see it coming." The expression on the Sultan's face ensured Jack had his attention. "Besides, my worthy friend; I am most certain you would miss the little tart. Perhaps a list of safe contacts to deal with and say, a quarter million U.S., same as last time? Perhaps for you to start some new venture?" The man with the stamina of nineteen men did not seem appeased with Jack's counter offer. Jack put out his hand, "I have nothing else to offer. All I am asking for are names, Id's, and last known locations. You get new business partners and additional funding." Hakim laughed whole-heartedly. "My friend, you are quite sly. And, a damn fool to find yourself at the mercy of the great Sultan Hakim." Grinning like the Cheshire Cat, he took Jack's hand, nearly crushing it. "We have a deal, Mister Jack. I will let you in on something else. A special gift from me to you." He leaned close to Jack and whispered in his ear. Don and Jane tried to mind their manners and let Jack negotiate but they could not avoid the horrified look that came over Jack's face at Hakim's last words.

Chapter 36

Her contacts assured her that Jack Owens would magically appear in front of her eyes. They told her, "It is Allah's will. "Alhamd lilah." Roya Abasi spent the past five days roaming the streets of the capital, keeping an eye on Jack Owens' known associates. She figured that her target would eventually meet up with one of them. It had been a long week with few results. Roya focused on the men, never thinking about the one woman who had Jack's complete trust. Not fifteen feet in front of her was the key to her success. Roya opened her notebook containing a cluster of photographs and confirmed her recall. ATF Special Agent Marcia Gainsworth stood facing her while having a heated conversation on her cell phone. Roya purchased a cup of coffee in a to-go cup and made sure the cover was only partially secure. She walked toward Marcia while pretending to be on the phone herself. She eavesdropped for a few moments catching enough of Marcia's conversation with what sounded like an ex-lover. She planned to embed herself directly into Jack's life but this situation appeared to offer a better opportunity for her to get close to him.

Marcia paced back and forth, her eyes becoming glassy, as tears started to form. "Damn it, Sharon. This is the third time you canceled since your transfer. I am well aware that it is a long trip to D.C. I deal with it all the time, why can't you?" She paused for a moment, wiping a streaming tear from her face. "You know what, just forget it! Forget us. This isn't working. It takes two to make a relationship work!" As she hung up, she changed direction again as she continued her nervous pacing. "Oh my God!" Roya's cry-out was received too late for Marcia to avoid the collision with the young woman. Marcia's cell phone crashed to the pavement. A coffee cup flew upward into the air, warm dark liquid cascading down onto both of them. The two women stood facing each other, their faces expressing the shock of the moment. Roya wiped her hands on her soaked coat and shook them off. "My coat is ruined." They both looked down as Marcia said, "My phone, too. I'm sorry, I just…" "It was an accident. A messy one at that. And your poor phone." Roya bent down to pick up Marcia's cell phone. As she did, her ankle twisted and her shoe slipped out from under her foot, causing her to stumble into Marcia. The trained agent's rapid reflexes enabled her to catch the woman and prevent her from falling to the sidewalk. "Oh my god, thank you. I can be such a klutz sometimes." Roya tried to stand but winced in pain. "Let me help you. We should get you seated. I can buy you another cup of coffee and grab a few napkins to dry off your coat." Roya smiled. "Sure.

Thanks." As Marcia assisted Roya into the nearby coffee shop, Roya asked, "Does this mean I have to buy you a new phone?" Marcia laughed. "No. It's a company asset. I can get it replaced."

The two woman spoke for the better part of an hour. Roya talked about her mom and dad splitting up, and how she was on her own at the age of seventeen. Marcia was impressed how a person with those odds stacked against her could manage to put herself through community college and then continue taking online courses to achieve her undergraduate degree. Roya Abasi told a most convincing and sympathetic story.

"After I got my degree in accounting, I worked various jobs. I always felt like the men had the upper hand at advancement. On several occasions, my managers had inappropriately approached me. The usual crap; dinner, drinks." Marcia touched her hand gently and then removed it. Roya was not sexually interested in women, but Marcia's brief touch was warm and genuine. Her ruse seemed to be working. She continued. "I fell for it once, thinking I could handle it. I never quite knew for sure if I reacted to the few drinks I had or if the asshole guy I was with slipped something in my drink. We ended up back at his apartment. By the time I realized what was happening, he was on top of me, his foul smelling whisky breath making me sick." Roya took careful notice of how her new friend was taking in all that she was dishing out. Marcia asked, "What did you do?" "I tried to push him off, but he was already inside me and had my arms pinned down. I let him finish and got out of there as fast as possible."

"Did you report the assault to the police?"

"No. I was so embarrassed. I wanted to forget it and never allow myself to be that vulnerable again. I called out sick for a few days, and when I returned, my coworkers were talking behind my back. One girl I was friendly with asked me if I was dating my manager. Her insinuation that I was sleeping with the boss for advancement. It made me sick. The twit obviously set me up, making it look like a date so I couldn't accuse him of any wrongdoing. I went to Human Resources and handed them my resignation, which included a full account of what had happened to me. They never called me, and from what I found out, nothing was ever said to the bastard." She paused, "I hate men." Marcia looked upset, but then tried to lighten the mood. "I sort of understand. Something similar happened to me with a guy who wouldn't take 'no' for an answer. Only, I punched the fucker in his nose and broke it in two places. He never looked the same after that. He messed with the wrong girl. His 'gaydar' must have been off that day." Roya looked embarrassed. "Oh, you're..." "Yes, I am; not into men." Roya had her right where she needed her to be. She made herself blush, a trick she mastered with lots of practice. "I experimented in my senior year of high school. Her name was Susan and it only last three months. I was super 'in the closet' and she was so much not." Her face turned beet red. Marcia asked, "What?" "The sex was, really good. I suppose we know our own bodies and what we like, so we're keenly aware of what would turn on our partners. Anyway, that was a one-time thing."

Marcia looked at her watch, "Oh, my. I'm really late for a business meeting." As she stood, Roya asked, "Are you a cop?" Marcia realized her sidearm showed as she stood. "Yes. I'm in law enforcement. I'm more of an investigator. It was nice to speak with you, Roya; and sorry about the coffee." "It's fine, a little water and it will be like new. I'll walk out with you." Marcia was distracted, something her training should have never allowed. She should have noticed that Roya no longer showed any symptoms of a twisted ankle. Marcia held the door for Roya to exit first. The fresh air had a bit of a chill to it; Marcia held her coat closed with her hand. Roya took her other hand in hers. "I really enjoyed talking with you, too. Can we get together? Maybe for drinks or dinner?" Marcia hesitated for a second. She considered for a moment that this might be an inappropriate situation, but said, "Sure. I'd like that. Give me your phone and I'll put my number in. Call me during the week." Awkwardly, Marcia gave Roya back her phone, and offered her hand. Roya gently took it and drew her close, kissing Marcia's cheek. "I'll call you." She looked back over her shoulder and shouted playfully, "What are the chances that such a silly accident would bring us together?" Marcia smiled and waved, "Bye."

Roya smiled a sweet smile. "Bye, Marcia." She felt like the beautiful Dionaea Muscipula. She envisioned the Venus Fly Trap plant as it lured its prey in, and clamped down on it.

Soon you will lead me to Jack Owens and allow me to fulfill my jihad.

Praise Allah.

Chapter 37

"One... two... three... four... five..." Alan Mayfield paced back and forth across the room as he slowly counted to ten. He stopped for a moment and drew in a slow and steady breath followed by a slow and controlled exhalation. He did this several times, trying to calm himself. A few years ago, Alan's uncle, who was a psychiatric social worker, noticed his nephew's random periods of intense agitation. He suggested several calming exercises. On occasion it worked, but lately the self-help attempts proved futile.

This woman who wants to cage me like an animal is haunting my dark soul.

"One... two... three... four... five... Damn!" Alan started to shake, and then looked around the room, fighting the urge to punch something. He focused on the smooth painted wall, searching for an available spot. The walls themselves, the surfaces, seemed to warp like a rolling ocean wave. "Ugh!" The pain, a consequence of his fist breaking through sheetrock, usually felt good and helped to relax him; not this time. Alan flopped into his desk chair and spun around a few times. As the room revolved three hundred sixty degrees, he watched as the holes and broken sheetrock that enveloped most of the visible surfaces, blurred past him.

"Katie Claire Owens."

"ADA Owens."

"ADA Katie Claire Owens!"

"Ugh!"

The vivid image of her face lingered in his mind's eye. Everywhere he looked, she was in front of him. Fantasies of what he would do to her saturated his dreams. Now, in his daydream, he visualized painfully torturing her, showing no mercy. He would demonstrate to her that his ministrations would completely liberate her from the hardships of life. Of course, death would finally free her. If it took days, or even weeks, she would submit to him as her master. Alan grinned; he thought, *OK, not weeks, she'll never last that long*. Alan Mayfield was truly confused over his demons. He often fantasized of his captive's complete submission. Then in an uncontrolled rage, his desires change. He wants them to fight his aggression with their own. If this damaged soul only knew what it was, that would satisfy him, he might find peace with himself. His victims, on the other hand, would suffer his wrath regardless.

The Internet, if you know what you are doing, can deliver a multitude of information about virtually anyone on the planet.

Alan typed "Katie Claire Owens, Lawyer" into his search engine, and sat back while pages of data flowed before his eyes. Busy work was good for Alan. As long as he kept his mind active and focused on something other than the obsession of the day, he could remain in control. *There is so much data on you my little miss. My eyes need a break.* In a small notebook that he pulled out of the drawer beneath the computer, he began jotting down notes. Lived on Long Island, two young boys, twins. He worked in silence except for the occasional mumbling to himself. "*How interesting.*" He tried to envision what the little tots looked like. He could have exploited his fantasy even further if they had been girls. "*Of course, they would look like her.*" His extensive web search found no pictures of the children, or the husband. He Googled "Jack Owens." *Graduated Emory with a degree in finance with a secondary in business law. Employed by AMR Consulting Group.* Alan shook his head in disgust. To himself again, he said, "What a nerd. This beauty's married to a traveling salesman." A further search, after an hour, pinged an article by some obscure Internet news site. "Husband of New York ADA vanishes without a trace." The article continued on to set the tone for a cheating husband who left his wife and job to run away with a mystery lover. *There has to be more to this*. Alan rubbed his temples, attempting to thwart off a migraine headache. "There has to be more to you Jack Owens! What man in his right mind would walk away from an intelligent, vibrant, beauty like her?!" His head pounded. He threw his notebook across the room, knocking over a small table lamp. Again, his mind held a vision of her leaning back against a doorframe, her skirt hiked up and her blouse mostly unbuttoned. Time was running out for her. He had to show her his version of true love.

He had to set her free.

Alan picked up his notebook from the floor, up-righted the lamp, and returned to his desk. His hand took on a life of its own, turning to a blank page and beginning to sketch. Katie Claire Owens began to appear before his eyes; just as he had imagined her. The pencil had a good eraser. He used it to remove a bit more of her blouse, revealing a bit more of her breast. "There, that's more like it. I think I'll have you pose for me; *just like this*."

"This is perfect, nice and sheer; with pretty buttons. White for her purity." Alan sorted through an array of women's apparel that hung in his walk-in-closet.

Some he bought to meet with his fantasies, others, if they were evidence free, he kept from previous victims. He opened the longer drawer on the right side of the closet dresser and removed a silky pleated skirt. "This will do. Not too short, but short enough to show some of what she has to offer." In his psychopathic vision, she would want to dress up sexy for him. She would want to submit to his every request. In return, he would deliver to her the final ecstasy before setting her free.

She will not show fear. Of this, I am certain. She will have fire in her eyes, but she will not yell out. There is nothing more sensual than a woman with incessant control of her emotions. This, of Katie Claire Owens, I am sure of.

Chapter 38

"Good morning, Miss Katie. Two eggs over easy on rye toast?" "You're the best, Rosa. I missed you so much." In unison, the twins recited, "We missed you too, Nana Rosa." Rosa smiled warmly as she handed Katie her breakfast plate. Steam aromatically rose from the hash brown potatoes and perfectly cooked eggs. Slices of orange with fresh parsley garnished the plate. "Oh my, you are spoiling us. It smells delicious." Katie touched Rosa's hand. No other words of appreciation were needed. They both recognized how much they cared about each other and of Rosa's love for the family. "Well, don't get too accustomed to it, my loves. I do have my other family to return to." She pouted along with the sad faces of the Owens clan. "Well, not until Mister Jack returns next week. Then, you are on your own to rebuild your family. Miss Rosa can't be the glue anymore for the two of you." She said it with such a serious face, Katie and the boys just stared at her. They all started to laugh at the same time.

"This is delicious, Rosa. Thank you."

The boys chimed in unison, "Yum."

Katie cleared the table while Rosa loaded the dishwasher. Rosa told her, "Leave it. You get going and drop the boys at school on your way to work. I'll finish here." Katie asked, "Don't you need the car today. What will you do?" "Ever heard of Uber? I want to walk around downtown and the seaport. I want to visit the Boston Tea Party Ships. The museums are supposed to be so interesting." Katie suggested, "You should also hit the Faneuil Hall Marketplace. It's a really fun, historic mall. There is both indoor and outdoor shopping. I love to walk around there." Katie pulled out a credit card from her purse. Rosa waved her off. "Please Rosa, I would love to meet you this afternoon and take you to lunch, but lately my days are crazy and it will never happen. I insist you go to the Salty Dog. The chowder is to die for; it's a must have appetizer. Later, when you get the boys, you can go for ice cream. Or, even better, go to Magnolia's Bakery." Katie paused to envision the delicious pastries then mumbled, "Yum, I want to go." Rosa took the credit card. She knew better than to attempt arguing this case with this lawyer.

"Come on, boys. Let's get going or we'll all be late."

Fifty minutes later, Katie walked into her building on Bulfinch Place and the hustle and bustle of the Boston DA's office. Detective Nick Lawrence was sitting behind her desk, in her chair. He leaned back into a reclining position, "Good morning, boss lady." His tone was more serious than usual. "Good morning, Detective. Haven't we had this discussion already?" Nick looked a bit lost. "Come on, Nick; about knocking before entering. I think it is obvious that extends to entering my office in my absence." Her chief investigator stood and gestured for her to take *her* seat. He walked over to Katie's office door and closed it. She was about to hit him with another reprimand, but he stopped her before any of the words were spoken. "I have something to discuss with you." Katie glanced at the closed door and asked, "Personal or business?" Nick leaned against the credenza, then immediately made a move over to one of the chairs in front of her desk. "Both." He sat down slowly as he continued to speak. She watched Nick's mouth as it formed words and projected them but heard nothing. Yet, she heard everything. Her heart pounded as her breathing drew insufficient air into her lungs. She fought hard to keep her breakfast down. Katie's eyes watered, blurring her vision.

"Katie!" Nick handed her a cup of water. "Here, drink this. We can go and get something stronger in a bit."

Detective Lawrence went over all the gruesome details of Ellen's murder, leaving out the obviously brutal details, since they would all be in the reports. He figured it would be easier for his boss, after she came to terms with the horrific reality of what happened to her precious intern.

Katie wiped tears from her face, "Was she…?" "It's all in here; when you're ready." Nick placed the report on Katie's desk. She made no attempt to reach for the documents, and appeared to be in a near catatonic state. Nick cleared his throat, hoping to break her out of her trance. After a brief pause he said, "The crime scene investigators found evidence in Ellen's apartment of a partial fingerprint on the heel of one of her shoes, and DNA was found on her neck. We believe it may have been from saliva." Katie asked, "What about witnesses?" Nick grinned, "Sure. A few said a man from the utility company was knocking on doors saying there may be a gas leak. Apparently, he hadn't entered any of the apartments, except Ellen's. Three tenants described him as tall, well-built man with tan skin, a heavy beard, dark glasses and a grey hat. Obviously a disguise. "Meet me for that drink later. We can talk it all out. You can rest assured I'll have everyone on this." As Detective Lawrence started to exit her office, Katie called out for him to wait a minute, and in a weak voice stated the obvious, "You *know*, it was him."

I know, it was him.

Katie waited a few minutes allowing herself to calm down. She walked over to DA Mahoney's office and knocked on the partially open door before she entered. The DA and Andy Smith from Public Affairs were having a meeting. They both looked up, surprised that Katie had walked in during a one-on-one meeting.

"I'm so sorry to barge in, but I need to speak with you." Katie was unfamiliar with the normal protocol of how DA Mahoney ran his office. DA Mahoney asked, "We're almost done here ADA Owens, can it wait?" Katie took a breath, "No, sir. I'm afraid it cannot." She directly addressed her boss's visitor. "I'm so sorry, could you please excuse us?" Andy glanced at the DA, and nodded as he walked out of the office.

DA Mahoney initially looked angry, but his face softened as he saw tears start to roll down his senior ADA's face. "Come sit down. Tell me what's going on." Katie repeated   all the details almost word for word, as Nick did for her. "I know this is the heinous work of Alan Mayfield." James sat behind his desk. Despite his hard line in the office, he was a genuinely good and compassionate man. He figured Katie could use a hug from a friend but office policy did away with most of the relaxed social atmosphere in the workplace, especially in this agency. "OK, so from what you told me, there may be viable evidence found at the scene. Have your investigators put a tail on your suspect so we don't lose him in the wind. If the evidence connects him to the case, he's ours. I know this became personal for you as of this morning. Don't let that get in the way of making a solid case stick." Katie nodded and in a soft voice said, "Thank you, James." DA Mahoney stood and took her hand. "I would suggest taking the rest of the day off, but I know you would refuse." Katie needed some time, but ADA Owens needed to nail this poor excuse for a human being. DA Mahoney said, as he sat himself back at his desk, "If there is anything you need, you call me." Katie wiped a lingering tear and nodded her appreciation. As she made her way back to her office, she stopped at Angie's desk. "Can you come to my office?" Katie said it quietly and did not wait for an answer. Angie, a bit unnerved at Katie's demeanor, got up and followed her boss.

As they both entered Katie's office, her cell phone rang. "ADA Owens." It was Nick, "They asked our office to notify her family. I elected to do it myself. I figured you'd want to come with me?" "Of course, Nick. I'll meet you downstairs in twenty. Thank you."

"Have a seat, Angie."

Chapter 39

The team's exfil went off without a hitch. Jack, Jane, and Don were driven by one of Hakim's guards to a prearranged rendezvous point a few miles south of Kandahar. The camouflaged vehicle waiting for them had the freedom to traverse the local desert region. That privilege came at a high cost, but it was well worth it. The police and other various factions recognized Hakim as a valuable team player who generously contributed to each of their causes. No one would see reason to intercept them. From that point, the two Humvee convoy made its way to an obscure dirt airfield. Six hours later, they were on the military transport aircraft and well on their way back to Washington.

The team sat on wide hammock-like mesh chaises hanging close to the floor in the middle of the wide-open cargo area. Don appeared to be asleep. Jane maneuvered herself to be closer to Jack; close enough for him to feel her body heat. Without any words, she leaned into him, her head on his shoulder. They sat for a few awkward minutes before Jane finally broke the silence. "I lost count; who saved whose life more, you or me?" Jack put his arm around Jane. "You. You definitely saved my life way more times than I, for you. Oh, and don't forget that time, Katie's crazy kidnapping. I was unreachable. You jumped through some amazing hoops to save her. You pretty much won her over after that." "Yes, I suppose that's true, Jack. However, you really saved my life in a way that is so much more than all those times combined. And the truth is; Katie still doesn't completely trust me." Jack removed his arm and sat up from his semi-reclined position. "But she knows that I trust you; completely. And, she's good with that." Across from them, Don cleared his throat, drawing their attention.

"So, Jack. You and the Sultan had quite the private discussion. Can you let us in on it, since we are supposed to be 'The Team'?" Don looked around, "I didn't ask earlier because that little plane afforded no privacy. There's literally just the three of us on this huge flying boat." Jane appeared to be napping. Without opening her eyes, she said, "They were mostly talking about me, right Jack? The pig wanted to trade me for that brat child he's raping. I can read gestures and lips very well." Jack looked over, at Jane. "If you read my lips, then you understood as he did, what I said. I told him, that you would give him the best sex of his life; just before slitting his throat. He promptly agreed to my monetary offer and a favor I may, or may not need to extend." Jane shook her head in disgust. She remarked, "As much as I would love to

269

maintain my killer reputation, touching him, or worse, letting him touch me would be disgusting; even for me." She grinned, "Well, for the old me." "I have to admit, Jane, you can be hard to resist. I knew you were trouble from that first infamous night I met you. You showed no interest in me, but I still had my sights set on getting you in the sack." He winked as if he were kidding. Both he and Jane knew he spoke the truth. As soon as Jack said it, he realized again, how awkward the moment had become. After all, Jane was there to seduce Jack's best friend, William, away from Katie. Jane's ultimate plan was to ease him into her web. Then, as it actually played out, replace him with his presumed dead identical twin brother, Carlton. Jane did all she could to estrange William from his friends and family, and especially Katie. That was then, and this is now; Jane is a different person. "Holy mother... Are you two still flirting? Why don't the two of you get a room or something?" Don figured he should have minded his own business. The look Jane and Jack gave him was intimidating. He tried to resist, but failed. "I'm just saying..." Don shrugged his shoulders, then got up and walked to the other side of the cargo area. He had limited knowledge of his two teammates' history. Early on, he heard all the bad stuff and some of the not so bad situations that constantly brought Jack and Jane together. He was also aware that Jane had saved

Jack's wife Katie from impending peril on at least one occasion. Donald's mind raced with thoughts of the bad things he heard about Jane, and fantasies of those horrors he could only imagine. Still, she had proven herself as an ally repeatedly over the past two years. He was about to apologize but Jack cut him off as the first apologetic word was about to roll off his tongue. Instead, he glanced over at Jane who offered a slight smile. She saw it in his face. Nothing more needed to be said.

"Listen. There's only one person that frightens me more than Jane, and that's Katie. Talk about a woman scorned…" He had Don's attention back. "Can we please get back to the business at hand? You wanted me to fill you both in on what Hakim told me." Jack glanced at Don while pointing to an open space next to Jane, "You had better take a seat; over here." The trio, who would try their best to save America, huddled close. The roar of the cargo plane's four turbo-props was deafening. It drowned out any possibility of eavesdropping from the pilots or the two security officers seated far up front by the lavatory and cockpit.

Chapter 40

Her morning was crazy; her mind frazzled, and her heart sad. Katie needed a break from all the hullabaloo of Bulfinch Place. The crazy pressure her new job came with afforded no free time, which she originally embraced as a welcoming distraction to all her personal problems. However, Katie needed a short reprieve. So, as soon as her morning meeting ended, she headed out of the office. With another hour before the lunchtime crowd inundated the streets and local businesses, Katie decided to walk around the local stores. Nordstrom Rack was quiet which made browsing around the store more comfortable. The red and white sign clamped to the center post of the rack she was looking through declared "50% off All Evening Wear." She already had two garments to try on. *Ooh, this is really nice. Jack would like this one*. Katie removed the sheer black dress with a low neckline and a lightly pleated bottom. When they first reunited after graduating from Emory, and after years of being out of touch, she was wearing a skirt similar to the lower half of this dress. Several times after they were *together*, Jack would joke that seeing her in that outfit was his special "Turn on." She imagined Jack, as he would first look admiringly at her. Then he would move behind her and seductively unzip the dress; letting it slide to the floor. In her mind's eye, she imagined him there with her. Instead of the privacy of the dressing room, Jack continued his seduction outside of it with customers obliviously going about their business. *Wow, now I'm an exhibitionist. Eh, it's just a fantasy.* Katie smiled to herself.

"Excellent choice. I could see you in that!"

Katie snapped out of her fantasy daydream and back into the real world. He stood there with the most serious expression on his face. "Shit!" As soon as ADA Owens displayed her surprise, she regretted the outburst. Angrily, she asked, "Alan Mayfield! What the hell are you doing here?" Alan Mayfield smirked, "Shopping. What would anyone do in a department store?" Katie fought hard not to allow the impending fury she felt building up in her, to cause her to say or do something she would regret later. She could not decide if it was fear or anger, she was feeling, or part of both. Regardless of which, she had to avoid showing either to this creepy murderer. She surreptitiously took a deep breath. "And I suppose stalking me in Trader Joe's the other day was a coincidence?" Alan shrugged his shoulders and displayed a boyish grin. "Oh, and the cafe last week! You had better keep your distance, Mr. Mayfield, or I will have you arrested on stalking charges." A few customers tried to disguise their eavesdropping and appear as if they were minding their own business, but they failed at both. A young man walked over, "Excuse me, Miss. Is everything all right? Would you like me to call security?" Katie gave the evil eye to Alan and told the concerned store employee, whose nametag read "Louis Stevens, Assistant Mgr." "No, thank you. I think this rude person is done here and ready to leave." Alan Mayfield said, "Whatever. We can catch up later." He winked at Katie then turned to Louis. His face expressed anger with an unfriendly scowl, "You should learn to mind your own business, son!" Then Alan quietly told the young man, "This isn't the movies, and in reality, the hero often doesn't survive. I think we will see each other again; real soon." He took a step backward and before turning and walking away made one last statement. "Katie, Katie, Katie. You shouldn't allow yourself to make the job personal. It's bad for your health." Alan took another step backward and added in a softer tone, "And for others, around you." He glanced at the assistant manager, and then pivoted Pee Wee Herman style, as if to mock them. Katie and Louis stood silently watching as Alan Mayfield brushed the racks of clothing with his hands as he moved through the aisle. Katie's deep-seated anger was too much to bear and she lost control. She shouted, but quickly toned it down, "You made it personal when you hurt my friend! I will make you pay one way or another!" The assistant manager gazed at Katie in awe as she watched her nemesis disappear down the escalator.

As senior ADA, there are expectations, which include a high level of professionalism and the ability to maintain self-control in any situation; especially when it involved the District Attorney, his office or any cases they were involved in. Alan Mayfield was a person of interest under investigation by her office and the FBI. All investigators including herself had to tread carefully so when the imminent arrest warrant was issued, there would be no conflicts to weaken the case against him. At that moment, when suddenly confronted by Alan Mayfield, Katie violated those expectations. Katie paced back and forth in her office. She was angry with herself for not keeping control of the moment. She also had concerns for the store's assistant manager, Louis. While the employee may not have realized it, Mayfield had threatened him. ADA Owens had an idea. She called Nick.

"Nick, I have a job for you. Can you meet me at O'Reilly's down the block for a drink? Say, around five." Katie Claire needed to do something. It was not that she had lost faith in the police or the FBI's ability to catch this evil person. All the red tape slowed them down. They needed evidence, and she had a plan to speed up the process.

Chapter 41

"So, here is what we have so far." Jack had prepared for two hours prior to the top-secret meeting. He drew, wrote, and erased on the five by six whiteboard. In attendance were Donald Graham, General Armstrong, Senator John White, and Marcia Gainsworth. There was no social talk, just subdued handshakes along with a few nods. The secure room located in the Pentagon's "Sub-level 2" had the latest technology for soundproofing. Its two-inch thick glass panels had blackout mesh between the panes. Using a control panel on the conference room table, an authorized person could remotely open or close the panels. Before Jack could continue, Senator White asked, "Will the President be joining us as discussed before your trip abroad?" Jack hesitated, not sure how to respond. The general saved him from an uncomfortable moment and gave him an easier path into the discussion. "We thought it best to keep this preliminary meeting to just the five of us; for now." Jack cleared his throat. They were all friends and trusted colleagues; he could be forthright with the sensitive issue at hand. "I think, General, we have to tell it as it is. Or, as we have been informed from our contact in Afghanistan." Jack leaned against the wall, his shoulder brushing against the whiteboard. "Damn." He picked up a dry erase marker and fixed the smudged text.

"As you all are aware from previous discussions, and the president's own divulgence, he had, or rather has, an identical twin brother. However, this situation started out differently from our other 'Twin' terror agents. In this unfortunate situation, and for reasons unknown to us, the president's parents placed the estranged brother in a foster home while waiting for the adoption process to complete. The boy was just three years old. We're not even sure the president himself knows the reason why. In any event, this estranged brother has reemerged. Our informant told a convincing story of a disgruntled sibling who felt rejected by his family for not trying to find him. As in most of these types of situations, he suffered abuse in some of his foster homes and probably has some symptoms of a dissociative disorder. The Taliban easily recruited him in his early adulthood. In recent years, he has flip-flopped between Isis and other terror factions. His main function was soliciting donations through various, less than legitimate campaigns, and raising operating funds for those terror groups. A few years ago, they began grooming him for a political future. He would be the next phase of their twenty-year plan, replacing his brother in the most powerful seat in the world." Marcia asked, "But they tried that last year, Jack. You faced extreme peril from that operation, and ultimately saved the day." Jack disregarded the flattery and for once, held back from making any sarcastic retorts. "This is true, Marcia. We avoided a seriously bad situation." He glanced at each of the others. "They are certainly aware that we expected another attempt at the presidency. After all, that is their ultimate endgame. We have to pray that they have no idea that we are informed of how they plan to do it. They probably think, we think, their golden plan was foiled and the twin conspiracy died with Vice President McDermott." Jack could see his small posse were taking a moment for recollection. Last year, his powerfully seductive wife Anastasia, a covert terrorist agent, was naively grooming the Speaker of the House, Ronald McDermott. Her mission was to replace the vice president with his *twin* operative. She and her leaders had this all planned down to every detail. With that, McDermott was not a terrorist; he just had a different political view on how to run the country. Even her introduction to her husband was part of the terror plan. Anastasia had an affair with the vice president, making her privy to sensitive information. It also made it easy for her to get close enough to assassinate him when the time was right, and make it look like a heart attack. As expected, through constitutional rule of progression, Speaker of the House,

Ronald McDermott assumed the vice presidency. Only, before that happened, his twin replaced him. Now the terror group had a man in the second most powerful seat with an agenda that would make *Allah* proud. The Black Widow, Anastasia, would eventually try to seduce the president into a compromising situation; hopefully leading him to a similar fate as his former vice president. Fortunately, President Albright, being a man of unquestionable integrity would have none of Anastasia's advances. Jack had already advised the president of a possible coup attempt, and worked with him to set her up and expose her phony husband, which lead to their ultimate takedown.

After a few minutes, Jack continued. "We are certain that President Albright is still the real deal. Surveillance teams have been keeping a close watch. He will never be out of one of our agents' sight." John asked, "What if they *do* lose sight of him? We can't cover him while he is in the White House." The general chimed in, "We have eyes *everywhere*. No one can get in or out of the White House or other government buildings without us knowing about it. In the unlikely event we do lose sight of POTUS, or suspect foul play, we will find him and discretely detain him. We will investigate anything that is even slightly suspicious. The plan is to catch them during the exchange. We thought it prudent not to inform the president of our plans, so he continues to act natural. Tipping our enemies off would foil any opportunity to finally bring this reign of terror to an end." Jack continued, "Jane has been instrumental in getting us this far, especially in Afghanistan. She is too recognizable, so she cannot be involved any further. She has been sent away for now." Jack glanced at the general, who had warned Jack to remain on board with his decision regarding Jane Austin, the ex-terrorist. Donald raised his hand as if he were in grade school. Jack raised his eyebrow acknowledging him. "What about the president's terrorist twin brother? Do we know where he is? Shouldn't we have him under surveillance?" Jack stood up from his leaning position. "That is an excellent question Agent Graham. Unfortunately, his brother fell off the grid shortly after his induction into this latest plot. I would assume they have him deep underground, in intense psychological and physical training. He is probably being updated on the most current political issues and the 'Who's Who' in the White House. Furthermore, the president's family will be at Camp David for two weeks before he plans to join them. We think this is the time they will attempt the assassination and exchange." Jack paused for one second. Marcia was about to make a comment but Jack continued. "One thing we need to alert our agents to look out for; if the president decides not to take his time off at Camp David and suggests his family remain there without him, this could be an alarm that indicates foul play." Marcia refrained from raising her hand this time as she asked, "Shouldn't we be concerned, being there is so much tension between us and North Korea, as well as friction between us and Russia? We should consider how vulnerable the United States is to a counterfeit president facilitating an order for a nuclear strike. This could lead the entire world into a massive nuclear war."

Jack acknowledged Marcia's most obvious concern. "Exactly! Moreover, the United States would never have the support of its allies. There would be major conflicts across the globe." General Armstrong added, "An action like that would allow the terror regimes to unite against their common enemies. They could ultimately destroy the world, as we know it."

Discussions continued well into the night. Jack had promised to call Katie as soon as he returned from abroad. Immediately, as his team had set their feet on German soil, local agents separated Jack and Don from Jane, and escorted them to a small private jet destined for Washington DC. Jane was escorted to a similar government plane and taken back home, to Canada. Jack had not spoken to his wife or his kids since before his trip overseas. John had already let him know that he kept Katie in the loop and she knew he was back on American soil, safe and unharmed. Before Jack left, he had given his wife a "burner" phone. After John's call, her instructions were to destroy it. Jack hated making Katie part of the covert stuff. She had been through a lot. She waited for him all this time, and then some. Still, his heart ached with fear that by the time this crappy mission ended, it would be too late for them, and she would leave him for good. He would not blame her, but he prayed Katie would give their marriage another chance. He checked his watch, 2:30AM. He decided to call her later in the morning.

Guards escorted him and Don to their rooms in a special military housing unit adjacent to the Pentagon. After his eight month ordeal in captivity, the guarded supervision and restricted movement around the facilities made Jack uncomfortable. However, Jack knew this was standard protocol for teams dealing with issues of national security. Besides, they were treated respectfully, and served a delicious gourmet dinner. The staff chef cooked Jack's porterhouse perfectly. Jack checked the hotel style phone in his quarters. There was no dial tone. Instead, he heard a slow constant beeping. The tiny writing on the front of the base read, "Internal Calls Only."

Sleep, Jack. You are going to need it. Jack's mind raced with all kinds of random thoughts. He found separating his personal needs for his family, and the country's business-at-hand difficult at best.

I will call Katie and the boys in the morning before the first round of meetings begin; or, there will be no meetings.

Chapter 42

The only time Jane could sleep peacefully through the night was when she lay in her own bed, with Pete holding her close. The latest adventure with Jack and Don wore her out, allowing her to doze off and on during the six-hour flight from Germany. Her disrupted sleep patterns brought with them the same disturbing memories of blood and death that often plagued her. With her head resting against the portal window and her eyes closed, Jane replayed various past events. One of her biggest regrets, the murder of her twins' dad, Michael. His death came at the hands of another ruthless female terrorist. Jane could have saved him, had she not chose to look the other way. Her cold-hearted upbringing allowed no room in her heart for love or compassion. Even if she had enough feelings to prevent his demise, the jihad took precedence above all else. Subconsciously, she switched channels only to move on to another heartless chapter. The death of a teenage girl leaving a concert venue who did nothing to Jane, except to offer her a cigarette and a bit of friendly conversation. The innocent teen fell prey to Jane's need to satisfy a hunger for physical violence. It was how she achieved self-gratification. She replayed the seduction, followed by the blackmailing of William's boss, back in the early years. Countless other seductions ruined lives and left untraceable bodies in her wake. The landing gear bumping down on the tarmac as the plane touched down woke Jane out of her nightmarish slumber. Upon awakening, the horrific dreams left but a trace of themselves in her memory, but just enough to pain her with the newfound remorse that finding humanity afforded her.

Jane's flight home to Canada arrived earlier than expected, getting her in around 10PM. The cab dropped Jane at Pete's place just in time to help him close the bar. The last customer paid his bill, and Jane locked the door behind him as he exited. She jumped into Pete's arms, wrapping her legs tightly around his waist and started unbuttoning his shirt. He hurriedly carried her into the back room, not even noticing how many times he painfully bumped into a chair or the edge of the bar or a doorframe.

Seduction was the most treacherous of Jane's sociopathic traits. In her earlier years as an assassin, she used it to compromise the most powerful of men, *and women*. With Pete, she shared her carnal expertise with genuine love and desire. "Hurry up!" Pete lifted Jane onto the table and proceeded to remove her camisole, pulling it over her head. Jane reached behind her back to undo her bra but Pete had already pulled down the shoulder straps exposing her still perfect breasts. He ravished her nipples with his tongue. She moaned and embraced his head with her hands, encouraging him continue his aggressive seduction. Pete worked her breasts some more before sliding his tongue up past her neck and finding her beautifully moist mouth. Jane managed to undo Pete's belt and unbutton his trousers. She grabbed his hips and pulled him close so he could enter her. From that point, she had control of the situation. Her tongue found its way back to Pete's mouth and wildly emulated his thrusting motion down below. Jane's rapid breathing and subtle moan was all Pete could take. Jane held him deep inside her. She could feel him still ready for more. Pete started a slow teasing motion in and out of her. He could feel her reaction right away.

"Wow! You really missed me." Pete caught his breath and smiled. "I really… did."

"Where are Jani and Mikael?" Beads of perspiration trickled from her forehead and down her cheek. A bead glistened as it slid over and off her lip. Pete slowed his movement even more but kept a constant rhythm, trying not to lose his concentration completely. "They're with Ron and Marci. We can get them in the morning." "Oh." She grabbed Pete's butt and pulled him firmly into her, holding him tightly until they both simultaneously climaxed again.

"Let's go home, stud. I need a replay of tonight's events."

Chapter 43

Angie arrived at the Boston DA's office at 8AM, same as every other day. She started a fresh brew of coffee in the kitchen area before returning to her desk to check her voicemail. Before today, Katie had not taken a day off that she had not planned ahead of time. Her communication was somewhat vague, but she clearly conveyed that Angie should hold her messages and forward all her calls to voicemail. She promised to be in by mid-morning.

"There he is!" Detective Lawrence snapped out of his drowsy mode. "Where?" Katie pointed. "Oh, jeez, Katie; I thought you spotted Mayfield." "Sorry, Nick. Been a while since my last stakeout." Nick laughed. "So you were on others?" Katie smiled, but did not answer. Nick said, "Well, at least he made it into work OK." They kept an eye on the employee entrance until 11:45AM. Katie remarked, "I suppose we're good for now. I wish we could get a detail to keep watch all day. We'll never be able to protect him if this ass sneaks in past us." Nick shook his head, "There's no way we can get this on the books. You know our butts are toast if the brass finds out what we are up to here." Katie agreed, "There's so many people around during the day, I'm sure he'll be fine." She didn't really believe what she had said; it just came out as the *thing* to say at the moment. "Let's pick up at..." Out of habit, she checked her phone for the time. "Say, nine tonight? He's probably off the clock by then. He would be out the doors at around nine-fifteen or so." Nick agreed and told her he would pick her up at her apartment. A homeless person, with his long unkempt hair sticking out from under his baseball cap, pulled down on the brim of his cap, seemingly to shade his eyes from the bright sunshine. He cautiously watched as the black sedan with cheap tin hubcaps pulled away from the curb. He waited patiently for another employee to swipe their ID badge in the card reader and enter the building. He waited for the door to begin closing behind the employee, but quickly grasped the handle just before it locked him out.

The morning flew by quickly. Angie had forgotten that her boss had not arrived at work at her usual time. She asked no questions as Katie rushed past her, calling out, "Good afternoon, Angie." ADA Owens had two meetings scheduled. One with her staff, and an update session with DA Mahoney. She considered mentioning her covert operation with Detective Lawrence, but reconsidered after envisioning her new boss's reaction. The buzz from her pocketbook startled her. The screen indicated "Unknown Caller." She had managed to keep her worries over Jack on the shelf while in the field. Now, back in the office, her stomach churned. "Hello? Oh, thank god it's you, Jack!" Katie spoke with Jack for ten cherished minutes. She was glad that he sounded optimistic and eager to march on with his "business at hand;" just like the *old* Jack. Their conversation made her smile even though she knew danger lurked everywhere for her husband, *and* their family.

At 6PM, she checked her calendar, noting a trial date for Friday morning. With everything she needed already prepared for the case, Katie packed a few files in her attaché and headed home to spend time with her boys. Rosa prepared a delicious meal of Paella Valenciana. After dinner, they enjoyed a desert of homemade Flan. Both boys yawned at the same time. Ryan's eyes were closing as he lay his head on the kitchen table. Rosa laughed, "Aye que lastima; you boys had a hard day in school?"

Katie tucked the boys into bed, asking them to promise to behave and go right to sleep. Katie cleared the dinner table and loaded dishes into the dishwasher while Rosa cleaned the pots and the stove.

"Dinner was delicious as always, Rosa. Thank you. I have to go out for a little while for work. Will you be OK? I shouldn't be too late."

****

Detective Nick Lawrence checked his watch. "It's 9:20. People have all but stopped coming out of the building. I think we must have missed your gallant young man leaving. Maybe he used the main entrance." "Let's give him five more minutes." Katie kept nervously tapping her foot, adding to Nick's edginess. She sensed his angst. "OK, Nick. Let's go in and see where he is."

"Well, it's obvious that he's not here." Katie ignored her partner's remark. "Excuse me, have you seen Louis Stevens?" The sixty something, dyed blond woman looked at Katie like a deer caught in headlights. "Louis? The assistant manager?" The light bulb finally lit. "Oh, the nice young man. Sorry, we have so many assistant managers. I think he left for lunch around 11:30. He must have not been feeling well; I don't think he returned to work. Everyone is getting the flu bug this season." She smiled sweetly and casually walked away. Katie looked at Nick whose face displayed his concern. The duo found their way to the employees' lounge. The store was shutting down; the staff had already turned off every other ceiling light fixture, which indicated it was closing time. Nick figured it was the prelude to going dark and locking the doors; there was no one left on the floor. "Well, this was a bust. Now what?" Katie's disappointment and worrisome look made Nick feel bad. "Wait! What's that?" Katie shrugged. "A storage closet, or pantry, let's check it out." Nick opened the door. "Hmm. Nothing much of interest in here except for a lot of crap and a mop." He moved a few things aside and disappeared into the darkness. "Oh, crap! I found your Mr. Assistant Manager." The half-naked, gagged and bound body of Louis Stevens was in the back corner of the closet, curled up like a ball. A ten-inch stiletto knife protruded from his chest. His shirt was soaked with the last ounces of blood oozing out. Nick sniffed the air allowing his keen analytic senses go to work. Besides the faint odors from the cleaning products stored in the closet, he detected the unmistakably pungent odor of chloroform emanating from the body itself. Nick whispered aloud, "How the hell did something like this happen, and no one heard anything? What kind of sick bastard are we dealing with?"

The detectives took Katie's and Nick's statement before letting them head home. Katie had tears flowing down her cheeks. Her glassy eyes blurred her vision. Nick mumbled just loud enough for Katie to hear his thought, "I guess the cat's out of the bag regarding our foiled operation." Katie disregarded his jumbled words. "How the hell did that fucker get past us and do this in a crowded department store?" Nick wanted to be sensitive regarding her feelings of guilt, but also had to say it as he saw it. "This guy obviously doesn't care about getting caught. He has a thing for sexually assaulting and torturing women. Stevens just pissed him off, big time. Probably more so because it was in front of you. You are his nemesis. Besides, who would have thought that Mayfield had the balls to nab Stevens in the middle of the day at work?" Nick realized as he said it that he was adding to Katie's guilt. "I didn't mean to say…" Katie stopped him. "He's dead because of me. I have to catch this psychopathic freak." "Wait a minute, ADA Owens! What do you mean by you having to catch him? You prosecute; I catch him. Got it?" Katie did not answer. She already had a mindset to lure this ass-wipe monster into a trap and end his reign of terror. Nick saw it in her face. "No way, Katie! No way! I will have nothing to do with you putting yourself in harm's way. I will go straight to DA Mahoney if I suspect you're doing anything out of your jurisdiction. I'll arrest you for obstruction if I have to." Katie half laughed, "Obstruction? Really?" She closed her eyes and said nothing else until he stopped at her apartment. She got out lethargically, "Good night, Nick." "Watch your back, miss, and remember what I said. Behave!"

After wiping her eyes and checking her face in her pocket mirror, Katie entered her apartment. Ryan and Kyle ran to embrace her with hugs and kisses.

"I love you guys, but why aren't you sleeping?" She didn't wait for any excuses. "Never mind; give me more hugs. I really need them, and lots of kisses." Rosa stood over by the kitchen area. Her facial expression said that she knew her Katie Claire was in over her head again, and in trouble.

Chapter 44

The media frenzy exploded completely out of control. Alan Mayfield, his identity known only to a few select law enforcement agents and the DA's office, now became infamous as "Jack the Ripper, back from the dead." Senior ADA Owens had to do something. This foul excuse for a human kept himself one step ahead of law enforcement. The tidbits of weak evidence he allowed them to find was his way of taunting them. How he avoided leaving any trace of DNA, even from perspiration, confounded her. Katie did her best to ignore the voices in her head reminding her of the one rule the law professors repeated continuously throughout her years of study; *never take it personally. Never!* "Well, it *is* personal!" Once again, embarrassed by her outburst, Katie sat behind her desk and took a deep breath, counted to ten and slowly exhaled, then focused on the closed door to her office. As expected, first a two knuckle knock, followed by the magical appearance of her assistant, Angie. "Everything alright, ADA Owens?" Her concerned look quickly morphing into a smile. "Yes, Angie. Thanks. I needed to vent. Sorry if I verbalized my frustration too loudly. This case, all the exposure in the media, is not helping us." Angie nodded in agreement, "I understand. It must be so frustrating that this mystery psychopath hurts people and gets away with being so smug about it. Someone should… take him out." She paused for a second before softening her tone, accompanied by a smile, "Can I get you anything, Boss? Coffee?" Katie told her "No, thank you." Angie nodded and left, closing the door behind her.

Someone should just take him out…

Angie's words rang so true in Katie's head. She tapped her pen on the desk repeatedly until her fingers went numb. It *was* personal. Alan Mayfield took her intern's life because she was an associate of Katie's. He took something that, in his mind, belonged to her. By doing so he intimidates her, makes her angry. This he believes empowers him. The poor assistant manager of the women's dress department is dead simply because he defended his customer, who happened to be Katie. Alarm bells rang in her head. What or who will be next? Could it be her, or her kids? If Jack were home, he would have taken care of it in a "Jack Owens" covert way. She, of course, would tell him to stay out of it. He would argue with her at first, followed by his agreeing to let it be. Then Jack would quietly "do his thing" and take this guy out of commission. Although she never voiced it to him, Jack was her superhero. In so many ways, her husband and his associates broke the law for the "better good." She, on the other hand, had sworn to uphold the law, regardless of the "better good." After the past few weeks she had to consider that perhaps the "better good" outweighed any oath that stood in the way of righting the horrific wrongdoings to society. Here she sat, behind her big fancy desk, contemplating morality and ethics, neither of which would stop Alan Mayfield.

Ever since the second attack, the media sensationalized the murders as the work of a serial killer. They positioned themselves across the street from Katie's building. Per DA Mahoney's internal directive, he issued a gag order. No one was to make any comments to the press regarding any of the related cases. At 1PM, ADA Owens took her purse and headed out of her office and toward the elevators. "I'm heading out for a bite and to run some errands, Angie." Angie took off her headset, "Wait. Do you want some company? I didn't bring my lunch today." Katie kept walking, and without turning around to face her assistant, said, "Oh, sorry. Not today Angie. I have some personal things to take care of. Rain check? Maybe tomorrow?" Angie was puzzled and disappointed. Ellen's murder was a result of her association with Katie. Katie was about to spin a web and pull the most unethical stunt of her career. In no way would she allow Angie to become tangled up in it with her.

"Hi, Phil." "Good day, ADA Owens. Enjoy your lunch." Katie smiled at the concierge and proceeded to exit the building via the revolving doors. She had never really noticed all of the security cameras that appeared to cover every square inch of the exterior and interior of the government building. Today they seemed as if they followed her every step.

Just like every day, the reporters and bloggers called to her for a statement. Just like every day, she waved them off. She had to time it perfectly, so as not to appear too obvious. She turned to the onslaught of cameras,

"Alright; alright. I do have something to say."

In this busy part of downtown Boston, you could suddenly hear a pin drop.

"The DA's office, in conjunction with other law enforcement agencies, are working around the clock to stop this monster." As Katie spoke, reporters rudely called out questions regarding people close to her and her office. One reporter shouted out, "What about Louis Stevens? Is it true that you also knew that poor young man from the department store?" Katie drew a slow, calming breath. Then, at that moment, she decided it was time to put her fantasy plan into action. In a split second, ADA Owens created a series of shockwaves; she knew there would be no turning back. "Yes. Mr. Stevens was a brave young man who came to my defense during an abusive confrontation with another customer." The reporter blurted out, "A customer who you interviewed as a person of interest?" This was it. "Yes. The same person who is still just a person of interest at this time." The mass of business people from the surrounding area grew rather large around her entourage of reporters. She continued. "All I can say is that whoever the person is who has committed these serial murders; he is an immature coward. He is obviously frustrated both sexually and mentally. His apparent need to prove his manhood by brutally killing an innocent young man shows just how deficient his manhood really is. I am going to use every resource my office has to get and detain him." She used and clearly emphasized "get" instead of catch or apprehend, the usual terms, knowing full well that simple word would catch Alan Mayfield's attention. Katie looked directly into the cameras. "I'm coming for you, *Alan Mayfield*. Let's see what kind of man you really are!" Mouths hung open as ADA Owens turned and walked back into the building. A mob of coworkers and others stood quietly, shaking their heads as she walked by. As Katie passed through the security checkpoint, the officer whispered, "That took a lot of balls; but I think you may have committed political suicide." Katie smiled and said nothing. She headed back to the elevators. For a brief moment, after stepping away from the chaotic rush of reporters and onlookers, she felt empowered. Now, less than ninety seconds later, she fought hard not to hurl her breakfast. As she walked into the elevator, she prayed her boss was still out to lunch.

Katie made it to her desk avoiding any contact with her colleagues. Angie was on a call, sounding as if she was arguing with someone. The rest of the office staff were busy doing their jobs, or at least they were pretending not to notice her return to the office. Katie felt the urge to cry. She considered taking half a sick day, but that would peg her as weak and that for sure, she was not. She said what she said, and now she had to deal with the consequences on two fronts. One at the office and one with a homicidal maniac. A serial killer for whom she had just challenged. She lifted the phone to call Jack. After two rings, she hung up. *He has his own problems. I need to deal with this on my own.*

"Angie, I have to run out. I never took care of what I needed to. I should be back this afternoon, but if not, I have my files for the court case on Friday. I'll work on them tonight." Angie told her, "You're my hero, Katie. I'll call you if anything comes up." Katie put on her coat and picked up her satchel filled with files, slinging the bag's strap over her right shoulder. Katie opened her office door, suddenly finding herself face to face with James Mahoney. The DA stood tall at six-two and towered over his subordinate. Kate sensed time freeze, along with everything else around her. In a monotone voice, Mahoney told her, "If you don't breathe, you'll pass out." He motioned for her to retreat back into her office. "We need to talk." They sat at her small conference table. The big man was stone faced. He held his anger well; part of being a successful prosecutor.

"Can you imagine the mayor and I having lunch at O'Doul's, watching the Celtics, and during a record setting three pointer, the game is interrupted for breaking news?" Katie felt beads of perspiration forming at the hairline on her forehead. "You're new here, and perhaps they did things differently in New York. You may have blown any chance of this guy getting a fair trial in Boston. What part of my instructions 'not to speak about this case to the press' did you not understand? If we catch him, he'll likely end up in a federal court and we will lose all control of the case." DA Mahoney scratched his head and then said, "I'm sorry, Katie. This is a rough start for you. I've been forced to place you on paid suspension until a review of this situation is completed. The mayor is fuming. I know the personal closeness of this case affected your better judgment, but this is what we, at a senior level, need to keep under control. Go home and prepare the best you can for an informal hearing before the mayor's council. Depending on the outcome of that, we will discuss your future here in this office." Katie apologized and confirmed she understood the consequences of her earlier actions. The DA stopped at her office door and turned back to her, "You said what we all were thinking. That took guts. But, wrong timing, wrong place. Be careful and watch your back. This guy Mayfield, or whoever, might very well have you marked as a target." Katie held back the tears bent on escaping her eyes. "Yes, sir."

I'm counting on Alan Mayfield targeting me.

Katie hugged Angie and told her to "Hold the fort. I'll be back as soon as this is all cleared up." They both knew that Katie's return was hopeful, at best.

The last order of business before the anticipated grand finale. Katie called John; he did not answer. She dialed the White's home number and Rebecca answered.

In fewer than ten minutes and without divulging her crazy plan, Katie arranged for Rosa and the kids to fly to North Carolina. After all the crazy things her senator husband and CIA godson have been through, Katie's request fell into Rebecca's unexplained but accepted category.

By the time Katie got home, the apartment was empty. She entered cautiously, her senses in hyperactive mode. All seemed safe. After loading her 9mm Glock and clipping it to her belt behind her back, she looked around trying to remember where she had put the Taser. "Ah, shoe box on the top shelf." This weapon had lots of baggage attached to it. Jane, the ally, used this in one of her devious assaults back in her reign of terror days. Jack had taken it from her at some point. Along with the shocker was a charger and an X26C battery pack. It had been years since it had been last used. She hoped it would still hold a charge.

****

Ryan won "Rock, Paper, Scissors" and got the window seat. Kyle sat in the middle and kept poking his twin brother while quietly chanting, "You cheated; you're a cheater." Every so often, Ryan would push Kyle away. Rosa tried ignoring them. Her heart had not stopped pounding since Katie made her request for them to leave town, "for a short vacation." Rosa also had enough exposure to the less than normal, more like explosive, Owens family adventures to realize that Katie Claire was up to something dangerous.

Kyle tapped Rosa's shoulder. Rosa smiled, acknowledging him. "I can't wait to see Aunty Rebecca. Can we play on the beach?" Ryan put his arm around his brother, "Can we, Nana Rosa?"

Chapter 45

Jack sat alone reading a case brief after the morning meeting that lasted past 1PM. His stomach growled from hunger. Marcia entered the small meeting room. "Hey." Jack did not look up from his reading material. "What's for lunch?" Marcia ignored his question and turned on the television. "Apparently, your dynamic wife is stirring up quite a shit-storm in Boston. The newscaster replayed a segment from the mid-day live broadcast. Katie was ranting about a maniac serial killer and tossing insults at him.

"Is she out of her fucking mind? When did this go live?" Marcia shook her head and shrugged her shoulders, "I'm guessing around one, or ten after." "I need to get to Boston. Can you keep things under control here?" Marcia offered to go with Jack, but he refused saying this was *his* and Katie's mess. He had to go and help her clean it up. Just as he was about to click "Purchase" for the airline ticket, his cell phone rang. Senator White called Jack about Rosa and the twins going to the Carolinas. This added information about his family only created more concern for the trouble Katie was facing. "Sorry, Jack, but the shit is about to hit the fan here. Our friends at the NSA have picked up chatter of an alarming nature. We believe there is a credible threat for Albright's assassination. You need to get your team to the secure room; ASAP!" John added, "I think this is it, Jack." John offered to send security personnel to shadow Katie until things settled down and she is out of danger. Jack told him, "No, I'll take care of it. I'll see you in twenty."

Jack called Jane's cell, Pete answered. "Hey, Jack. How are you? I'm glad you're finally back home and safe." Jack politely replied with his appreciation for Pete's concern, and then abruptly asked for Jane. He apologized for being terse; telling her husband it was an urgent matter. "Hold on, Jack. I'll see where she's about." Two minutes passed before Jane came to the phone. "Hey, buddy. What's going on in the world of Jack? How's the hunt going?" Jack simply said, "It's going. I have another issue that requires 'Jane to the rescue.' I'm not sure what the threat level is, but my wife, Katie, may have gotten herself in a pickle." "I expected your call, Jack. Katie is all over the news up here too. You did not really answer me, but if *you're* not going to her rescue and are calling me…. for sure, I'm on it. I'm not sure when I can get there though. It's a good fifteen or so hours drive to Boston." Jack told Jane to hold on for a minute. The dead silence on the phone made her start to pace. Pete staring at her did not help. Jack broke the silence with, "OK. General

Armstrong arranged for a private plane to fly you into Bedford. This is off the books and Hanscom Field has no government checkpoints; so no red tape to deal with. A friend owed him a favor, who happens to live not far from Attawapiskat Airport. Wheels up in one hour." Jane glanced over at Pete to see his stressed expression just before he walked out of the room. "I can do that, Jack." "Thank you, Jane." "Listen, Jack. I have repaid my debt to society many times over by now. You are going to owe me big time for this. Pete is not a happy camper." The momentary silence was deafening; Jane knew her simple words struck a sore spot that would never heal. Jane cupped the mouthpiece of the phone with her hand and quietly said, "Ok, Jack. I can never make up for what happened to William. Back then, I cared less about anyone. He was a resource needed only to achieve my jihad. I am not that person any longer. His demise means something to me now and I feel, really feel awful about that; and the many others too." Her words were sincere.

"Anyway; I got this, Jack."

"I know you do, Jane. Tell Pete that I'm sorry, and I'll make it up to him."

Intelligence information suggested an imminent attack on the president's life sometime in the next few days. The details were still quite vague. President Albright's family were already vacationing at Camp David and he missed them. He had plans to visit with them for the weekend. The group agreed that his traveling indicated a possible threat to security. The meeting broke at 9PM sharp. Jack got a secure text from Jane that she had Katie under surveillance. She wrote that if anything serious occurred, she promised to "have Katie's back". Jack tried calling his wife, but again, he got her voicemail. He was angry with Katie for putting herself, and possibly the boys, in danger. The first thing he learned at the farm was anonymity. Due to the circumstances surrounding Jack's covert operations, there was no way to avoid Katie's involvement. He feared that too much of him had rubbed off on her.

Marcia put her arm around Jack's shoulder, giving him an affectionate hug. "We have a few hours before checking in again with the operations team. I'm going to meet a friend for drinks before calling it a night. Why don't you join us? Besides, you sure look like you need a few." Jack politely declined his partner and friend, telling her he wanted to keep a clear head. "C'mon Jack. You need this to unwind. It will help you relax and perhaps get some sleep. Jane will call if anything happens; the night team will do the same if we are needed before the 5AM re-grouping. Besides, it's important to me that you meet my new friend."

"OK. OK. Tell me about this friend."

"Awesome! I'll drive."

Chapter 46

"Jack, this is Roya Abasi." They spoke for a while; the two woman seemed enamored with each other. Jack politely asked the usual questions. Roya told the story of how she and Marcia met. She continually touched Marcia's hand as she spoke. It appeared very sensual. Jack always found this to be a covert tactic of seduction. Nonetheless, he tried to push his suspicious nature to the sidelines. Marcia ordered a pitcher of margaritas and Nachos Grande for the table. They all laughed, and everyone seemed to be more relaxed as the evening progressed. Marcia seemed genuinely smitten with this one. She had become completely undone after the breakup with her ATF girlfriend, Sharon. Marcia once confided in Jack that Sharon was "the one," her "forever soulmate." Jack was happy for her and over time had become fond of Sharon. Something was not quite right with her new *friend*. Jack could not put a finger on what concerned him about Abasi. She was considerably younger than Marcia. Probably a good eight to ten years. Looks-wise, she was attractive enough. Roya appeared to be small framed but in excellent physical shape. Jack figured her for a gym rat. He tried to shake his guilt of picking on Roya to drown out his concerns for Katie. Jane would keep a close eye on her. He trusted Jane more than anyone; especially for Katie's situation.

"Good to the last drop!" On the job, Jack's partner displayed a serious by the book persona. She seemed to work hard at letting her guard down when it came to her personal life. At the moment, Marcia seemed so happy; whether it was the new girlfriend or the green Mexican potion, he was glad to see her letting loose. Roya leaned over and whispered in Marcia's ear. Marcia blushed, and Jack thought he heard her giggle. Jack caught Roya's quick glance and her smile directed at him. He wondered what she said to his partner that brought so much color to her face.

"I think we need another pitcher." Marcia checked her two compadres for their agreement. Jack stood up; his chair wobbled and almost tipped over behind him. "I don't know if that's a good idea my friend, we both have work in a few hours." What he couldn't say was that they could be called in at any moment. Roya reclined back, her silky blouse spreading a bit to show more of her modest but firm cleavage. Jack did his best to appear to not notice, but was sure he had failed. His only way out of the awkward moment... "OK. I have to hit the head." He considered the company and that perhaps his phrasing could have been better. Marcia made her way to the bar; Jack to the men's lavatory. Someone was exiting as Jack arrived at his much-needed destination, located at the rear of the establishment. He pushed open the door with his foot before it had a chance to shut. He entered a stall and as he stood in front of the commode, he heard the door swing open behind him. Without turning away from his current business he said, "Occupado! Solo dos minutos y estaré terminado."

"Oh. I think we'll be more than two minutes."

Jack zipped up quickly and turned to find Roya standing there. She used her foot to kick the door closed and pushed the button lock. Another of her blouse buttons was miraculously undone. She was quite perky. "My girl seems to be madly in love with you. She is definitely not bi-sexual. She just cares so much for you. I figure, the only way for me to take her heart, is to be willing to share. I want to sample the goods. Besides, she agreed to us, the three of us, going back to her place tonight." She looked him up and down as if she was doing an inspection. Jack felt like a piece of meat in a butcher's shop window. "Wait. Marcia wants both of us to go back to her apartment?" He knew that Roya had to have gotten mixed signals from Marcia. This girl did not know Marcia as he did. Roya's hands were quick; she began to caress his privates before he had a chance to stop her. He tried pushing her away but before he could tell her to get out, she pressed her body firmly against his and grabbed his butt, holding him tightly in place. Her lips met his as her tongue wildly explored his mouth. Jack would have prayed for a moment like this ten years earlier. Or, not.

He pushed her away firmly; hard enough that the back of her head hit the tile wall. His eye caught a shiny object as it hit the floor and clanged.

"What the FUCK?" Before he knew it, she punched him in the throat followed by a well-placed knee to his groin, causing him to double over and nearly lose his balance. *That surely killed the mood of the moment*. He fought the intense, blinding pain and grabbed at her hair. He yanked downward with all his strength. Roya hit the floor with Jack on top of her. She struggled to hit him again but Jack had enough of her. He landed one solid punch square in her nose. Blood splattered everywhere. She was out cold. He thought that perhaps she was dead.

  Marcia had already poured herself another margarita while she waited for Jack and Roya to return. They had both been gone for more than ten minutes. Marcia learned right away that Roya was a surprisingly promiscuous young woman. Marcia wondered if she was teasing Jack. Then the thought of Roya seducing Jack made her angry. She would never jeopardize her friendship with Jack, nor did she have any sexual interest in him. *Roya had better be behaving herself; and Jack too!*

  Given Marcia's ridiculous fantasy about Roya and Jack of just a moment ago, her heart nearly stopped as she saw Jack approaching. He looked like a bus had hit him. Then she noticed the awkward limp, and blood on his face and shirt. "Oh my god, Jack! What the hell happened?" A few people stared, but most were too drunk to have much concern for what they perceived as a guy who must have been in a bar fight and lost. Jack, out of breath, could barely speak, so he pointed to the restrooms. Marcia jumped up and made her way to the rear of the bar. Jack took a gentle gulp of margarita and painfully swallowed it before following her.

At first, Marcia was horrified and speechless, and then she saw the dagger lying on the floor. She looked at Jack displaying a horrified expression. Neither said anything. Marcia helped Jack carry her out the back door. Two employees looked on questioningly. Marcia flashed her badge, and shook her head in disgust. "One of ours. Had too much to drink" she told them without missing a step. Marcia asked Jack, "Where do we take her?"

He already had that figured out.

Chapter 47

It took nearly two hours of interrogation (*Jack Owens style*), before Roya Abasi "cracked." As Jack drove the thin bamboo wedge beneath Roya's toenail for the last time, she cringed and cried out in agony. Their terrorist captive gave up the location of the cell that directed Roya to find and assassinate Jack. She also had limited, but useful information on the target and timing of the planned clandestine attack against President Albright. Marcia worked hard to hold back her tears of disappointment and embarrassment. She hated the fact that in spite of all her years of training for undercover work in the field, she had allowed herself to be "played." She finally understood what the phrase "Blinded by love" meant. Marcia wanted to know what they should do with Roya now. "She's an enemy of the United States and she has my DNA all over her." Jack nodded and then paused for a short moment of thought. "She has both our DNA on her. Get her in the shower. Hand me out her clothes." Marcia stripped down naked before doing the same to her very recent, ex-lover. Roya was barely able to move. As the shower rained over them, Marcia scrubbed Roya hard from head to foot. Blood from Jack's earlier defensive assault colored the shower stall floor crimson.

Roya whispered to Marcia in an attempt to seduce her once again. Marcia's response being, "Don't waste your last breath on bullshit." As if an alter ego had overtaken Marcia's psyche, she suddenly snapped and screamed angrily, "Damn you, Roya!" Marcia's hands suddenly wrapped themselves around Roya's slender throat, her thumbs applying strong, steady pressure to her Adam's apple. Roya struggled lethargically as she attempted to push Marcia off her. Jack's earlier "interrogation" techniques had left Roya nearly paralyzed. Her efforts to free herself were as futile as Marcia's grip was relentless. Marcia squeezed the last bit of life out of Roya. Tears rolled down Roya's face as her arms fell limply at her sides. Marcia wept silently as she slowly stood up and stepped out of the shower stall. She took one last look before turning away *and never looking back*.

Upon their return to the Pentagon, Jack and Marcia disclosed little of how they obtained the information Roya had given to them. Neither Jack nor Marcia spoke of those last moments in the seedy, *off the beaten path*, motel. Jack made a call, and they left the mess for another covert team that specialized in cleaning up situations like Jack and Marcia's. Whatever "cleanup" meant, they didn't want to know. Before signing her name to the official report, Marcia did one last read-through. She concentrated on one section in particular of her ten page typed report to be sure she had it covered precisely as it *should have* happened. She prayed her version matched close enough to Jack's story.

Marcia's "Once upon a time" official statement read:

"I was approached by the foreign agent who attempted to befriend me. Her methods were classic and rather obvious. I played along, and called my partner (Agent Jack Owens). After several social meetings, I suggested she meet my single friend, Jack. After a few drinks, we lured the suspect to a safe house where we proceeded with the interrogation. Two of Roya Abasi's handlers must have followed us. They ambushed us during the interrogation. One of the assailants jumped me and we both fell to the floor where a struggle ensued before I could disable him with a Taser. Jack disarmed the other combatant, also engaging in a fierce physical confrontation. At some time during all the chaos, Abasi escaped. By the time I was able to draw my weapon, both of Abasi's associates had fled. We were in a public establishment and did not want to risk harm to bystanders by engaging in a gun battle. We had obtained the information from Abasi that we needed. Her capture would come in due time.

Jack's version read somewhat differently (by design), but the contents perfectly aligned with Marcia's account of what had happened. Both of their official reports disclosed Abasi's admission of her plot to assassinate Jack. Neither included the more important intelligence they uncovered. That would be shared only with the team, two levels below the pentagon.

Jack looked at the atomic clock on the wall and noted the time as 2035 hours. "All right. We have just barely eleven and a half hours to get our ducks in a row and set up the sting to catch these crazy bastards. We need to take them alive if possible." Jack directed his next remarks at the general. "Sir, our information indicates that the terrorists have a failsafe plan not to be taken alive if something should go awry during the operation. They may have the ability to blow the helicopter and all inside." General Armstrong wrote some notes in his logbook. "Well then, we had better have the element of surprise on our side. I will convey this to our naval partners in this operation. We are keeping extremely tight surveillance on the president. I can assure all of you that he has not been compromised. Not even his own Secret Service detail are aware of us shadowing them." Donald snorted as he asked, "So, we don't even trust the most trusted of security at the White House?" Jack, John, and Marcia all chimed in, and in unison replied, "Hell no!" Donald Graham, embarrassed, retorted…. "Of course not. This crazy world is so fucked up."

They spent another two hours planning a strategy for how to neutralize the terrorists before they could cause any harm to the president. They also discussed the ramifications of the entire operation. The group all agreed that allowing President Albright to appear to follow his normal routine would enable them to catch the jihadists "in the act" and eradicate them for good. "We could all be charged with treason by using the president as bait." They all shared Donald's concern, in theory. In reality, they would be heroes *if* their plan played out perfectly. The only caveat was keeping the president absolutely safe. Armstrong cleared his throat making sure he had everyone's attention. "OK. I ran this by my Intelligence team and they raised the same concern. As you may or may not be aware, the construction project at the White House presents a security risk, so Marine One is flying out of Andrews Air Force Base. We will substitute a double for President Albright with one of our own guys, a military investigator with top security clearance, Larry Morford. He is almost a dead ringer for POTUS, at least with sunglasses and a hat. He has the height and the build; *and* the receding hairline," he quipped. No one seemed to catch his rare attempt at lightening the moment with his dry sense of humor. "We used him before to divert crowds of onlookers and the media after the election. I already ran the plan by Morford, and he is ready to step in. He's a decorated American hero who more than once volunteered to 'Walk Point' during his many deployments into combat zones. He is no stranger to dangerous missions. We will attempt to delay the President by thirty minutes by telling the president he has an urgent call regarding a family matter. This will allow us to update him privately on the mission and make the exchange. We will have Morford in dark glasses and on his cell phone as he approaches his transport vehicle thereby avoiding any direct conversation or close contact with his security detail. By the time our doppelganger arrives on the tarmac for Marine One, the Seal teams should be in place and ready to breach. The arrival of POTUS's motorcade will distract those inside Marine One. Jack already knew from last year's encounter, that Albright was a team player. He would undoubtedly commend their actions. Just over a year ago, Albright's adulterous lover, Anastasia McDermott, poisoned the vice president. Anastasia belonged to a jihadist cell that played a major role in the "Twin" terror plan to disrupt and dismantle the American government. Under false pretenses, she seduced and eventually married the up and coming political prodigy,

Speaker of the House, Ronald McDermott. Anastasia's affair with the vice president under the pretense of a working relationship, gave her unlimited private access to the second most powerful man on the planet. McDermott also had an estranged *twin* brother. When the timing was right, his jihadist-raised sibling replaced him. Then the Black Widow carried out her plan to poison her lover and move her fake husband into the number two seat of the most powerful government in the world. All her hard work eventually paid off. Her next move was to get President Albright into the same vulnerable position. To Albright's credit and her chagrin, he rejected her advances. Jack had already briefed President Albright of their suspicions. Persistence and swift action by dedicated agents foiled the diabolical plot to infiltrate the top power position in the White House. To the rest of the country, and the world, the White House simply suffered a sad loss of a beloved vice president.

A loud peal rang out from the secure phone. General Armstrong lifted the receiver. "Armstrong here. Are you fucking kidding me? Negative! Stand down until the Seal team arrives. Whatever you do, do not let that bird fly." The general hung up and quickly explained that the president had changed his plans, and decided to leave for Camp David to visit his family this evening. Jack and the others, almost simultaneously, glanced at the atomic clock. Senator White exclaimed, "What the hell! At this late hour? What! The commander couldn't sleep?" The general continued, disregarding the senator's outburst. "He is en route now and about fifteen minutes out." Armstrong's face drew serious color, "There's no possible way now to insert Morford for the president. We have to call off his transport and update the president of the situation." Armstrong picked up the phone again to call the Naval Commander. He rapidly dialed a series of numbers, cursing once due to a dialing error and having to start over again. He rambled a bunch of code words, and ordered an immediate deployment of the Seal Response Team. Armstrong then called the White House who informed him that they had been trying to reach the motorcade as well as his protection team with no success. Jack made his way to the securely locked glass door with the rest of his team right behind him. Behind him, the general slammed down the phone as he shouted, "Shit! The bastards have compromised his personal security detail! They're jamming all the communication channels." Armstrong nearly choked as he added, "We need to move! Now!" The guards remained at attention, disregarding Jack's banging for them to allow him to exit the conference room. The guards waited for the only authorized person to grant approval as per protocol. The general walked over next to Jack and signaled to the armed guards outside. The buzzer sounded as the door locks clicked open. The general quickly strode down the hall, leading the way. "I have a convoy waiting for us. Let's get over there! The Seal team is only ten minutes out." Agita nearly choked Armstrong as his mind raced with multiple scenarios of this mission, each playing out in the worst possible way. Never in his career did he experience "cold feet." Jack could tell the general had something else troubling him, perhaps it was his grumbling or his repeated clicking of the button on his satellite radio that gave it away. Their eyes met as the general raised the radio closer to his mouth. "No way, Armstrong! An unplanned military breach of Marine One would cause massive collateral damage and blow our chances of ending this reign of terror. If we don't take at least one of them alive, my eight month ordeal, Afghanistan, this mission, it's all for nothing. We must let this play out as we planned. Our Seals are fully prepped for this mission. They will get there in time. They *will* eliminate the enemy." The general paused and with trembling hands, lowered his radio.

Jack's heart pounded. They all remained silent during the fifteen-minute ride to the rendezvous point at Andrews.

Chapter 48

Alan Mayfield arrived home tired and frustrated. He entered his small, rather dreary second floor rental apartment in a brownstone on Boylston Street. His frustration at maintaining restraint over his compulsive urge to abduct and assault another victim put him on the delicate verge of an emotional episode. He had the perfect opportunity less than an hour earlier. He had stopped at a local fast food burger joint. It was moments before closing time. The staff were already mopping the floors and cleaning the equipment. Alan ordered a double burger with fries and a soft drink. The girl's look told him he might need to find another food place for his meal. She called out, "James, you forgot to lock the doors again!" She glanced behind her while shaking her head and mumbled, "My fiancé is going to kill me if I'm late again." Then she said to whoever was in the back, "One last order; Double with fries." She looked at Alan, "Anything else?" He just smiled and shook his head. "That'll be $7.29." Alan handed her a ten and asked, "Did you set a date yet?" She looked at him, bewildered. "Your engagement ring; it's a beauty." The girl shook her head. "No date set yet. I told him I wouldn't give him what he wanted unless we got engaged. I made him sweat it out

for a while, but he caved. So, no date. But, I got the ring."
Then she smiled and handed Alan Mayfield his change, his double burger and fries; and an empty, fill-it-yourself cup.

Alan sat in his car eating the burger and cold fries. The cold fries really pissed him off. Even worse, his cola was flat. The long tubular fluorescent lights slowly shut down one after another. The manager, who also doubled as the crappy grill cook, let the server out before he exited with her and locked the door. They waved good night to each other, and he headed down the street on foot. The sassy young woman made her way to a car parked around the side of the restaurant. She was ripe for the snatching. Alan noticed her perfect long legs that her short, just below the butt uniform nicely showed off. He imagined his hands as they moved upward from her ankles, caressing her legs and thighs along the way. *No!* He had to resist! That bitch of an ADA and her goon were on his case. He had to stay below their radar. His hands begin to tremble. Alan started his car and headed home.

As he inserted the key into the front door, he sensed that something wasn't quite right. Alan stopped and turned toward the street. A car slowly pulled away from the curb, directly across the street from where he stood on his front porch. He could tell that the driver was a female with light, shoulder length hair. *The bitch is tailing me*!

Alan cautiously entered his apartment. All appeared as he had left it earlier that day. *Wait*! He thought, perhaps some of his drawings were out of place on his desk. As if someone had picked them up to look at them, and then sloppily tossed them back onto the desk.

****

Katie drove to her home and waited. She was sure the maniac would be banging on her door at any moment. If he had not noticed her stalking him, which she was certain he had, her subtle rearrangement of some of his personal items surely would raise his level of angst. After an hour of pacing and listening for any unusual noises, she drew a calming breath and popped a frozen mini pizza into the microwave. Allowing herself only a half glass of Chianti, Katie looked at the portable TV on the kitchen counter, deciding whether or not to watch Jeopardy. She decided not. As 11PM approached, Katie Claire could not keep her eyes open. The stress of the day, along with her anticipation of Mr. Mayfield's guest appearance wore her out mentally and physically. Both her mind and her body needed a rest.

The burst of sound from her alarm clock jolted Katie from a deep sleep. She jumped out of bed and quickly scanned the room for her firearm as she silenced the alarm. Panic ensued, but quickly waned as she located her Glock on the nightstand. "Shit. Fuck!" She rarely cursed. Alan Mayfield had gotten under her skin. This really pissed her off. She swore she was not going to let that happen. "Are you kidding me?" Both the dog and the cat were still asleep at the foot of the bed. The cat yawned without opening his eyes.

After checking her outfit in the mirror, Katie went back and touched up her tired eyes with a bit more makeup. She planned to approach DA Mahoney, first to apologize, and then to ask him to reconsider reinstating her. If not, private law practices paid a hell of a lot better. Jack had pushed her in that direction in the past. *Perhaps he was right. I'd be able to practice law, my way.*

Her Glock holstered behind her, hidden beneath her blazer, she mentally readied herself, petted Lacy and waved to Sir Oliver Jones who meowed his goodbye.

Jane spent the night in her car. She cursed several times, swearing how much Jack owed her again. She barely had been home for a week after their trek into the desert. Pete was pissed again, but like the other times, said nothing; she just knew it. During her days of covert jihadist plots, back at Emory College, Jane had deceitfully befriended Katie. Actually, she made it appear as if Katie had taken her under her wing. They spent time together on campus, in bars and shopping at the mall. Jane hated to shop but loved to shoplift. At the time, she was downright evil. Jane thought she knew how Katie Claire Owens ticked. *Damn it, Katie. Where the hell are you? You should have started your day by now*. Jane checked her watch, noting the time as 9:20AM. "Damn, girl." With an uneasy feeling, Jane exited her rental car and headed for the apartment building entrance.

Katie cautiously scanned the hallway in both directions. *This is so silly*. She tapped her foot nervously. The elevator floor indicator showed "B". She figured it would be two or three minute before it found its way up to her. She tapped her foot again, anxiously.

The creaking sound of a door opening behind her made Katie turn quickly. Her frail eighty-seven-year-old neighbor, Mrs. Johnson, leaned out. She looked terrible. Katie knew she had some medical problems and ended up in the hospital a few weeks earlier. "Are you OK, Mrs. Johnson?" She was shaking terribly and barely made eye contact with Katie. "No. I need help; please." Mrs. Johnson looked as if she was about to collapse. Katie put her satchel down and ran over to the elderly woman, grabbing her arm to steady her. As she got closer, she could see tears in the woman's eyes. Mrs. Johnson had the look of abject fear on her face; Katie's whole body went numb. In that split second, she had to fight off a rush of panic. His arm suddenly shot out and grabbed Katie, pulling both women into the apartment. Once inside, Katie managed to pull free, but Alan Mayfield held a short stiletto blade to Mrs. Johnson's throat. He shouted, "Don't try to run or I'll kill the old lady." In an automated response, Katie reached behind her back and yanked the Glock out of it's pancake holster. Alan shoved Mrs. Johnson directly at Katie. Both women fell to the living room floor. Before Katie knew it, her serial killer had his booted foot stepping hard on her wrist. Katie feared that he had broken it. Alan kicked the firearm out of her hand and it skidded across the floor.

"I thought I'd like to have you all submissive and terrified. You, ADA Owens, have engaged me in something new and exciting. I find your eagerness to challenge me incredibly exciting. My job now is to tame you, like breaking in a wild Mustang." Katie was afraid; more like terrified, but she was not going to give him the satisfaction of knowing it. She stopped struggling beneath the crushing weight of his foot. As he eased off her wrist, Katie made an attempt to get up. Alan bent down and swiftly backhanded her in the face with such force that blood splattered from her nose. Alan then grabbed Mrs. Johnson by the arm and with his knife at her throat, forced her to sit on the couch while warning Katie not to move. He used his knife to cut off the electric cord from a table lamp, and secured Mrs. Johnson's wrists and ankles, while warning the terrified woman not to speak or move. He then turned his full attention back to his prize captive, who lay helplessly on the floor.

With his knife now at her throat, Katie lay still as her abductor kneeled over her and began moving his hands over her body, starting at her ankles and slowly up her inner thighs. "We will have to do something with these. Although, they are quite lovely." He was referring to her netted stockings. "C'mon, miss. Where's that spunk now?" He flicked open the clips, releasing the stocking from her lace bikini panties. His disgustingly fetid breath on her bare skin made her want to puke. Suddenly, he stopped. "You'll enjoy it more if what I do to you is a mystery." He held her firmly just above the collarbone and partially over her throat. She could not move her upper body. His left hand pulled out a red silk blindfold. "Let's put this on you. If you play nice, I just might let the old woman live. Stay put and do not move or make a sound. We are going to have so much fun!" Alan placed his knee on her chest and leaned forward, immobilizing Katie with his body weight as he secured her blindfold. With all that was happening, she hardly noticed the searing pain in the small of her back. As he applied more pressure on her chest, the pain in her lower back intensified. He slowly and methodically slid his hand from her throat down to her abdomen. "Here we go. This could get messy. I hope Mrs. Johnson has a strong stomach." One of his hands, she was sure his left one, held her firmly over her pelvis. Katie had to respond, she had to gain control and throw him off his game. "A real man would actually be arousing me right now. Turning me on. Your hand there, caressing my skin, should start to make me wet. A real man would be turned on and have a raging hard-on by what I'm saying to you now. But, you're not a real man, are you; Alan? You're nothing but a sick, perverted serial rapist and murderer." She could sense the fury building up in him. His hand pressed harder on her fragile lower abdomen, aggravating the pain in her back. She continued, "What happened to you? Did your mommy abuse you? Did your mommy make fun of your tiny example of manhood?" The pain from his hand intensified. He yelled, "Shut the fuck up!" His hand, still applying extreme pressure, made its way upward and over her breasts. The pain was becoming unbearable.

Suddenly, she heard a ripping sound as she felt cooler air engulf her upper body. He had viciously ripped open her blouse, and now his tongue ravished her belly, breasts and then her neck. Pain again and an oozing; this time on her neck, just above the shoulder. She winced, fighting to keep control and not give him the satisfaction of knowing he hurt her. Alan had *vampired* her. He bit her neck, drawing blood, while inflicting a hickey. Katie fought hard not to pass out. She was seemingly weakening to his assault. Her only defense now would be to make him think he "broke" her. Katie relaxed her body. Alan grasped both her wrists and pushed her arms above her head. He licked her lips. "Keep your hands above your head. No matter what! Do not move them! His hands began exploring beneath her undergarments. Unlike before, he was being gentle. She was running out of time. His MO had him killing his victims during what he perceived to be their moment of ecstasy. She needed her hands by her sides, but his instructions not to move were frighteningly clear.

Jane finally gained entry into the building. She frantically pressed the call button, but the elevator remained in the basement. She heard banging noises from the elevator shaft and thought someone might be moving in or out. Jane quickly looked around and found the doorway to the stairwell. She rapidly started her ascent to locate Katie, taking the steps two at a time.

Katie started breathing heavily and moaning the way she would when Jack was making love to her. The only difference being, that at this moment she was faking it. With Jack, she never had to.

"Oh, my god! What's happening to me? This isn't right." Her legs began to quiver.

"I told you not to speak or move."

"I want to see you the way you see me. Take off my blindfold."

"No. I said quiet!"

More heavy, fast paced breathing. His hands moved over her body and back down between her legs.

"Oh, please stop! Stop! Stop!" She arched her back and tried to squeeze her legs together as she faked fighting off an explosive orgasm. "Please stop! Don't make me do this."

"Oh, my god!" *Heavy breathing*

"Please… Stop." *Heavy breathing*

"Oh, my god!" *Heavy breathing*

She could sense he was on the verge of doing something; perhaps preparing to slit her throat. Suddenly, one of his hands gripped her left hip. Panic hit her again once she realized he was going to flip her over and launch his sexual assault from behind. She would lose any chance to gain control if he succeeded. His other hand now gripped her right hip. This was it. She felt the motion of her body as he swiftly attempted to roll her over, face down. She needed to act instantaneously or she would lose the last opportunity for surviving this assault. *It was now or never.* Katie suddenly found herself in mid-air. Her right hand reached behind, and as she landed face down, she fiercely kicked her feet straight out and into Alan's groin. She had fortuitously found "blind" luck. As she doubled over in excruciating pain, fifty thousand volts delivered from the concealed stun gun taped to the small of her back brought her assailant down quickly. She tore off her blindfold and quickly retrieved her Glock from across the room.

Jane finally reached Katie's floor. The loud commotion of shouting and screams of pain drew Jane directly toward Mrs. Johnson's apartment. The door was slightly ajar. Jane kicked the door open and sprang inside ready for action. In front of her stood Katie, scantily clad and disheveled, holding her firearm in one hand while repeatedly kicking a bloody faced man on the floor. Katie looked more surprised to see Jane, than shocked from her own awkward situation.

"What the hell are *you* doing here, Jane?"

"Saving you?"

They just stared at each other for a moment. Jane said, "Jack is so going to kill me."

Katie returned to the present moment and realized poor Mrs. Johnson was still lying on the couch, her hands and feet still bound. Katie untied Mrs. Johnson while Jane grabbed a throw blanket from the living room couch and put it around Katie. "Let's get you to your apartment so you can get cleaned up." Then, quietly she said, "I'll take care of the old lady and this sorrowful bastard."

"No, Jane. You probably shouldn't be here. I'll call 911 and follow the process through. My job here is done." Jane grinned. "You set him up, didn't you? That whole television interview in the street?" Jane shook her head in disbelief, "All part of your plan to this outcome. Crap, Jack is going to kill both of us." Katie wiped a tear from her cheek. "Poor Mrs. Johnson. I didn't plan for any harm to come to her." Jane put her arm around Katie. To her surprise and relief, Katie did not cringe or push her away. "She looks like she'll be O.K., Katie."

The police came to haul Alan Mayfield away while an ambulance whisked Mrs. Johnson off to the nearest hospital for evaluation. Jane waited in Katie's apartment. She tried contacting Jack to update him on his wife's situation and the wild events of the day. The obscurity of his whereabouts after calling several of his associates meant things were happening in DC. She was glad the teams were making progress. After all Jane had done in the past two years, she had hoped to be more involved in the final take-down of her former comrades. Her part in Jack's rescue and her involvement with him and Don recently in the desert should have proven her loyalty. Mostly, she wanted to be a trusted member of the team. Jack had her "Six," just as she will always have his. Jane's upbringing and brainwashing set limits on what types of relationships and social situations were comfortable for her. She would wait for Katie to return to the apartment and stay with her until Jack made his way home, or advised otherwise. Katie waited for the police at the crime scene next door. She endured two hours of interrogation by the Boston ADA's office, by the same staff she used to work with, as well as FBI, state police, and CSI agents. When they completed her interview, although she said she was feeling okay, she was driven to the hospital to get her wounds checked out and treated.

The news media had a field day. Some reporters maligning her by insinuating she practically asked for the attack by making her earlier statements. They had no idea how close they were to the truth. As the newscasters embellished their stories, hundreds, perhaps thousands of women and men gathered in the streets around the DA's building in downtown Boston that evening. The crowd cheered Katie as a hero who single-handedly saved the city from a serial killer.

A little after 4PM, the unmarked police car that had first taken Katie to the hospital and then to Police Headquarters for her written statement, dropped her off at her apartment building. Jane was standing with her arms open when Katie entered. She held Katie gently until the tears slowed down. "Thank you for being here for me, Jane." She took a calming breath and said, "I need to call my boys."

****

"Hi, Rebecca. Yes, I'm fine. Everything is OK now. I'll tell you everything when I see you. Can I talk to the boys?" Katie told Ryan and Kyle how much she missed them and loved them. They whimpered, "We want to come home, mommy." Tears rolled down Katie's cheek. Fighting to control a trembling voice, she told the boys, "In a few days, mommy and daddy will come get you. We can play on the beach if you like."

Chapter 49

General Armstrong had made his call to the Department of Naval Special Warfare Command. He brought the Special Operations Force Team commander up to speed with as much information as the commander's security clearance permitted. The original order was for all the teams to have "boots on the ground" at Andrews, at 0900 hours. Fortunately, as one of the elite immediate response divisions of the United States military, the general's unexpected call hours earlier for an *immediate* deployment raced across high-level channels with lightning speed.

The unplanned cover of night made the clandestine operation a bit easier to launch. With less than two minutes to spare, the Navy Seal team was in position, covertly surrounding the Sirkorsky VH-3D Sea King that would become "Marine One" as soon as President Albright stepped aboard. The rotors were already spinning as the caravan of SUV's arrived.

"Tomahawk has arrived." "Roger that."
"Team-1, confirm ready." "Team-1, ready."
"Tac Team-2, confirm ready." "Team-2, ready."

President Albright gracefully and unwittingly stepped out of his heavily armored vehicle, code named "The Beast," escorted by two secret service agents, and proceeded to the air stairs. His mind now clear of the earlier pressures of political quagmires and governmental chores, all he wanted to think about was seeing his family. The usual entourage lined the asphalt corridor, saluting, waving, and nodding their respectful gestures as Albright approached the stairs to Marine One. Jack, General Armstrong, and the rest of the team quietly made their way onto the tarmac standing off to the side, out of the president's view. Their presence would be out of place, and possibly alarming to the president. They had to avoid anything that might tip off the terrorists of their compromised *jihad*. Based on the intel obtained from Roya's interrogation, there could be enough explosives on the helicopter to blow it and a good deal of the tarmac around it as well, causing massive injuries and death. The president's life was at stake here, among many others.

During the crazy Monte Carlo Rally style race to Andrews, Jack quickly checked his phone for messages from Jane. To his chagrin, there was nothing. No messages from her nor Katie. His absence in Boston during Katie's time of need weighed heavily upon him, but Jack had to focus on the mission at hand and get his priorities in order. When on a mission, Jack never let his personal life or anything else get in the way of his business at hand. That keen ability to compartmentalize, partly due to the intense training early on at the "Farm" in Virginia, had helped keep him alive. However, something changed since his torturous kidnapping. His family had become his first priority. *This will be my last mission in the field. I hope they can forgive me.*

Using caution to remain out of the aircraft's visual and video sights, navy seal team members stealthily breached the Sea King through its rear cargo hatch. The clicking of static in his earphone startled Jack, forcing his attention back again to the current moment. Jack took a step backward to where the general stood. They began whispering back and forth. Marcia and Don looked on, wondering if they were arguing. This was the most intense atmosphere any of these seasoned agents had ever experienced. They could barely hear the general's quiet but curt order to Jack, "You better get the timing right! POTUS is not to set one foot on that stairway!" Jack stealthily made his way back to Marcia and leaned in close, whispering instructions in her ear. He seemed a bit off balance as he leaned into her so Marcia grabbed his arm to steady him and for her own reassurance. She glanced at Jack, who now solemnly nodded; his way of saying to her, "*You got this!*"

"Team-2 in position."

One of the president's detail proceeded up the stairway ahead of him. A moment earlier, the agent told his partner, "I'll take the point and secure the craft." Following protocol, the agent emerged from the aircraft and signaled "All Clear," then disappeared back inside. Clearly a breach of standard procedure. The normal protocol would be for the point agent to remain at the aircraft's portal to assist the president as he reached the top of the air stairs. As the president took his first step onto the metal stairway, a woman came running up from behind him. She shouted, "Mr. President, you forgot your briefcase." Marcia handed the thin leather attaché to Albright, who appeared momentarily addled. He started to say it wasn't his, but never got a chance to finish his sentence. Marcia suddenly tackled him to the ground, covering his body with her own. Simultaneously, two members of Seal Team-1 quickly restrained the secret service agent still behind the president. The other four team members flew up the airstairs. Two shots rang out as Team-2 approached from the rear of aircraft and took control of Marine One along with the agent and other hostiles inside.

"This is Bravo One. Marine One is secure."

"Roger that Bravo One. All is secure on Marine One."

As the radio static cleared, the commander of Seal Team-1 tapped his microphone button again, and in a solemn tone declared, "That was close. *Way too close*. We neutralized the hostiles in the process of them arming an explosive device. All teams, good job. Mission accomplished!" He paused to compose himself. "Command, I'm sure this will sound crazy and I know POTUS is secure down below, but I'll be damned if he isn't sitting here right in front of me, pale as a ghost."

"Copy that. Proceed using prearranged protocol. Secure all hostiles for transport, including the POTUS impersonator."

As the Seals disembarked from the helicopter with their prisoners, Jack and his team looked on. At first, it was unnerving to them all to watch the parade of terror masterminds as the teams took them into custody. Then, the elation of their success overshadowed all else. The interrogation of these evil men would take place somewhere so secure that even Jack and his team might never know its location. What happens to them after that...?

The commotion from behind drew their attention. The president pushed off his military detail as he exited his SUV. There he stood, in his almost perfectly pressed double breasted suit. Marcia's tackle surely the reason for a few of the obvious creases. Like a mirror image, his estranged evil twin brother looked back at him with a stone cold expression. All could see the pain President Albright was experiencing. The brother he never knew, his true bloodline, had a heart of stone and a soul filled with hate and evil. The Twin stared back at his brother with his soulless eyes. In a desperate tone, Albright said, "Oh, my brother. Surely, you can believe we did not abandon you. A deviate person took you from our family as a lifeless newborn. I always sensed your presence on this earth. If only you had approached your family. If only you could have known the glorious love and affection of our family. POTUS drew a sad breath and turned back to his vehicle. He stopped and told his security detail to wait. Albright walked over to the covert team.

"General, good job." He shook the general's hand. Armstrong nodded and saluted his Commander in Chief.

"Jack." President Albright embraced Jack in a heartfelt hug. In a soft-spoken voice he said, "Once again, we meet at the moment of peril." Jack replied, as the embrace morphed into a handshake, "We beat them again, Sir."

"Indeed we did, Agent Owens. Whatever happened to keeping me in the loop?" POTUS brushed some dirt off the arm of his suit. "As soon as the pain of being tackled abates, we are going to discuss that. Perhaps over lunch at the White House." He grinned as he took Marcia's hands in his. "You scared the bejesus out of me, Agent Gainsworth. My backside is going to hurt for at least a week. Still though, I suppose I should at least say thanks." The president leaned close to Marcia and whispered in her ear, "for knocking me on my ass." He let go of her gently and gave her a polite wink. He shook Donald's hand and then Senator White's. "John, why don't you and Rebecca join us at Camp David next month? The women can catch up and we can discuss bi-partisan politics while fly-fishing."

"Thank you all for your service. Today will be marked as a monumental day for good triumphing over evil."

President Albright's last words before leaving meant a lot to all the military and intelligence agents who participated in the entire operation. The president meant what he said, except that none of the day's actions would ever make it into the news media or historical journals.

Epilogue

Jane eventually got through to Jack. He had twenty questions for her, each starting with "Is she safe?" "But… is she safe?" Jane kept telling Jack to find a television, which finally, he did after ten minutes of arguing with Jane on the phone. "Over there, Jack." Marcia pointed to Reese's 1900 Pub & Grill. He looked on in awe as the newscaster repeated the details from the earlier morning's live broadcast. A banner rolled across the bottom of the television screen… "Boston ADA takes down Serial Killer." Jack listened as more and more information flowed from the female news anchor's lips. First, "ADA Owens, the brightest and newest senior member to join Boston's elite prosecuting team." Then, "ADA Owens is suspended pending investigation." Then, finally, "Katie Owens, Boston's heroine." The rhetoric morphed into a debate as to whether the DA's office should allow her to return to her position as senior ADA. Jack asked the bartender to change the channel. He turned to Marcia, who knew better, and said nothing since they arrived at the bar. She sat quietly, and sipped her well-deserved extra dry martini. "All this in the week I was in DC? Who is that woman? I am going to kill her! And Jane? What the hell was she doing during all this? She could slaughter a whole city with a dagger and her looks; but keeping Katie out of trouble? I guess that was asking too much!" Marcia slid her half-filled martini over to Jack and signaled for two more.

Jack called in a favor, and later that afternoon, boarded a private jet headed for Boston. He and Katie agreed to leave the events of the past week alone for the time being. They caught the 9PM flight to Raleigh, Durham airport and reunited with their boys. The family sang songs the boys loved during the four-hour drive to South Carolina, and enjoyed a few days on the beach. Jack watched while his boys played in the sand. Kyle dug out sand while Ryan filled the moat with water. Jack took a moment to reflect on the past. He closed his eyes, while envisioning him and William twenty-five years earlier on the same beach, building sand castles and occasionally fighting as to who was in charge. He missed those innocent times, and so enjoyed watching the twins.

Two weeks later, Jack had lunch with President Albright. He asked Jack if he would mind leaving the Central Intelligence Agency to work in the White House as Special Investigator reporting directly to the president. "I know it is mostly a desk job, Jack, and you would deal with only domestic issues. However, it's not a bad way to finish off your career while still serving your country and your president." Jack had already made up his mind, but asked the president if he could have a few days to talk it over with Katie. President Albright put his arm around Jack; "How are you and the Mrs. doing?" Jack told him, "It's a work in progress, but we are both determined to get our family back together. We are planning to take the boys to Disney for a family vacation. We will see after that." President Albright smiled. "Sounds like a good plan, Jack. Perhaps accepting my offer and taking this position will help reinforce your wife's faith in your staying close to home and out of trouble. I need your answer by the end of the week. The business of running the country must go on, my boy."

DA Mahoney asked Katie Claire Owens to resume her duties as senior ADA. She politely and respectfully declined. She would never know if his request was genuine, or if the media hullabaloo forced his hand. Katie decided to take Jack's advice from more than a year earlier, and go into private practice. She encouraged Jack to accept the president's offer. She and the twins moved to Washington DC, where she started a small law firm with two junior associates and a soon to be certified paralegal named Angie Rodriguez. Jack occasionally does some private investigation work for her firm. She and Jack maintain separate residences while they work on renewing their relationship.

General Armstrong received his fifth star and eventually retired, knowing he made a difference in securing his country's safety. He and Jack still keep in touch often.

Senator John White and his wife Rebecca still live in North Carolina. Each afternoon, Rebecca continues to brew her famous sweet tea. She and John sip it slowly, while sitting on the back porch enjoying their beautiful gardens. They visit with the Owens family as often as possible.

Marcia finished out the year, and took her twenty-year pension. She now lives a happy life in Aruba with a very dear *friend*.

Jane and Pete celebrated their twin girls' fifth birthday. Jane does not go back to the states often, but does keep in touch with Jack and Katie. She keeps asking them to bring the boys to meet her girls. Katie thought perhaps the Owens family would plan a trip north in the summer.

Jack still has nightmares recalling his ordeal in the desert.

Satan looked down upon Jack Owens. No words came from the demon's mouth, but Jack heard what he had to say...

I have many dreams, each uniquely bizarre. The one that stays with me day in and day out is the one I had always feared the most would come true.

It did come true, but Jack Owens always believed that good *would* triumph over evil. Each time he has the nightmare, the pain of it eases a bit more. Each night his dreams end where he smiles, knowing the evils of the Twin Terror Plot have been checkmated for good.

Jack Owens has his family back and he will never leave them again. He and Katie Claire date regularly. The renewed intimacy between them grows stronger every day.

Jack Owens bit the devil's head clean off, and buried it deep within the sand; *Beyond The Desert Sun*.

The End

Note from the Author:

I hope you have enjoyed reading "Beyond the Desert Sun." The Jack Owens trilogy had come to conclusion leaving me with an emptiness; sort of like losing an old friend. I had originally planned three books for this project. The last book, "True Deception," had three different epilogues written before I decided to leave an opening for Jack to possibly return some day. After two significantly different novels, "Crossing America," followed by the psycho suspense thriller "Becoming Alice," Jack Owens convinced me to give him one more chance at saving the western world, as we know it, from the evil terrorists.

To all my faithful readers, thank you for your positive comments and support.

While the world may seem at times in turmoil, human nature is to find peace and enjoy life. For most of us, that is a truism. While some of my fictional work may push boundaries, I try to keep it *real* and embellish purely to entertain my readers.

I welcome and encourage my readers to comment on my books and ask questions; especially, if clarity is needed for any part of the story. The best way is to visit my website and leave me a comment.

Please visit www.waynelasnerbooks.com for updates on all books as they become available.

Visit www.Amazon.com and search for "Wayne Lasner" to see all my published works.

Acknowledgement

Creating a story and "penning" it to paper (actually on computer) is the most rewarding activity I can think of. People ask me what inspires me to do this. My answer is simple; the characters themselves are culpable. Formed from my imagination, they come alive in a daydream that inspires me to write about them.

I would like to thank all my friends and family for their continued support. To all of you who have read my books, your positive feedback is the driving force behind my continued creative process.

While I take great pleasure in creating stories for others to share, it is not all fun. There is tediously hard work that requires many months of research and multiple rewrites.

With more gratitude than I can possibly express, and once again, thank you, Mark Goodman. None of this would be complete if not for your relentless effort in editing and most important editorial contributions.

A special thanks to my son Brandon for his artistic contribution to the "Beyond the Desert Sun" book cover.

Other Books by Wayne Lasner

The Jack Owens Series

>   The Twin
>   Rage
>   True Deception

Crossing America

Becoming Alice

Available in Paperback and for Kindle at Amazon.com

Keep up to date with all my work by visiting my website at **waynelasnerbooks.com** and by liking my work on Facebook at **www.facebook.com/waynelasnerbooks**